PAINTED LEAVES

Also by John Fink

LIBEL THE DEAD

and in the Gillespie family annals
THE LEAF BOATS

PAINTED

LEAVES

JOHN FINK

ST. MARTIN'S PRESS
NEW YORK

Fink, John.
    Painted leaves / John Fink.
        p.   cm.
    "A Thomas Dunne book."
    ISBN 0-312-13137-2 (hardcover)
    I. Title.
PS3556.I475P35   1995
813'.54—dc20   95-1736
                                    CIP

First edition: June 1995
10 9 8 7 6 5 4 3 2 1

For Marjorie, Don, Therese, and Jim,
far-flung members of the clan

with appreciation for their help
to Jerry L. Butler, master police officer,
Dr. Turner Gray, medical examiner,
and Dr. Michael Hoffman, psychoanalyst

and special thanks to Pam

1

Ordinary suicides as everyone knows, are seldom mentioned on the "Ten O'Clock News," especially not around the holidays when there are so many of them. Even celebrities who kill themselves often get short shrift. But tonight there had already been several radio and television bulletins, and the two detectives entering the tall, fog-shrouded condominium building on North State Parkway were not surprised to see a TV microwave truck standing by. It was 7:00 P.M., with plenty of time before the telecast. The truck bore a large number 2. And the dead woman on the twenty-fifth floor was not just any celebrity but one of Channel 2's own.

The late Marlee Roberts, with her auburn hair, wry smile, and don't-mess-with-me gaze, had long been Chicago's most prominent television news anchor, and in three hours thousands of viewers, informed of her death by the early bulletins, would be tuning in to find out why she had slit her wrists. Some would be stunned or horrified, some merely curious. But a surprising number would be honestly griefstricken, perhaps imagining her as an angel on an old-fashioned greeting card, with a rose in her hair. The image would be appropriate, for at thirty-five Marlee had given the impression of being an old-fashioned girl.

To remind viewers of this once-in-a-lifetime opportunity to mourn her, Channel 2's news director, alerted at home, had ordered the microwave truck dispatched before he began the short drive downtown.

A hard-charging newcomer to Chicago with a three-pronged name, Howard Damen Custer III had been saddened by the news. He had known Marlee Roberts since their college days and would miss her as a friend. More significant, as far as his job was concerned, she was the biggest draw on the "Ten O'Clock News." In fact, her presence on the anchor desk had been one of his primary motivations in leaving Los Angeles to take up his new post at Channel 2. Her sudden death would create a sensation, and Howard Custer knew a ratings-grabber when he saw one. So now, behind the wheel of his silver Corvette, he already had someone clearly in mind to replace her.

With traffic slowed to a crawl by deep fog along the wintry Lakeshore, Howard car-phoned a young but capable reporter he had hired soon after his arrival in Chicago. A dark-haired beauty of some distinction, Karen Kohl lived directly across the street from Marlee in a two-bedroom rental apartment almost as familiar to Howard as his own. He was surprised, and a bit chagrined, to find her in. It was Monday, her day off, too, and he had been calling her without success all afternoon.

"What are you doing there?" he said accusingly. "Where have you been?"

Karen replied coolly, as if she was not sure she liked his possessive tone. "Where were *you*? I finally gave up and went to my health club."

That voice. It always did him in, when she dropped into that lower-range alto. It reminded him of how domineering women could be. He felt excited by women like that. "I told you I'd call," he whined. "Why did you go out?" "Well, I thought you'd changed your mind." A pause. A defensive snarl. "I don't change my mind." "You do, all the time. I thought you weren't coming." "Well, I was." By now Howard was fuming. At Karen, at the traffic he was stuck in, at everything that continually conspired to keep them apart: his wife, his two children, his job, and middle-class Midwestern morality.

He sulked for a moment and then, brusquely, as was his fashion (though usually not with her), he told Karen about Marlee, hearing her gasp and wail, "Oh, no!" then listen in silence as he went on. When it came to some piece of business that directly affected her, no one could listen as hard as Karen.

He told her to join the crew of the mobile unit in front of Marlee's apartment house for a series of special reports that would interrupt regular Monday night network programming. Heard another sharp intake of breath. Was amused to recall that one of tonight's programs was "Murphy Brown," the prizewinning show about a female anchorperson who was hard as nails. Marlee had been hard as nails, too, but a lot sweeter than Murphy Brown.

More like Karen. Karen could be sweet, and someday she too would be hard as nails. But not yet. Not quite yet.

"Thank you, darling," she said, now chastened and willing. "I appreciate your confidence in me." And without pause, sounding less innocent, "Why aren't you sending Jimmy?"

"Because he doesn't live across the street. Now, get over there. Fast."

"I will. And I'm sorry if I sounded rude."

"Don't be sorry. Be great." He hung up and called the newsroom to tell the executive producer of the "Ten O'Clock News" that Karen was on her way.

"Karen?"

The name, the question hung suspended between them like the old-fashioned telephone lines in the tiny Illinois town where Howard had grown up.

"She'll be good," he replied. "Anyway, she might as well get her feet wet on a suicide." Actually, Karen had done live reports before, but only under supervision. Everybody knew she needed more experience. Everybody would wonder. Did everybody know about Karen and him? Fuck 'em, Howard thought, saying, "It ought to be a good show, right there in the middle of the Gold Coast," adding quickly, "on a very sad occasion."

The assignment manager had come on the line. "We aren't going to see much of the building, Howard. The truck says it's all fog out there."

"Fog here, too. Well, fine, that's exactly the way we want it. Nice and ghostly." Preparing to sign off, he realized why he had ghosts in mind. Not Marlee. Later in the week, he was taking his two small sons to see *A Christmas Carol* at the Goodman. Astonished as always by the magical way his mind worked, he breathed, "God bless us, every one," and hung up.

The assignment manager, who was already giving instructions to his staff, asked for clarification too late.

Though he could not be called handsome, Howard Custer's looks and drive had been known to stir interest and even admiration. His ungainly features had a certain intrepid intensity, matching a combative energy that at times seemed to verge on the uncontrollable. That image was partly deliberate, partly something that just got away from him when he was very excited or angry.

As the traffic suddenly came unstuck and the silver Corvette shot into the fog, Howard felt merry and bright, almost giddy. *A Christmas Carol,* he was thinking, by Charles Dickens, one of his favorite authors. Marlee Roberts. And one of the Dickens characters, Jacob Marley, and Marley's ghost. He laughed as he cut off a fortress-size Cherokee wagon. Laughed because it was the season to be jolly. Because he was in love and in control. Because it was Howard Custer's time to shine.

Ten minutes later, ambling happily into the cavernous Channel 2 newsroom, his great tweedy overcoat flapping about him, Howard cried, "Hi, everybody. Bah! Humbug!" awakening a dozen or more startled colleagues from their self-conscious state of depression and mourning. Ooohs, frowns, shudders, and nervous laughter followed him as he strode past the assignment desk into the writers' area, trailing a scarf as long and woolly as Bob Cratchitt's.

"Okay, listen up!" His voice sliced and diced the air, and involuntarily, as the invisible fragments fell, people ducked. "So it's a tragedy. I'm as sorry as you are. So Chicago's lost the best female anchor it ever had. Well, I'm probably even sorrier than you are. We're all sorry as hell about Marlee. So let's do what Marlee would have wanted. Let's run with it!" Critically, he examined the dazed expressions around him. His voice rose, cracking a little. "Don't you see what we've got here, for Christ's sake? It's Christmas, there's a London fog out there, and God love her, we've got Marlee's ghost!"

It might have been a religious revival meeting. Somebody gave a tense little scream, and somebody else said, "Jesus!" Across the room someone began to sob.

Pleased by this display of creative distress, Howard gestured a young woman wearing rimless glasses out of her chair and sat down at her computer. He had been here for six months, and so far he had failed to see in his underlings the kind of rabid, self-motivated frenzy he always enjoyed in himself. At last, he felt, he had struck a responsive nerve.

As his fingers moved feverishly over the keyboard, the assignment manager and the executive producer leaned down for a closer look at the screen. Howard's head of brown curly hair bobbed to the rhythm of the keys, and his determined brow, beady eyes, and hawklike nose gave him a glowering look. He was well known for his concentration at the computer in his office, at which he sat for hours and hours, working up memoranda and letters and God-knows-what else. Now, on the screen, rapidly multiplying letters glowed like the lighted windows of an endless train coming out of a darkened tunnel:

> With Christmas only a week away . . .
> (Howard tapped out with scarcely a pause)
> the city is covered by cold and fog . . .
> and today it is cloaked in mourning . . .
>
> If Charles Dickens . . .
> London's most admired journalist . . .
> were reporting this story . . .
> he might remind us sadly . . .
> that at this hour . . .
> the best of times and the worst of times . . .
> Chicago can never forget the shining spirit of
>   Marlee Roberts . . .
> a young woman of great talent and good cheer . . .
> who took her life earlier today. . . .

Charles Dickens might add that perhaps . . .
before death came to her . . .
Marlee Roberts remembered happier Christmases. . . .

A snow-covered pond on the rolling hills of Iowa . . .
The cold air alive with the scent of holly and
  woodsmoke . . .
Up the way, a farmhouse . . .
filled with aromas of roast goose and pudding . . .
and sounds of carols and laughter. . . .

That's where Marlee Roberts . . .
who died today . . .
first knew what she wanted to do in life . . .
to help make this world a far, far better place . . .
than most of us have ever known.

"Blah, blah, blah," Howard said as he traded places with the bespectacled writer. "Tuck in some more warm-and-cuddly, but don't screw it up. Keep it literary, okay? Elegiac."

The writer squinted up, her eyes shining with tears. "I don't think the Iowa bit will fly, Howard. Her bio says she was from Jersey City."

"Half of Jersey, you can't tell it from Iowa," he shot back, bouncing away. "Don't give me details, give me Dickens."

By eight o'clock, news reporter Karen Kohl had gone on camera three times, the fog thickening around her. Gamely, she had read from the TelePrompTer what she considered to be the best of Dickens and the worst of Dickens, for each version of the script had been more sentimental than the last.

But at 8:10 P.M., word got out that the chief of the Chicago police department was on his way, and she began to scramble for details. If one thing is known to be true in the news business, it is that the city's top cop does not make house calls during a suicide investigation just to pay his respects, not even to the likes of Marlee Roberts.

Howard, who was having a tuna on rye in his office when he heard this, cried, "Something's going on—I can taste it!" On one of the TV screens high on his wall, he watched as Karen broke in on "Murphy Brown" to report this new development, the first of any real significance. He noticed that she seemed uncertain. She stared fixedly at the camera and spoke too fast, and he thought he detected a pleading look in her eye. His confidence in her shattered, he went down the hall and barked at the assignment manager, "Get Karen some backup. She's too new, she can't handle this." His gaze whipped around the vast room. "Where's Jimmy? Anyone seen Jimmy?"

"He's off today," the assignment manager replied. He reached for the phone. "I'll send her a couple of legmen." Then he hesitated, staring at the monitor. "Hold it. We've got competition."

As they watched, a second microwave truck lumbered out of the fog-laden darkness. Then another. Soon three trucks were stacked up behind Channel 2's alongside the twinkly lights of the Pump Room, the well-known old restaurant and watering hole.

"They can smell it, too," Howard said, and suddenly his agitated mind composed an image of Marlee as she had looked at her best, robust and glowing. "I knew it couldn't be suicide. She would never have killed herself." Peering into the upturned faces around the assignment desk, he asked plaintively, "How did Jacob Marley die in *A*

Christmas Carol, does anyone remember? Was it liquor? Gout? Was it suicide?" He shrieked, "Somebody! Was it murder?"

A researcher went to find out. But at least one other thing is known to be true in the news business. Self-indulgent flights of fancy die aborning, their wings iced over, in the face of harsh reality. Reluctantly, Howard put aside the Dickens connection.

At 8:20 P.M., the police chief arrived at Marlee's condo and went upstairs without a word. In reporting this, Karen's delivery was nimble, precise, and well paced. Howard felt enormous relief. And when, a few minutes later, an assistant offered the opinion that the newsroom was becoming ravaged by nerves and fatigue, he was so gratified by this demonstration of creative tension that he declared a fifteen-minute recess.

On his way out, he stopped by the control room to watch Karen summarizing what she had gleaned from random cops, building employees, and bystanders. This time her manner was doggedly intense, but Howard saw it only as a facet of her impassioned ambition and undeniable beauty. "She's good, isn't she?" he asked hopefully of no one in particular.

The executive producer turned to him with raised eyebrows. Putting a finger to her lips, she said, "You might think so, you might not. But look and be amazed."

Howard peered at the screen, frowning. Had he missed something? He saw that perhaps he had. Could this be the Karen Kohl he knew? The same white-skinned, raven-haired, long-legged kid who had clung to him at least once a week in the quiet of her bedroom, whispering her adoration and her yearning to become a star? He knew she had ability, not to mention hard little nipples and a quick, hungry mouth, but where had this fervent, almost frightening communicator come from?

No longer encumbered by either Dickens or the facts—there were few—Karen Kohl had gone rampantly Shakespearean. Her ordinarily cool, crisp voice had dropped into that florid lower range. It spoke all the right words, and with an urgency that was all-consuming. In her eyes as she looked into the camera, he saw what had never been there for him, a feeling of absolute possession. She owned the camera. She owned the viewers at home. My God, he thought, she even owns me. For a moment, he felt the kind of terror theatergoers feel as they cling to their armrests or purses and suck in their breath.

In the ghostly fog, she might have been a stressed-out, gore-drenched Lady Macbeth, hinting in five-foot blank verse at appalling things to come.

The scene on the monitor wasn't the fall of Macbeth or the Battle of Agincourt, but it was close. Behind her, the cordoned-off street between the two famous old Ambassador Hotels looked as if the media were preparing to cover yet another CNN-size invasion by United States Marines massed within the surrounding mist, impatiently waiting for the fog to lift before cutting down everything in sight.

2

With seventy-five minutes to go before the "Ten O'clock News" and what looked like a big story breaking, the capacious newsroom was curiously gray and empty. Everything seemed to be happening offstage, as indeed it was.

A mile north, Marlee Roberts's apartment building was aglow with activity. The medics had come and gone. The medical examiner and the evidence technicians were busily deciphering the pitiless encodings of violent death. Across the city, Channel 2 reporters were (a) soliciting testimonials from city officials and friends and family of the deceased, and (b) sampling the reactions of the viewing public, building a record of Marlee's place in its vague and larcenous storehouse of memories.

Down the hall from the studio, the day's collected newstapes were being edited to make room for whatever might result when the police chief came out onto State Street, and old Marlee Roberts tapes were being melded into colorful cameos of her career and her personal legacy. Now the news director, tired of making decisions about all this, was about to return to his office.

But in the dimly lighted newsroom, all was quiet. It was like a mortuary, or a tomb. Two or three pale wraiths drifted from desk to desk, distributing year-end summaries of employee benefits or resounding company achievements. And in a far corner, the assignment manager had just settled down for a somewhat lighthearted private phone conversation.

His place at the assignment desk had been taken by a shadowy figure who leaned back into the dim glow of a stray spotlight, tipped a broad-brimmed hat over his eyes, and carefully put his feet up. Surrounded by the computers, scanner radios, and other not-yet-outmoded accoutrements of the space age, he seemed an anachronism, a Ghost of Christmas Past got up as a disreputable reporter from "The Front Page."

The figure seemed less out of context here, however, than it would have at the brightly illuminated anchor desk at the far end of the room. Isolated in the surrounding gloom that appeared to be the futuristic set of an entirely different movie, possibly "Star Trek XIII." Unmanned cameras poised before it, blank television screens clustered at its rear, the anchor desk seemed a wide, glittering podium for setting sail through the undiscovered universe.

Ordinarily the desk might have been occupied by one or more anchorpersons, a weatherman, perhaps a sportscaster. They would have been fretting over their lines, tightening up the script here and there, getting their cues straight: when to pause, when to smile, when to look deathly solemn. Out in front, in among the snarling black cables, the floor director might have been putting the camera operators through their usual choreography for the big broadcast, when not a moment of the clock could be lost or a signal from the control room misinterpreted, and the place would be full of stagehands and sound technicians and production assistants.

But this was no ordinary night.

The floor director and the cameramen were fortifying themselves in the cafeteria. The sportscaster, whose scathing wit played well only when Marlee was there to give it her smile of dubious approval, was fortifying himself at the bar around the corner, wondering if he would have to change his act. The weatherman had no such problem, since, by and large, no matter how chatty and engaging he might seem, he interacted only with highs, lows, isotherms, and such. Down the corridor in his weather lab, he was studying the possibility of lakeshore fog being replaced, toward morning, by lake-effect snow, and idly wondering if he could score big with the news director by working Dickens into his forecast. These able journeymen were staying clear of the set until the last possible moment. They had liked Marlee Roberts a lot and were feeling the natural nervousness about loss and change that had overtaken everybody. They were not hiding out, they were simply staying clear.

But Stanford Grigg, the senior anchor, was frankly and unapologetically hiding out. He was deeply upset and mortally afraid. A handsome, cadaverous black intellectual whose precise speech and flat, trip-hammer laugh were as familiar to viewers as his sparkling brown eyes and frozen smile, over the past eight years he had come to lean more and more on Marlee Roberts, and now that she was gone his dependence had become complete. Tonight, no matter who else would be at the anchor desk, the weatherman, the sportscaster, or Christ Jesus Himself, Stanford Grigg felt he was going to be up there alone and abandoned. He wasn't ready for that, not yet. But he was getting ready. Sitting in his little windowless office with his door locked, he pressed his knees together as he always did at the anchor desk and told himself over and over that he was getting ready. "Dammit, man," he cried out when the producer asked through the door when he intended coming onto the set, "can't you see I'm getting ready?"

On his way from his office to the newsroom, the news director heard this exchange and hurried on. He had consoled the general manager by phone and was no longer worried about the g.m. He wasn't worried about Stanford either. Stanford was a pro who could be counted on to turn in his usual uninspired performance regardless. Howard hated watching Stanford Grigg on the "Ten O'clock News." He was too stiff, too predictable, too old. God, he was almost sixty. Howard wanted to get rid of him. Marlee would never have permitted this, but Marlee was gone. Now there remained only the awkward impediments of Stanford's unmistakable race, his age, and of course his all-around competence.

Walking into the huge, shadowy newsroom and seeing not only its emptiness but the brilliantly lighted, infinitely more concentrated emptiness of the anchor desk always put Howard Custer at peace. It wasn't the emptiness that did this, or the shadows, or the silence, but the knowledge that, at the snap of a finger, he could instantly fill the place with racing, frantic people. Right now, though, everything that needed doing was being done, and Howard wanted to be alone with his thoughts.

Leaning over the anchor desk, he tried not to feel too much like a genius. His genius was why he got so angry when others couldn't keep up. It was why Stanford Grigg had to go, and why Marlee, in death, undoubtedly understood that. If she had been sitting here, he would have been eyeball to eyeball with her. Eyeball to eyeball with Marlee, Howard had always blinked, and he did so now because it was such a tender moment.

Marlee, he told her, we'll miss you, cupcake. (He would not have dared to call her that in life.) That's why we're not replacing you right away. Not replacing you will remind viewers of their tragic loss, and in this way your absence will give us a win during sweeps week. Just by sitting here alone, poor old Stanford will do that for us. Of course, I'll have to replace you eventually. I'd like to replace Stanford, too, but not right away. I know you really wouldn't want that, and besides, I want to see how the new girl does. I'm still not sure about her, but if she does okay, then I can think about how to get rid of Stanford.

Howard hesitated. Am I making a bad mistake? he wondered. Will Karen really be okay? Can I trust her? He felt his jaw tighten. My God, he thought, who else is there to trust?

He said to the woman who wasn't there and would never be again, Okay, Marlee, that's it, cupcake. Slapping the desktop, he strode across the newsroom as if it might be a graveyard, whistling.

3

At the assignment desk, the semirecumbent figure shifted in the gloom, tipped back his hat, and watched the news director approach. Jimmy Gillespie was not a hard-drinking man. But tonight he had been drinking, partly because Marlee was dead, and partly because, as her friend and Channel 2's senior investigative reporter, he had waited at home until seven o'clock to be assigned to the story and no one had called.

Furious and grieving, he had put on his hat and walked six blocks through the cold fog to his favorite tavern, on North Avenue, growing more and more morose. There he had bought a round of drinks for the half dozen hard-drinking print journalists in the place and raised his glass. "To Marlee," he had said, noting the way the light sprang off the oak bar into his Scotch and ice, hanging there like firelight, exactly the color of Marlee's hair. "May she fly away before the boogeyman comes, and may she make it to heaven in spite of him," which was an old Irish toast he hoped would suffice.

He had no doubt that Marlee would make it to heaven.

But old shibboleths from childhood still clung to him, such as the one about the church not approving of suicide. To Jimmy, that was as incredible as the fact that Marlee had slit her wrists and bled to death, or that it was Karen up there on the TV screen and not him. He had repeated the toast with the next round of drinks and the one after that. Then he had taken a cab to the station to find out why he had not been called.

The news director, coming across the room, was whistling—what? The tune was familiar, but Jimmy couldn't remember the words.

Anyway, he was more interested in the way Howard's face was randomly lit by soft flickerings from overhead, and the way his puckered lips, whistling, drew his lean, beaky features into vertical line, making his narrow face an ax blade. This observation was not necessarily meant to be unkind, for although they did not always see eye to eye, he and Howard were old acquaintances. They, along with Marlee, had met fifteen years before, in journalism school at Northwestern, the university on the lake. It fringed Evanston, the first suburb north, where Jimmy had grown up, more or less. The other two had been outlanders. Marlee, with her ready smile, well-rounded legs, and renegade Jersey accent, had won his heart immediately. Howard Custer had been something else again. He was from a little place in downstate Lincoln country called Mattoon, which he had upgraded to an exurb of St. Louis, even though St. Louis was 120 miles away.

At college, Howard was off-putting. Howard was crass. It took months for them to establish an arm's-length relationship. In the end Howard's biting sarcasm and intimidating arrogance came to seem only a peekaboo disguise for his underlying need for love and an even deeper self-loathing. Jimmy had kept his distance, and from Marlee, too. Her warmth and assurance overwhelmed him sometimes, walled him off just as Howard's negativity did. He felt if he got past those walls of hers, he might blunder into something breakable in himself or in her. It had occurred to him once or twice since that, in spite of his outwardly easygoing nature, he might be a little off-putting himself.

So now the lovely Marlee was dead and here came the same old Howard, tripping across the newsroom doing his best to look unbothered and nonchalant. What he always looked like to Jimmy was a hawk or an eagle in perpendicular pursuit, about to strike. But what always struck first, in Jimmy's experience, was the scream.

It wasn't an actual scream, of course, but it was a startling outcry. It held anguish and urgency, anxiety and contempt, and whoever was on the receiving end invariably felt like a particularly defenseless kind of prey.

Howard screamed.

"Where are your people?" he shrieked. "What's going on? Where is everybody?"

He's mistaken me for the assignment manager, Jimmy thought, because I'm sitting in the assignment manager's chair. And sure enough, from down the way where the assignment manager had been talking on the phone, came his hasty response. "Still on break, Howard. Back in five."

Howard stopped where he was and cried, "Back in five? I want them back now. We go on in an hour, for God's sake!"

In the ensuing silence, Jimmy could hear the phone being put down, the chair pushed back, the footsteps leave the room. Carefully, he took his feet off the assignment desk and sat up. Howard said uncertainly, "Jimmy, is that you?"

He put both hands on the arms of the chair and hoisted

himself upward. I am not drunk, he told himself. The room oscillated violently. Christ, he thought, I'm not sober either. He considered the mathematical possibility that if you turned your body too quickly at the age of thirty-five, your accumulated bulk—in his case, 190 pounds spread over six feet—might screw you into the floor. So, very slowly, he looked around, a grin lighting his handsome Irish face. Give them a big smile, his father had always said, and 90 percent of them will think you know what you're doing.

Apparently reassured, Howard came toward him. "What are you doing here? I thought it was your day off."

Jimmy licked his lips. "Karen's day off, too, isn't it? How come she got the call?"

Howard seemed to waver. "I'm sorry. You pissed?"

Wiping his mouth with the back of his hand, Jimmy pondered this complicated question. "If you mean am I drunk, no I'm not. I had a drink because Marlee's a friend of mine. If you mean am I sore, the answer is yes. And for the same reason." He tried to take off his topcoat. It stuck somewhere around his elbows.

The other man dropped into a chair. "Look, I wasn't around when it happened. Karen called in, and somebody told her to run across the street. We tried to get you." He began picking something out of one eye, and Jimmy thought, He always does that when he lies. He sat down, too, leaning back on the coat and pinning his arms at his sides. Oh, Christ, he told himself, I'm pissed. "Now I'm worried," Howard said with a shaky little laugh. "A suicide Karen can handle, but what if it's murder? My God, this is her first big assignment. Believe me, I wish you were out there, buddy. I wish you'd been home."

"You should have thought of that earlier." Jimmy sighed, feeling helpless. Prometheus bound. "Don't worry, Howard, it's not murder." He struggled with the coat but it wouldn't budge. "Howard, nobody kills somebody by slitting their wrists. Christ, you can still run around with your wrists slit."

Howard said, "Her first major gig, she'll be jumpy. She might even freak out. Jimmy?" One hand went up to his forehead, blotting out his right eye. Cyclops, Jimmy thought. "I miss Marlee, too. I'm like you. Let's have a drink later."

"I don't know, Howard."

"Jimmy?"

"What?" He saw the hand come down. Howard's lips were so tightly compressed that the cords in his neck and jaw stuck out.

"Tell me the truth. She's hopeless, isn't she?"

"Who?"

"Karen." It was a whine. The sort of whine Howard's voice always had when he couldn't make up his mind about someone.

Jimmy shook his head. "No, she's not hopeless. She's been in the field with me for three, four months. She'll be fine." He lurched forward in the chair and his right arm came free. "Look, if it will make you feel better, I'll give someone out there a call."

"Thanks," Howard said. He had an ingratiating, almost insinuating way of saying thanks. He stood up and looked off at the anchor desk sparkling in the distance like the site of the Holy Grail. It always reminded Jimmy of the altar in church. He always half-expected a robed priest to appear and genuflect before it.

Howard cocked his head as if listening. He said softly, "You really think she'll do well?"

As if in miraculous reply, lights began to blossom here

and there across the newsroom, then came up glaringly. Jimmy shut his eyes. He heard the sounds of people filling up the room, the buzz of conversation rising. Close by, a woman's voice inquired, "Howard?" and he looked up, seeing Howard flinch as if she had hurled a javelin.

It was Dorothy, Howard's secretary. She was in her late twenties, black, and built like a Chicago bungalow. But a *pretty* Chicago bungalow. Her hair, pulled tight into a neat little knot at the very top of her head, seemed to draw up the corners of her vivacious eyes, making her look Spanish or French or Egyptian. Even oriental. It was usually impossible to tell from her expression whether she was amused or outraged, but sometimes she smiled like an angel. Right now Dorothy's eyes were wet, her expression dangerous.

She said sternly, "They want you right away in editing."

"What now?" Howard said. "Can't they handle it themselves?"

With more than a touch of sarcasm, she replied, "They try, Howard. They think they got it right, only they got to hear it from you. I told them I'd get you in there."

Howard sighed and turned to go. "Dottie, do me a favor? Tell the control room where I am and make sure everybody's back, okay?"

Now out of his coat, Jimmy picked up the phone.

"That's two favors," she said, "and it's not Dottie. Dottie's the word for loony tunes. Dorothy, that's my name, unless you want to start going by Howard Damen Three."

He swung around. Stress seemed to have invaded his sinuses, making his nostrils flare. "Sorry. It's the strain of the evening . . . Dorothy." He smiled thinly, as if his jaw ached, then set off across the newsroom, bumping into people and apologizing.

Jimmy was having trouble hearing the guy on the phone

because now Dorothy was shouting. "And don't you put you-know-who up there, no matter what you think of her. She's not ready to take Marlee's place, not tonight and maybe never!" Here and there people glanced up expectantly. Howard kept going, not looking back. "Nobody wants to see her at the anchor desk, not anybody here or anybody out in television land, and that's the truth!" As he went out the door, she stamped her foot.

Jimmy put down the phone and somebody said, "You through?" The assignment manager stood looking down at him. "If you are, I need my chair back."

"Sure," Jimmy said. He got up, picked up his coat, and took Dorothy by the elbow. She did not resist, but he thought he could feel how full of energy and rage she was.

She said, "You better watch it when you take hold of me. I almost hauled off and hit you."

"I know, you're a raging inferno." He escorted her down a long row of mostly empty desks, happy to be holding onto her because he wasn't sure he could walk straight. "Why don't you just ease up on Howard? It'll lower your blood pressure and improve your love life."

She batted her eyes flirtatiously. "Only you could do that, Jimmy Gillespie, but you're so blind." A look of suspicion crossed her face. "Have you been drinking?"

"Of course, haven't you? Who were you yelling about, Karen?"

"Sure was. Don't you know how he thinks? That's who his eye is on."

Tell me something I don't know, Jimmy thought. Last summer, introducing Karen to Howard and then returning twenty minutes later to pick her up, he had opened the door and found the two kissing enthusiastically. Howard had bounced away, explaining airily, "Just sealing the pact." And once she was on the job, in September, it had become obvious to everyone that they were trapped in the same force field, not just alert to each other but becoming mutually possessive. People exchanged knowing glances when the conference rooms that Howard and Karen entered became instantly charged and steamy. Scandalous, because both of them were married then.

He said to Dorothy, "It'll pass. Don't let it get to you."

She glared up. "Him making her so nervous she kills herself. And Stanford doesn't have long to go. You getting set to take Stanford's place?"

"Who, me?" Jimmy laughed, but this kind of talk made *him* nervous.

Dorothy shrugged. "You're already a weekend anchor. You got more experience than anybody here but Howard the Third. Besides, he likes you, Jimmy, you know he does. He liked you the minute he came here. I can tell by how his eyes blink."

"So? We know each other from way back."

"So? He'd get rid of me if he could." They were entering a crowded area and she began moving fast, bumping nobody because they got out of her way. "Only good thing about being a secretary in this place, you do your job you can stay clear of politics." At Channel 2, secretaries were hired independently, in a kind of pool arrangement, and assigned by the head of the pool. They could not be dismissed without proof of incompetence. Dorothy did her job well, and for months had been bucking for advancement.

Jimmy said, "I thought he was going to make you a junior executive. Assistant to the news director or something."

"Un-huh. He's been promising me that for six months. He hates me because I keep telling him he doesn't act right, the way he talks to people, lays his weight around. He'll put her in, that Karen, you see if he don't. Maybe you, maybe not." She flashed him a look. "You're drunk, Jimmy. You don't know him like I do. I don't drink. I keep my eyes open, see what he does. Always flashing that pardon-me, shit-eating smile that makes the general manager think he knows all about everything, only he doesn't. Always bent over that computer of his, filling it up with stuff and nonsense. I see how he talks to Stanford. Makes Stanford so angry he can't even speak. Makes him almost crazy."

Jimmy left her at the control room door. "Howard's just hyper, Dorothy. Anyway, listen. They're saying now . . ." He waited until he had her full attention. "Marlee may not have killed herself, Dorothy. This could be a homicide."

Dorothy looked up, her large eyes richly brown and troubled, like the waters of the Nile, or the Danube, or perhaps the Yangtze. "Oh, lord," she said. "It wouldn't surprise me any if he was the one that did it to her!"

4

The condominium's oldest and most garrulous employee, the night doorman, had been questioned by cops in uniform and cops in plainclothes, and he felt wrung dry. This was just as well because, before being permitted to return to his post, he had been warned not to say anything. Still, with more and more gold braid parading past him to the elevators, and the media and the curious gathered outside the glass entryway, his excitement was building again. It was the kind of high he remembered from celebrated crimes of the past—the Richard Speck case, for instance, the one with that loony who killed all those Filipino nurses, or the murder spree up in the northern 'burbs a few years ago. What was the name of the family, Gillespie? Times like that, he'd had to imagine what a homicide investigation was like, but tonight he was part of one. Not only had he found the woman's body, he might have talked to the killer on the phone.

Before he went home, he would probably be questioned some more. The detective who seemed to be running things, the older one, hadn't asked him anything yet; he didn't know why he was taking so long. He pictured telling his story upstairs to the chief of police. He wondered what the next week would be like back home in the neighborhood, after being interviewed by television reporters and getting his mug on the screen.

Actually, if you left out the few really hairy moments, like looking into the woman's bathroom and finding the body, there wasn't a lot to say. But it was a damn sight more than happened to most of those who hung by the doors of apartments and condominiums of life without getting a peek inside.

What the doorman had told the police was this:

The phone call had come shortly before six o'clock, a brief message from someone who sounded like an undertaker, saying that there was a body on the top floor of the twenty-five-story establishment. The building manager had left for home, so after trying to raise the tenant on the intercom the doorman had posted one of the maintenance crew at the front entrance and gone upstairs to have a look. Crank calls were not unusual. Neither were bodies in a place so full of the Gold Coast's elderly. But the two-bedroom apartment in question was occupied by a popular TV anchorwoman who looked to be only in her thirties and far too healthy to have a heart attack.

After some delay, he had unlocked the door and stepped inside. He had called her name a few times, finally concluding that if there was a body it would probably be in one of the bedrooms. So he had gone down the hall, seeing the closed bathroom door. Now, this was the tricky part. If he knocked and she screamed, he could get chewed out tomorrow by the management. If he went away, he might be chewed out for not doing his duty. So he had knocked and waited, wondering if early retirement was in the offing, then knocked some more.

Finally he had opened the door a crack and looked in, seeing the blood on the white tiled floor and one wall. Opening the door some more, he had seen more blood, and finally he had taken a deep breath and peered around at the tub. There she was, her naked body half submerged in water that swirled a vivid reddish-rust, like her hair.

"That's very poetic," the younger detective had told him. "Tell me, did it turn you on?"

"A little bit," he had admitted, but then, he said, he'd begun to feel sick. All in all, it had been an ugly sight, one not to his liking.

Badly shaken, he had returned to the living room and dialed 911. Then he had gone back downstairs. Before the police could respond, he had recovered sufficiently to report all he knew to several other building employees and at least a dozen residents.

These reports, spreading rapidly as gossip, had provided the media with two fairly substantial but seemingly contradictory rumors. One rumor was that Marlee Roberts had told her doorman that she was expecting a visitor. The other was that no visitor had arrived. If, as the waiting reporters had agreed, the police chief's presence in the building suggested homicide, the first rumor seemed to be the one to go with. It had been put on the air, cautiously and without confirmation, just after 8:30, about the time the doorman was being brought back upstairs for further questioning.

One of the policemen on the twenty-fifth floor was feeling comfortable with both rumors. A middle-aged sergeant named Kirkpatrick, he had worked out of Violent Crimes for the past seven years. For an older cop, he appeared to be exceptionally fit. Even the pouches beneath his eyes looked muscular.

If you wanted to see what life really looked like, it was said, you had only to look into Kirkpatrick's eyes. But fledgling cops and police reporters who took this advice did so at their peril, for the sergeant's eyes had a slight cast and were the color of old Chicago ice, and those who peered into them were never quite the same. They came away as if returning from a far-off land that was cold and harsh and where nothing, to be true, needed to make sense. No, the idea that Marlee Roberts had been killed by a visitor who never arrived was not hard for the detective to accept. In fact, he was addicted to such paradoxes. Through them, he came close to experiencing what he seemed to be lacking, a sense of humor.

Sergeant Kirkpatrick didn't find much of anything funny because his life was his work. Violent death simply did not amuse him. In the same way, he was not interested in departmental politics, although he had learned to accept death and politics and humor as things others couldn't live without.

So he wasn't surprised when the captain, who was the commander in charge of sixth area Violent Crimes, phoned the chief of police or when the chief decided to make the announcement himself, on the scene. If the chief wanted to be the one to tell the press, and if the commander wanted the chief to have no doubt that this was murder, the sergeant could understand that. That's why he had called in the crime lab, because, as he told the captain, there had been a question about the medical examiner's preliminary finding of suicide. The question, of course, was his own. So was the thought that was working its way to the front of his brain, that Marlee Roberts's death might possibly turn out to be the work of a serial killer.

The chief and the commander were waiting. But before giving them the final word, the sergeant needed to have a chat with the principal witness and then reach an accord with the medical examiner. Then it would be up to the top brass to decide what the right blend of police work and politics should be. And to take the consequences if they got the mix wrong and it blew up in their faces.

With the examiner and the technicians still busy in the bathroom, and the living room full of brass, Kirkpatrick entered the spare bedroom to question the doorman. He nodded at his partner, who had already filled him in. The younger man's expression seemed somewhat aggrieved. Maybe he's sore, the sergeant thought, because he feels I've been holding out on him. He sat down opposite the doorman in his maroon bandmaster's uniform and began.

5

"I'm told the deceased called you at five o'clock or there-abouts. What did she say? Her exact words?"

The doorman's pale eyes stared at the sergeant without focusing and the jaw twitched several times, ruminating. " 'Roy, I am expecting a guest. Don't bother to ring, just send them on up.' "

"Not 'him up' or 'her up'? Nothing to indicate who it might be?"

Another search of the memory. "No. All I knew was to look for somebody who was coming. Male or female, old or young, even more than one person, I have no idea."

"But no one came."

"No one came." The eyes, the husky voice were doom-ridden.

"The call that came later, telling you there was a body. Anything strike you about it?"

"Like I told the other officers, it was a tenor voice, or you might say a high baritone. As a matter of fact, I remember going up in the elevator and thinking it could be one of the young guys in the garage. Giving me a hard time, you know—"

"He said what? The man on the phone."

A look back through the ages. " 'There is a problem in twenty-five F. It's another body.' "

" 'Another body.' He said 'another'?"

"That's what I meant by a guy from the garage. We had a death about a month ago, an old lady, and I thought—"

Kirkpatrick was on his feet, saying he would have more questions later. He returned to the hallway where the medical examiner was waiting, eager to go home. A small man with a mustache, the examiner gave him a beseeching look and said, "Kirk, I can go either way."

"No, you can't." The detective put an arm around his shoulders and led him along the corridor toward the crowded living room, stopping halfway where no one could overhear them. "In about a minute I've got to give the chief an answer, Eddie, and I've already made up my mind." They were standing close, so close he could see pores and wrinkles and smell the garlic on the other man's breath.

The examiner said, "She could have killed herself."

"With those wrists? All that blood?"

"I've seen worse."

"Not with a suicide you haven't. Or if you did you were wrong." The detective could see he had hurt the examiner's feelings. "Pardon me so much, Eddie. You were misled."

"Why are you so set on this? This is an important case. I can't—" The examiner caught his breath. "Is that it? She's a celebrity? Is that why you're doing this?" His eyes took on a glow, as if he was about to defend the sanctity of his office.

Kirkpatrick said, "I only say this. Remember the girl on Clark Street, a few blocks down, early October? Same wrists, same spattered walls. You said suicide, I didn't argue. Remember the one on Pine Grove, mid-November? Same thing. I didn't argue. Look, I don't care. A thousand homicides a year, I have enough to do. But this one, there's only one way you can go. I need you to be solid on this. There are too many eyes looking at it, and I won't change my mind."

"Kirk, I can't remember every single case."

"Just think about this one. The slashes are too deep and too many. They even got some tendons. And three, four deep ones on each wrist, she wouldn't have been able to do that. They go straight across, no hesitation marks. Eddie, you know that hardly ever happens." By hesitation marks, he meant those superficial tracings of a sharp blade on skin that indicate an ambivalence about cutting life short. "And all that blood on the floor and walls. There was a struggle."

"There could have been. But how—?"

"Suicides do not slash their wrists like that and run around falling against walls, then step into a warm tub. Then the phone call."

"A friend. He found her and didn't want to get involved."

"What's your excuse?"

"Don't say that. We have to be very careful in these matters."

"Careful enough to have a second look? She was murdered. And if she was, so were the other two. And in the same way."

The examiner's eyes widened. "You're not thinking serial?"

Kirkpatrick glanced around. "How do you know you've got a serial killer, doctor? You see the same thing in each case. And what was the phone call all about? 'Another body.' Number three. He wants us to know what he's doing. He wants to get caught. The commander thinks so, too."

"I see." The examiner glanced toward the living room. Then he looked into the sergeant's eyes, and the corner of his mouth turned up in a kind of spasm. "It could be murder. I don't think it is, but pending results of the autopsy, I'd have to say it probably is."

"Pending the results of the autopsy," the detective said, "I'm glad you agree."

In the doorway, Kirkpatrick stared across the living room at the captain, caught his eye, and nodded. The commander in charge of Violent Crimes turned and made his way toward the gathering of gold braid and shiny blue shoulders in the far corner to tell the chief what they had already decided was true, that Ms. Roberts's death was in no way a suicide but the work of a killer with an unvarying pattern and a psyche as ugly as a steel trap, one who had killed twice before.

It's always nice, the detective thought, to have undisputable evidence, or, in the absence of that, some kind of miracle. As in this case, wounds that cried out, accusing the perpetrator of all manner of hideous things. And on top of that, a witness who could shed some light, like a doorman who had talked to the visitor who had never arrived. Oh yes, the visitor had been there all right. He had just arranged to arrive unannounced.

Watching the chief head downstairs with his entourage,

Kirkpatrick felt along his cheek for the stubble that told him he needed a shave. Then he went to find his partner, thinking of the gray body floating in the rust-colored water. What you see is what you get, he told himself. And what you don't see, sometimes you get that, too.

6

Jimmy Gillespie had few illusions, even when he wasn't snockered by a mercifully rare combination of too much grief and booze. Ordinarily he was not a serious drinker. Nor was he deeply religious or inclined to give others his heart. Those illusions he had he planned to keep safely at home, buried deep in the sock drawer next to his seldom-made king-size bed. Out of sight, out of mind.

He certainly held no romantic notions about his work, which these days mostly involved the police. He was aware, for instance, that no love was wasted between the media and the forces of the law. He thought this was unfortunate, because they both served as prime irritants in the oyster that was Chicago, producing the pearls of peace and enlightenment that made it the envy of the civilized world.

If he sometimes saw cops as a lunatic fringe devoted to keeping dark secrets, he also knew that they regarded most reporters as dangerous turncoats who, given too much trust or leeway, could blindside them cruelly. Jimmy acknowledged that there were some reporters working the police beat who were neither polite nor fair, but he was prepared to defend their dignity, their professional integrity, and their right to ask embarrassing questions, even when they overdid it.

His working philosophy was: If it got the job done, why not? As long as they didn't target sources maliciously, zealous reporters were only doing their job. And if the forces of law and order occasionally were caught in the crunch, they had only to remind themselves that the role of the press was to inform and clarify, just as theirs was to serve and protect.

The media's mission, after all, was predicated on the public's right to know, its penchant for demanding why and why not, and above all its insatiable lust for a scapegoat, preferably one that had been banged around a bit, then dragged up and down the block until it was rubbed raw and nicely bloodied. If the scapegoat happened to be the police, okay, get mad. But why blame the media? That was like letting the mugger go free and arresting the guy who had called the cops.

Jimmy Gillespie had no illusions about the fascination of violence. He would have liked the world to be without it, but when he encountered it he found it alluring. In the past three years he had often looked into the eyes of Detective Kirkpatrick at the scene of a gruesome killing and felt no pain, only a little shock of recognition that said Yes, this is the way things are. He had seen the face of life—not to be confused with Sgt. Kirkpatrick's—and found it cruel and not too bright.

Whatever had happened to Marlee was only the latest example of that. Three years ago had been the worst. Jimmy had been working across town at Channel 5, as day assignment manager. Each morning he would send out Channel 5's fleet of mobile TV studios to tape the day's outpouring of news. One day he dispatched a microwave truck to Skokie, where a young woman's body had been found in a pond. Jimmy had lived in Skokie. His father still did. But he gave no thought to this until he saw all the newsroom faces looking up at him. The faces had hard round eyes, and the eyes were asking tough questions: How are you going to handle it, mister? How are you going to deal with the fact that your twenty-eight-year-old sister is dead?

Three quick family funerals later, the eyes finally had stopped staring. He thought it must be because, by then, he looked so awful. There should have been actors in masks to walk him through it, and a chorus to explain it, and philosophers in wraparound garments to give it meaning. But there weren't, and his sister Hope and the others were gone and it was all a muddle and a mystery. Walking into the Channel 5 newsroom after that was like trudging through the rubble of a forest fire he himself had somehow started. That's when he knew he had to stop sending out the TV trucks, because each time he did so he recalled the catch in the throat and all those upturned faces.

Because life was a kick in the gut, a mystery and a muddle, a fog in the night. And now the police chief was getting ready to come downstairs and stir the ashes into flame again.

Jimmy, brooding in front of his dead computer, knew what the chief was going to say, that Marlee had not died by her own hand. Sometimes, like now, he thought of Marlee as family. And that if life was a series of losses and disappointments, then that's what families were for, to mark them by.

He was by no means a complete pessimist. He knew that even huge losses didn't make it the end of the world. He knew that Marlee had a family out there, just as there were plenty of Gillespies left, even doddery old Dutch, the father of them all. Patricia and Frank (Marcus Franklin Gillespie, Jr.) and all their adolescent offspring. Emily and Raymond, the younger half-siblings from his father's famous second brood.

Of his brothers and sisters, only Patricia was still in Chicago. Frank was in Washington, into politics. Emily was at the University of London, getting an advanced degree in architecture. Raymond, the youngest, the one who at first had seemed most deeply wounded by the family tragedy, had gone out east and found himself a bride. Though Jimmy was known for his resiliency and stubbornness of character, he had been the slowest to come back from grief. The world to him was still shut down. It felt like yet another wall he couldn't get over.

For a while he thought he had climbed it. Before signing on as investigative reporter at Channel 2 News, he had made a deal with Howard Custer's predecessor: to report directly to the news director, to make an occasional documentary of social significance, and to be considered for the next anchor job that came along. That's what he had always wanted to be, a news anchor. But by the time Howard came along, two and a half years later, little had changed. The wall remained high and wide. He had gone through lots of women, casually, even carelessly, and his social life had the feel of a chancy crapshoot. The anchor job? Don't ask.

With Howard, though, things began to look up. They also began to look down.

Howard Damen Custer III, once the campus smartass, had made a serious splash as an overseas network correspondent in Africa and Beirut, winding up in Los Angeles in a cushy but boring administrative job. He had married a Hollywood costume designer, had two kids, then set his eye on the news job in Chicago as the next, somewhat ugly but challenging step up the slippery ladder he had been climbing forever. And only his old classmates, Marlee and Jimmy, could see what a panic the man had been in since Day One. Jimmy saw it because he had learned well what panic was. Marlee had come out of the womb understanding it. Encountering Howard again had only made her more watchful, and more protective of herself and others.

But even she couldn't fall on all the grenades Howard dropped into the antiquated machinery at Channel 2 News, meaning to destroy it so he could start over from scratch. Though Marlee made sure nobody got fired, everybody took a licking. The "Ten O'clock News," until then relaxed and somewhat sedate, became fast and garish and occasionally hysterical. Rock 'n' roll with a touch of slash, slash, burn. Hard copy, completely brittle in Howard's hot little hands.

Panic.

Marlee had said it the first time Howard walked in the door. His foreign-correspondent Burberry, hanging nearly to his ankles, might have been a western marshal's trailcoat concealing his favorite shotgun. At the first runthrough, it was as if he had whipped his coat open and started blasting away.

"Just read the script, for God's sake," he had screamed at Stanford Grigg. "This isn't foreplay, this is the real thing. You're supposed to be a stud, so get it on. Read it, don't . . . masturbate!" As he turned away, Stanford turned a rare color, some combination of puce and green, humiliated like a proud violinist who has had his bow taken away and been handed a chainsaw.

Marlee's frown had grown dangerously deep. "Well," she had said, putting her script aside, "let's not *panic*." She had excused herself and left the room, Jimmy guessed, to find a drink.

So far he had been puzzled at having been asked to sit in. Howard had merely said, "Be there." Now the news director handed him Marlee's abandoned script and said, "Get up there and read it." He did. He had no qualms about it. He didn't feel that Stanford needed taking care of. Stanford had been on one anchor desk or another for sixteen years, one of the first African-Americans anywhere to read the news in prime time. But, as with Jackie Robinson in baseball, it hadn't been his racial identity alone that had gotten him the job. Stanford was no James Earl Jones, but he knew what news was. He had come out of the local ranks of the pioneer TV news readers—Clifton Utley, Len O'Connor, Fahey Flynn. Even so, Jimmy knew it lay outside Howard's powers of good taste to treat Stanford like a legend. It was even possible that Stanford was sick of being regarded as one.

So Jimmy had read the script effortlessly and flawlessly, hitting the stopwatch on the nose. "Not bad," Howard had said mildly, and turned to Stanford, who was staring at the control room as if he couldn't believe someone wasn't going to ride out on a white horse and put a silver bullet into this sorry excuse for a news director.

"See how easy it is?" Howard had barked at him. "Now, do it again, and this time try to forget who you are. The words, Stan, the words. The shortest distance to the viewer is from your mouth to his ear. Reading the news is a no-brainer, Stanford. It's just there, like a punch in the teeth, okay?"

The older man had quivered, then read it, his features rigid, his voice in a vise. Twice he lapsed into a fey kind of sob. And when he was through, he looked up angrily and said, "May I go now?" This time, because he was furious and maybe wanting his dinner, his voice had been like a razor's edge without a nick in it.

"That's it!" Howard had screamed. "Did you hear it? My God, Stanford, you're beautiful when you're mad."

Afterward, the news director had taken Jimmy aside and said wearily, as if he had fought all the wars and birthed all the babies, "Thanks. I knew I could count on you. Stick close and we'll both get what we want."

"Meaning what?" Jimmy had said, for once a little amazed that he couldn't detest the man with some of Stanford's passion.

Howard had put a hand on his arm. "Come and see me tomorrow. We'll talk about it."

Jimmy had tried to see him for three days running and never got close. But a month later he was the regular weekend anchorman, cohosting the show with a succession of young reporters on Howard's tryout list. So far Karen Kohl had not been in the running, and he wondered why. She had done some anchoring in her previous job. What was Howard saving her for, other than his private pleasure?

Now the days were gone when he worried about viewers seeing him on the anchor desk and saying, "That's the Gillespie boy up there, the one whose family was involved in all those terrible killings." He was simply the Saturday and Sunday voice of the "Ten O'clock News," his sole purpose to inform and clarify events by reading the words on the prompter. And the only ones out there who mattered were those who got randomly caught in the crunch, the shooters and muggers, the schemers and grifters, the deliberately subversive and the well-intentioned, all the way from public servants in City Hall to mafiosi in Maywood, on up to and including, at this very moment, the chief of police. Who, perhaps imagining that all he had to do was serve and protect, was innocently coming downstairs to speak his piece and go home, leaving Marlee Roberts to the ages.

7

Howard has dragged Jimmy into the control room to watch Karen Kohl strut her stuff. Howard is strangely excited. He has been on the phone with Karen, and he hints that the chief is about to be deliciously sandbagged. And from the look of her on the screen as she awaits him, Jimmy thinks Karen is just the doll who can do it, God bless her. And God forgive us for the sins we are about to commit in Thy name. Grievous sins, you might say, world without end. Amen.

The TV picture is first rate, despite the fog outside. Jimmy tips back his hat and stares up at the bank of monitors showing a crowd of reporters confronting the chief. He's a good cop, Jerry Davis, appointed only last year after a long career in Traffic, Robbery, Arson, and Personnel. He has a folder full of commendations, some for bravery in the line of duty, and Jimmy wonders if he is about to earn another. He also wonders what Howard wondered earlier, whether the stern-jawed young woman who shoves her way to the front of the pack with her cameraman in tow is the same starry-eyed, distractable person he undertook to break in last fall, whose main talent until now seemed to be screwing Howard.

A hush falls over the Gold Coast as the chief makes his formal announcement: The police are investigating the possibility that Marlee Roberts's death may be homicide. At this time, certain evidence indicates that she did not die by her own hand but was murdered by someone who sought to make it look like suicide.

Why make it look like suicide? The question whips through Jimmy's head and back again, like a boomerang.

The reporters and cameramen lunge at the chief, who looks as if he is about to be clubbed to death by microphones as he heads for his car, saying only, "It's too soon to tell," and suddenly it's over.

Except that his aides have been too busy holding off the bobbing cameras to see what Karen is up to. Leaving her cameraman behind, she gets there first and blocks the chief's path.

"By God, she's doing it!" the news director cries, as if he is witnessing something juicily X-rated, such as the chief's naked, hairy body vised tightly between her unforgiving thighs.

The camera, held aloft, zooms in over the heads of the chief's grim-looking entourage, and Karen says sweetly, "Chief Davis, tell us why you think it's murder," and shoves her mike at Jerry's startled eyes.

Jimmy hears the chief's heavy breathing, which climaxes in a superaudible, almost pornographic expulsion of pent-up air as he huffs explosively into the world's collective ear. "Tell-tale evidence," he grumbles, because he can't very well say nothing at all to such an innocent question. "Clear and unassailable evidence. The nature of the wounds on the body, the condition of the premises. The medical examiner has a lot more to do on this, and we'll have to see what the autopsy shows. I can't be more specific at this time."

He nods in conclusion and even smiles a bit as he ducks his head toward his car, but Karen takes back the microphone and asks, "Has anyone suggested it might be the work of a serial killer?" The chief's eyes widen. He opens his mouth to say something, but she stiffs him with another question. "If that's a possibility, can you tell us why?"

Jerry clears his throat. He seems to have a bad case of laryngitis. "The evidence. The evidence I spoke of. It's similar to—" Someone whispers in his ear. "No, no, there's no evidence whatever of serial crimes. There are a number of other cases we're looking into, that's all I can say." He nods with finality this time, then casts a furious glance at the camera.

She waits. The mike doesn't quiver. Finally the chief continues, now in an almost avuncular tone, as if, besieged by a mere broad, his only choice is to condescend. "Believe me, I wish I could say more. We should have some answers in the morning." He doesn't add "little girl" and he doesn't say "honey." But Karen's eyes narrow and Jimmy thinks: Scapegoat!

"Here it comes!" the news director's shrill voice breaks like a teenager's. His knuckles are white.

Karen's hair and eyes are ebony. Her skin is ivory. She's an orthodox icon, a Greek tragedy starting to unfold. "Chief Davis, how can the department justify withholding evidence of possible serial killings? People have a right to protect themselves. Is that what you call promoting public safety?"

Jerry backs half a step and blinks. "Wait a minute," he roars. "I didn't . . . you said . . ." He is nearly engulfed by the camera as she pursues him relentlessly. He treads water, his blood pounding. Her persistent voice is like the theme music from *Jaws*.

"So what you're telling us, chief, is that a dangerous killer is at large, someone who could possibly strike again at any time, is that right? And the police have chosen to say nothing about it?"

Jimmy thinks, Back to you, Jerry, and God keep us all. The chief's bulging eyes lurk in anguish beneath the decorative gold braid on his visor. His jaw clamps as the purposeful voice of the interviewer insists, "Exactly how long has the department been aware of this menace, Chief Davis?"

He's all alone out there, Jimmy thinks. He's been blindsided. He's angry. And right now he's wondering, Sly little fox, who is she anyway?

Oh, Karen, I didn't see you coming either. I didn't know how good you could be.

The chief's reply, when it comes, is transparently intended to save his ass. "Young lady, it's hard to pick up a pattern until you see it being repeated, if I'm not being too obvious. We still have a lot of work to do. Now if you'll excuse me. . . ." He glances around for assistance, his lips puckered in a feeble attempt at a smile, and the news director giggles like a child.

Karen's dark eyes flash. "But chief, why did three women have to die, one of them an important member of the news community, before the pattern became clear? Aren't the police supposed to see what's happening before it becomes obvious to everybody?"

The chief nods, not at her but off-camera, and from somewhere a gruff voice says, "Please step aside, miss."

The camera is backing away, getting jostled a bit as it gives viewers a wider shot: the car door opening, and

Karen leaning toward Jerry's massive backside as he gets in, gloved hands protecting him, warding her off. She asks sharply, "Can you tell us about the witness—?" but the door shuts firmly, a reminder that the night is cold and not very friendly.

What's happened to the fog? Jimmy wonders. He tries to ignore Howard's fingers gripping his shoulder, Howard's head leaning past him, his exultant expression.

The car pulls away. Karen turns brightly to the camera, making a few brisk remarks that seem oddly inappropriate. Too brisk, and better left unsaid because they're about Marlee. The end of Marlee, the very last.

But then she does something that seems impossible to plan or to fake. In the middle of a sentence, very delicately, she chokes, sending out a little trail of white vapor. It comes floating upward as if signalling the death of a pope. Or the election of a pope, Jimmy can't remember. He hasn't been to mass since high school except when somebody died.

Karen's eyes are suddenly filled with tears. Real tears! She says quietly, in that deeply saddened Lady Macbeth contralto you'd never believe was there if you hadn't heard it, "All of us at Channel 2 News loved Marlee Roberts," and chokes again, ever so slightly. And it's as if she has told her audience of maybe half a million viewers, I love you all, each one of you—just like Michael Jackson. And it's amazing, because all at once, with her white-on-white skin and dark eyes and coal-black hair, for an instant *she looks just like him.*

Quickly, she sends everyone back to a program already in progress, a couple of gawky Alaskans trudging through the endless snow, trying to explain something to each other, and Howard rises and claps his hands. "Yes!" he cries, throwing a fist into the otherwise subdued, almost stifling quiet of the control room. "Yes! She did it!"

He clutches Jimmy's arm just above the elbow as they leave. "Did you see how she got the drop on the top cop, made him sweat and kept her cool? And the tears—can you believe this? I knew it, I knew it, she's a natural!" He is walking fast. "Get her in here right now. Do this for me. I want her on the anchor desk with Stanford when we go on." Jimmy feels the news director's hand on his back now, not quite pressing him, not quite daring to shove. "Do it, Jimmy. Now."

Jimmy turns and stares. "We air in fifteen minutes."

"Tell them to put her in a cab. Go!"

Jimmy goes, and as he does so hears Howard say to the executive producer, "Shoot it wide, wider than usual. There's going to be an empty chair between Karen and Stanford. I want a soft spot on it. Intro from Stanford. I'll get something written so he'll know what to say."

"What about Karen?" the producer asks. "Will she know?"

"She'd better. She's on her own. Now go and explain it to everybody."

Twelve minutes to go, and Jimmy is on the phone at the assignment desk, telling the truck what to do, when, as if a trap door has been sprung on a gallows, Stanford's face slams down on the anchor desk. The sound is like that of an unabridged dictionary falling from a considerable height. Fierce winds seem to blow through the newsroom, immobilizing everybody. Then people begin moving and shouting, and an improvised tag team starts working on Stanford.

"What's the ruckus?" the voice on the phone inquires.

"Stanford's fainted," Jimmy replies. "But don't panic. Howard's here."

8

Howard dragged Jimmy into his office past a thoroughly alarmed Dorothy. "You killed him. You killed Stanford!" she cried, and "She won't make it. She won't get here on time, you wait and see!"

But by the time Howard had poured them a couple of drinks, there the two anchors were up on the wall, in a wide opening shot showing the spotlighted, forlornly empty chair between them: a hastily recoiffed Karen, a bit pop-eyed but fresh as the dew, and a distinctly woozy Stanford, who was heard to murmur as the familiar Victory-in-Space theme music ground to a halt, "I'm ready."

From Howard's fatuous smile of approval as the show got under way, Jimmy concluded that nothing could stop Karen now. She was flawless as she recounted the evening's events, Marlee's supposed suicide, Marlee's almost certain murder, and more to come: the possibility of a serial killer on the Near North Side. Stanford's performance lacked its usual exactitude. Looking a little cock-eyed, he made several miscues, mispronouncing a couple of everyday words and twice stepping on Karen's lines. But for a man who had been blindsided by stress he was doing amazingly well. If his skills had temporarily left him, his long experience had not. Once the camera caught him staring down at the empty chair. It held on him for a full five seconds until he looked up, realized he was on, and said mildly, "Pardon me, please. Some things you don't forget." The moment might have been planned.

Viewers could only have warmed to Stanford, he looked so stricken. And they must have seen Karen not as intrusive but as Marlee's rightful emissary in the land of the living, her vicar here below. Hadn't she taken on the chief of police in Marlee's behalf? And hadn't she said it for all of them, how much Marlee was loved, and with tears in her eyes? Tears that, on tonight's special hour-long edition of the "Ten O'clock News," still welled up every now and then?

Though Howard insisted that nothing was settled, that Karen would stay on for only one week and then he would decide, Jimmy had no doubt that she would be up there from now on, her expression one of permanent surprise, her smile hard as diamonds, the most sentimental of rocks, her tears turned on or off at will. As the taped tributes to Marlee were rolled, and the taped highlights of her career, he felt his resentment growing. Why, he asked himself, should the keeper of the flame be someone who has known Marlee for less than six months? And isn't it ironic that Karen wouldn't even be here if it weren't for me?

The vehemence of his feelings surprised him, and as the weatherman, in predicting the likelihood of snow on Christmas Day, got in a passing reference to Ebenezer Scrooge, he wondered if he was being fair. Marlee's replacement was bound to be a female, that was preordained, so why not Karen? He studied her reaction as the sportscaster lobbed a mild witticism to Stanford. She looked straight at the camera, let her eyes grow wide, and set her teeth in a show-window smile. It wasn't Marlee's knowing, half-amused gaze, but the sportscaster seemed reassured. Jimmy was startled by what she had just done, it was that good. It was the look of a well-bred young woman who has been goosed at a country club dance and is determined not to show it, no matter what it takes. It implied neither approval nor disapproval. And best of all, it worked.

"Yeah," he told Howard as the show went to commercials, "she's doing great. Howard?"

"Yes?"

"One thing bothers me."

"I know. She hates Stanford. Do you think it shows?"

"No, I mean about the interview. With the chief."

"Too rough for you? I know he's a friend."

"Well, he didn't deserve it, but no, I mean the part about the serial killer."

Howard nearly sprang from his chair in animated protest. "Hey," he said, grinning broadly, "that was great! That was all ours."

"Great or what," Jimmy said, "I want to know where she got it. Nobody out there told her. The chief didn't tip her. He didn't want to talk about it, practically denied it. So where did she get it?"

Howard drained his martini. "She didn't say anything to you?"

"She didn't say anything to anybody. I checked with the guys on the truck. It was news to them. The producer said he got a call from the *Tribune* afterward, asking him where it came from."

Howard got up to replenish his drink. "You've been in on all her assignments. You ought to know."

"I know it, but she's said nothing. Zip." Jimmy was drinking Scotch and smoking one of his father's cigars, a first-rate medium-size Corona. Dutch kept them on hand for distinguished guests who never came around any more, so whenever Jimmy went out to see him he carefully removed one from its cedar-lined box, precisely for occasions like this.

Howard came back and sat down. "Okay then, we'll ask her. Not tonight, tomorrow. The general manager wants to take her to lunch. You come, too. Afterward, we'll ask her." He glanced at Jimmy. "Don't bring it up in front of the g.m. Let's keep it tight right now."

"What for?" Jimmy stared back, letting out a curl of creamy smoke. "You know, don't you?" He sat up straight. "You talked to her before the interview. She told you, didn't she?"

Howard looked away, giggling, and smiled down into his drink. "Well, let's not make too much of this. All I knew was she had something hot and wanted to go ahead with it. I told her to use her own judgment. See if the chief fell in with it, that was the setup she had in mind. If he did, we had something big. If he didn't, nothing lost." He looked at Jimmy. "Turned out, he did and we did."

And you're off the hook either way, Jimmy thought, because you didn't ask her what it was. "So where did she get it?"

Howard shrugged. "Oh, she said something about digging into a couple of cases in her spare time. She checked them out with the cops and worked out her own conclusions. Just theories really. So when the chief came on the scene, it was there in the back of her mind."

"What cases?"

"You'll have to ask her that."

Stanford was doing the sign-off now, one last word about the empty chair. As he said good night, Howard laughed and glanced over at his companion. "My God, Jimmy, lighten up! Let's drink to Karen."

"Marlee," Jimmy said, putting down the cigar and picking up his Scotch. "Tonight let's just drink to Marlee."

The general manager's lunch the following day was full of lighthearted celebration, with a few solemn asides in Marlee's memory. Jimmy thought it was odd that Stanford wasn't there. Inexcusable really, because the high spirits had less to do with Karen's sudden ascent than with the overnight ratings. Channel 2 News, which for months had lagged far behind the competition, had zoomed ahead, and the g.m. was ecstatic. He leaned forward, lights bouncing off his head. His Baldness, Dorothy called him. Mr. Big.

"Keep it up," the g.m. said, eyeing Karen and then Howard. "Keep it up."

"We will," Howard said, grinning.

"Good. How?"

There was a stunned silence, which Jimmy sought to fill. "Well, one thing we don't want is a repeat. We'll have to come up with something completely different."

The g.m. stared at him, puzzled, then gave him a searching look. Howard turned his attention to the overhead lighting.

Back in his office, taking off his jacket, Howard said, "I'm going to forget you said that, buddy," and sat down behind his desk, yawning.

"So am I," Jimmy said. He looked at Karen. "I got a call from Kirk this morning. He wants some information."

"About what?" she asked.

"Your serial killer."

Howard said, "Kirk?"

"Sergeant Kirkpatrick, Violent Crimes. He's in charge of the case." He returned to Karen. "He wants to know where you got it."

"Was he very upset?"

"Hard to tell. He found it curious last night that everything he was thinking you were thinking."

Karen looked down at her crossed ankles, very smooth in silk or whatever passed for silk, very trim. "Okay, but it's really you asking." She looked up. "You're sore because I didn't fill you in."

Jimmy looked at Howard, and Howard, plainly impatient to get this over with, said, "Jimmy's supposed to be told what you're working on in the field at all times, you know that, Karen. Come on, put it out on the table. Let's get on to other things."

A little indignantly, Karen said, "Well, I haven't been trying to keep any secrets!" She shrugged. "I got interested in these two cases, that's all. They weren't news so it wasn't worth mentioning. And it was all on my own time, most of it."

Jimmy said, "Why these two cases?"

"I knew them. Slightly. I guess, in a way, they were . . . friends. Kind of."

"And they just happened to be the same two cases Kirk picked up on?"

Her ivory skin turned sunset pink. "I didn't know that, not until later." Then her indignation spilled over. "Oh, tell him to ask his partner! Ginko, you know Ginko. He likes me." She shot a glance at Howard, who was all attention now. "We're buddies. I told him about them and Ginko filled me in, and then he let it drop that Kirk had his suspicions."

"So why didn't it come out at that point?" Howard asked.

"Because, Howard, nobody really had anything to go on, not until last night."

Jimmy said, "That they weren't really suicides."

She nodded. "Same thing as Marlee. I found Ginko last night in Marlee's building, and he said that's what Kirk was thinking."

"Because of the wounds."

"Wounds, blood, the whole shot." She looked around the room, then at Howard. "You have a cigarette?" Startled, Jimmy looked at him, too.

Howard, somewhat abashed, opened a desk drawer and fished out an open pack of Camels. He brought it over to Karen and then sat down beside Jimmy on the couch.

Jimmy said, "You guys smoke?"

"No," Karen said. "Howard doesn't. I don't either. Except once in a while, I . . ." She broke off to light up, then changed the subject. "It wasn't exactly like Marlee. These two girls had plenty of reason to kill themselves. I was almost sure they had, at the time."

"Killed themselves why?" Jimmy asked.

"Unhappy. You know, very unhappy. No money, poor housing, ill health. Emotionally damaged from childhood, probably beyond repair. On drugs. Prescription drugs. Antidepressants, anti-everything. Not girls either. One was older than I am."

"Friends, you say?"

She said coldly, "Is that so unheard of? I met them, I found them . . . sort of interesting. They dressed well, seemed normal enough at first. Well, the first one did. And then she introduced me to her friend, and I said, 'This can't be right.' Her friend was obviously a weirdo. I stayed clear of her. Then Clara—that's the first one I met, the one who introduced me to the others—she set me straight. She told me all the bad news, how sick she was, and how poverty-stricken. She's the older one. She wasn't ashamed of it. She needed help, that's all, just to eat. And then I got to thinking, you know, I could do a documentary. On lost people. Not missing, not homeless. Just lost. Why not? But with one thing or another, I just kept postponing it. My divorce, and . . ." Another look at Howard. "Anyway, I didn't bother to tell you about them. I wasn't hiding anything."

"And then there were none."

"They died last fall, about a month apart. Not Clara. This friend of hers, and the weirdo." She looked down at her ankles. "To tell you the truth, it was Clara gave me the idea. She was sure they'd been murdered and she was scared. She still is." She looked at Jimmy. "It could have been suicide, who knows? So far it's just a theory."

He said, "So basically you agree with the chief's position. You put the screws to him last night just for kicks."

Howard said, "You're straying. . . ."

"No," Karen said, "it's relevant." She stubbed out the cigarette and glanced at Howard. "Just for kicks, yes, I suppose. And for good old Channel Two News."

"And so what's your feeling now, about what's happened?" Jimmy said. "Three murders, one killer?"

"That's a possibility. Clara thinks that. She even thinks she knows who killed them. You talked to Kirkpatrick, what does he say?"

"He thinks it's a possibility. Has he talked to this Clara?"

Karen let a moment go by. "I don't know."

"Don't you think you should find out? If she thinks she knows who killed them—"

"She doesn't know. It's her fears. She's afraid of . . . everything!" There were tears in Karen's eyes, and Jimmy thought, My God, just like last night. Only who had she really been weeping over, herself or Marlee? And who were the tears for now?

Howard said, "Okay, that's it, let's call a halt. Karen, the Clara thing could be important whether she knows anything or not. I mean, exclusive interview, right? With the woman who knew the other two?"

"Right. I guess."

"So does that clear the air?" He turned to Jimmy. "That do it for you? It's getting late, pal. We got to cover the news."

Jimmy said, "I think I should take over Clara at this point. Make sure Kirk knows about her and follow up."

"Fine. Karen will put you in touch." He gave her a big grin as they all stood up. "Okay? Ready for tonight? Another big show?"

"As I'll ever be," she said, grinning back. She turned away and began applying lipstick.

Going out, Jimmy said to her, "I wasn't too hard on you, was I?" and she gave him a peck on the cheek. He left her and Howard smiling absurdly at each other in front of the couch, its black leather glistening, smiling up, too, maybe for old times' sake.

Karen. She was conducting herself like a seasoned pro, but once or twice he had seen a glimmer of self-doubt. Was it possible that there were times she felt frightened of . . . just everything?

9

Jimmy passed along the word about Clara Turner to Detective Kirkpatrick, along with her phone number and a word of caution about her possibly fragile state of mind. On the phone, it was hard to tell how interested Kirk was. He seemed more concerned with the source of the information.

"How did they meet?"

"I don't know."

"You're slipping, Gillespie. Time you got back to work before you forget how. Where did she come up with her serial killer last night? I want the truth."

"Partly Clara's idea, partly yours."

"Mine?"

"She and Ginko were shooting the shit one day."

"He told her? That Polish blabbermouth. It's a crime he learned to speak English."

"It could happen only in America."

"She should have talked to me. I would have told her it's none of her business what I think until I say it is."

"She wasn't planning to use it. It just slipped out when she saw the chief's beady little eyes."

"Yeah, and then media-fried his beady little brain. Is that how people move up in your business, by being the worst they can be? How can you expect us to be straight with you after a thing like that?"

"Because Channel Two's the only game in town."

"Not any more, you're not. She's on my list."

"We're number one in the overnights."

"Tell her to enjoy it while she can. I'll be down there one of these days to talk to her. I want to know where she was at five o'clock."

"Kirk, be serious."

"You too, Gillespie. We're going to look at everybody in the place. Who knows? It could be an inside job." Jimmy couldn't believe what he was hearing. It sounded like Trivial Pursuit II: The Chief Strikes Back. "We'll try not to take too much of your time."

By stretching his imagination a little, Jimmy could see how it was with Kirkpatrick. Play rough with one of them, all the boys in blue woke up the next morning with bruises. As for Karen, he thought he understood her, too. Maybe her ambition was a bit unbridled, but he had been touched by her reaching out to the women she called lost, exposing her emotions by just that much. Exposing some vulnerability, too.

Stop it, he told himself. Don't go down that path.

He was remembering his first impressions of Karen last fall, when he took her under his wing: bright, quick, almost too attractive for her own good, and his. Embarrassing now, recalling how gaily he had introduced her to Kirk and his partner: "Karen Kohl, the firemen's friend, every cop's dream of what all police reporters will look like some day." She didn't mind. She wasn't a feminist exactly, not when it came to fitting herself into a new job. But Kirk must have thought he was drunk. He ignored her. She and Ginko, though, hit it off right away.

After work, for three nights running, Jimmy ran her by the tavern, where she schmoozed with the newspaper crowd. He even took her out to meet Dutch one September afternoon. His father was entranced by her quick-eyed beauty. In a mood to entertain, he led her on a walk around the park across the street, where the autumn leaves and high prairie grasses soon had her insisting they do a feature on the place. Jimmy demurred. "We don't want the whole world coming out here," he told her, and Dutch, catching his drift, fell uncharacteristically silent. She must have known about the Gillespie family tragedy, but hadn't yet made a connection with the park. No need to mention that this was also a place of death and rude memories.

But something about her caught and held that afternoon. Maybe just seeing her, fresh and alluring, against the background of his faraway youth and all that had happened later, like envisioning a new start in the very place where things had gone bad, wiping out the sorry past of dead leaves and gray skies, and replacing it with something refreshingly new.

Whatever it was, against his better judgment he had allowed himself to wonder what it might be like, making love to her. Bad news, he knew, because there she was, a newly married lady already fooling around with Howard. Getting entangled like that could only play out one way. And then, in her first month on the job, the topper: her sudden divorce, still not final. Her husband had wangled a transfer to Indianapolis and left town. The split had nothing to do with Howard, apparently. He appeared to be genuinely surprised, and all at once had begun acting very married.

Perhaps feeling bereft by the failure of her marriage, Karen had turned to Jimmy. Once, waiting in a car for some detectives to show up, they had discussed the pitfalls of early weddings and divorce and wound up holding hands, like children, only his knuckles rested on her hipbone. He could feel her belly rise and fall with her breathing. It had shaken him, rattled him, getting that close to her.

A few nights later, his gonads doing a hot little dance, he called her from the office, where he'd been working late, going over old tapes for a documentary. "I thought I might stop by on my way home," he said. "We could talk about it."

There was a short silence. "Well," she said, "come by if you want to, but don't expect to be entertained. I'm doing an article proposal for *Cosmo,* and I want it to go out first thing in the morning." She had done a few pieces for *Philadelphia* magazine and at least once a week sent off a query to some national publication, so far without success.

"Maybe I can help."

"I doubt it. It's about lonely women."

"In whom," he said, "I am well versed."

She laughed and told him her door would be unlocked. He found her at her computer in the spare bedroom. She was in a commodious flannel robe, with her hair wrapped in a towel and her face, when she looked up, creamed and shiny. Impulsively, he leaned down and buried his face in an enticing arc of skin between neck and shoulder.

"Don't *do* that," she wailed. "I can't be distracted," then swiveled her office-style chair around and, as he straightened up, looked him over. Suddenly, with a playful, Christmas-morning smile, she reached out and grabbed his rigid cock, which he had somehow been unaware of until her fingers closed around it. Had he walked all the way from the studio like that?

They fell into the unmade bed vacated by her husband and she drove him wild encasing him in rubber. He entered her in a rush and she cried, "Stop, we can't do this!" He expected her to mention Howard, but she said, "If we do, I'll fall asleep, and I'll never get that proposal in the mail."

He looked down at her, thinking she must be out of her mind. Then he quickly withdrew, getting up on his knees.

"Wow!" she said, staring. But it wasn't a comment on his manhood, its size or throbbing intensity. Rather it was an expression of her amazement that he had been so unselfish as to unimpale her in the midst of his pleasure. Yeah, Jimmy thought, why did I do that?

She returned to her computer and Jimmy went home. Every now and then he wondered why, in her gratitude that night, she had not found an alternative way to reward him. He decided it simply had not occurred to her. Or maybe she wanted his sacrificial act to be complete. Did she always demand entire compliance? Had she driven her husband batty this way?

In any case, she didn't speak of it, or of *Cosmo*, and nothing like that had occurred since. She seemed to have put all of her energies into making herself a bankable talent, and he was not about to dilute them.

Hey, he told himself, don't take that path either. She didn't invent the rules of the game.

The truth was he was just plain pissed. It still irked him that she had beaten him to the anchor desk, especially since he helped pave the way. At the same time, he felt a kind of blind admiration: He had never known anyone to rise so far so fast.

So where had she come from, this vulnerable, slim-limbed predator he was responsible for bringing to

Chicago? Why, from a place he had never visited before last spring: Wilkes-Barre, Pennsylvania. W-B PA.

That was what really rankled him. If his younger brother hadn't decided to get married, he would never have stopped off in Wilkes-Barre on his way to New York, or seen the leaf in the window or met Kathleen, and there might never have been a Karen Kohl at all. Simple as that, and as irrevocable.

There it was again, that old devil predestination.

Jimmy had stayed in Wilkes-Barre just long enough to meet Raymond's fiancée and to let his brother know that yes, though they had been born of different mothers ten years apart, they did have a special relationship and yes, he would always be there for him in times of need. Getting engaged, however, didn't seem to be one of those times. The wedding would not take place until the following March, but Raymond and Gwendolyn had already made the adjustment. They were living together in Cambridge, Massachusetts, where they both would graduate from law school shortly after the wedding. They had received offers from firms in New York City, the ultimate legal maze, he from a sprawling corporate firm in Manhattan and she from a nonprofit environmental outfit across the Brooklyn Bridge. Incredibly, they already had their eye on a two-bedroom apartment in Brooklyn Heights.

So what, he asked himself, am I here for? Ah, what indeed.

Well, it was the beginning of May, sunny but cool, a tumultuous Pennsylvania greening against which Gwendolyn Beckham stood out like a sturdy spring flower. She was just what his brother had said, an attractive, level-headed blonde, and from a family that outnumbered even the Gillespies, though only about half of them were on hand.

Like Raymond, she was the youngest, with eight brothers and sisters, most of them married and all, it seemed, a shade bigger and bolder. Like Raymond, she was lean as a rail, lifting and swinging her sisters' kids like sacks of meal or big loaves of bread, as athletic and taffy-haired as a Viking. Like him, she had lost a parent years before when her father had died. The Beckham kids had practically raised themselves, but under the steady gaze of a mother who, these days at least, gave every indication of believing that this, more or less, was the way life turned out for everybody.

If the Beckhams weren't Irish, they were at least from the same corner of the globe, England and Wales, and, like the Gillespies, they were Catholic. They didn't go to the big church at the end of the block, its creamy bulk banded in alternating light and dark marble, its broad dome golden against the blue Pennsylvania sky, but to a newer one over the hill behind the house where the wedding would be, its siding painted a blinding white, like the snowy whiteness of nuns' garb, the whiteness of geese.

The Beckham house rose from its hollow like a stately, dove-gray Mississippi paddlewheeler churning downriver between bluffs. Jimmy was given a small third-floor bedroom whose windows looked out from beneath a four-sided Dutch gambrel roof, the kind the seemed to characterize every fourth house in Wilkes-Barre. The room was crammed with books that trailed down off the shelves into stacks on the floor and then onto more shelving in the hallway. It had a distant view of the mountains, rounded and rugged as the backs of wild ponies but too small, he was told, to be the Poconos, and too far north to be the

Greens or the Whites, so what were they? He settled for Appalachian. Pleased to be in the thick of a big family again, he sank into a narrow bed as deep and engulfing as a passing thunderhead and slept extra hours.

The second morning, with Gwendolyn and Raymond already off to the outlying shopping malls, he decided to run downtown. Tight-packed houses kept him from seeing much of the mountains, just as their green flanks concealed what lay there: deep below, played-out mines that for nearly a century had made Wilkes-Barre a booming source of anthracite and, on the surface, stripmining scars that for the past three decades had marked the region's decline.

If the town languished, its houses looked shipshape and its hilly residential streets suggested an eternal busyness. Like restless, eager shoppers, the streets rose and fell topsy-turvy in every direction, lugging their houses like packages under both arms, until, gasping for breath, they stopped dead at the top of Hazel Street, on the edge of a precipice with no place to go.

There they were, the bordering mountains in the far distance, with the rest of Wilkes-Barre clustered here and there on the slopes of the great river basin. Directly below, the land seemed to have been quarried flat into a broad-bottomed reservoir holding railyards and manufacturing and, off where Jimmy supposed the river ran, an uninspiring clutch of church spires and midsize business towers.

Two decades before, one June, the Susquehanna, bored by flowing endlessly to Chesapeake Bay, had sought other avenues of expression. Thousands were evacuated, and downtown Wilkes-Barre, Gwen's mother said, had steeped for days in its dark brew. Then, as if by magic, the waters disappeared, leaving a massive cleanup. At the time, it was the country's worst nonmilitary disaster. These two monu-

mental withdrawals, the quickly ebbing flood and the ago-
nizingly slow departure of the coal fields, seemed to sym-
bolize the city's sense of loss and its lowered expectations.

Since the rest of Hazel Street seemed to have vanished,
too, Jimmy took Park Avenue for half a mile and then a
concrete slab of a bridge that was unadorned and massive
enough to have made Josef Stalin proud. Coming off it, he
sat for a while watching basketball practice in the high
school gym where Gwen and her brothers and sisters had
played, loading up their living room with team trophies.
Then, trotting again, he cut between two stalwart churches
and through a parking lot, slowing to a walk at Main Street,
and that's when he looked up and saw the leaf.

It was right at eye level in a bookstore window, a large
post-oak leaf curled at the edges, pale brown streaked with
vivid red, like an October sunset. But the autumn colors
were shiny and he saw that they had been painted on. He
concluded that the leaf had been hammered out of metal
and must be for sale.

He decided he had to have it. Not only because it was
like those he used to sail on a pond as a kid, but because it
was painted. This made it like something out of his dreams.

When he was ten, having sailed hundreds of leaf boats in
the pond a few blocks from home—oak leaves like this one
that lumbered out like unwieldy treasure ships, sometimes
floundering on dangerous shoals, and willow leaves that
darted here and there like sleek racing hulls—he wondered
how it might be to race an entire fleet in all different colors.
Painted leaves? Why not? So he had daubed one red, just to
see. But too impatient to wait for it to dry, he had put it
down on the water and watched, aghast, as the oils spread
out around it in a luminous slick. Dismayed at the prospect
of fouling the pond, where tiny transluscent bluegill hov-

ered amongst the algae, he had ended the experiment.

Even in his twenties, whenever he visited the pond and the wind was right, he would put a few leaves on the water and watch them sail out. Not now, though, not since his sister's death. How could he? Her body had been found in the pond.

10

The young woman in the bookstore looked like a mere slip of a girl. She wore a red-patterned, full-pleated dress with old-fashioned puff sleeves and starched cuffs that barely left room for her delicate wrists. But she was far from tiny, and not the least bit shy. With her pleasurable abundance of red hair, a smile that glowed like her skin, and a voice that came from the diaphragm, she obviously wasn't one to be trifled with. Moreover, she was busy, getting ready for customers.

"Yes?" She sounded friendly, but daring him to waste her time. She was married, Jimmy could see that from the sizeable rock on her finger, even as she was telling him the leaf wasn't for sale.

So he told her about the leaf boats and she said, "Oh, well then, take it. I only painted them as decorations. They're from my yard."

This took him aback. "You mean it's real?"

She laughed. "Which one do you want?"

It turned out that there were half a dozen leaves in the window, moored among the books. He picked out the first one he had noticed. While she found a box for it, so it wouldn't be crushed, she told him she owned two stores, this one and another in one of the malls, that she was worried about making a success of the business, that her mother helped behind the counter and her husband, an investment banker, kept the books and that when she got a minute of spare time from her two preschoolers, she did paintings like those on the walls, cloud shapes that merged and drifted as if weather, good or bad, was all there was. To prove it, she gave him a card that said Kathleen Reilly, Paintings & Books.

Jimmy gave her his card in return, and she said, "How about that? My cousin's in television. She's moving to Chicago as soon as she gets married. Can you find her a job?"

He said that might be a problem unless she was something special, and Kathleen said, "Oh, she's very good. She's been anchoring the news in Philadelphia for three months. The only reason she's leaving is the guy she's marrying has a new job out there."

Jimmy said, "Tell her to call me. I'll be glad to give her some names."

"Oh, thank you. She'll really be pleased."

Several other customers came in, and then her two tiny kids, a boy and a girl, towing their grandparents. Jimmy hung around for a while, selecting one of the paintings and a couple of books. He told her he'd stop by in the morning to pick them up, along with the leaf. "Oh, good," she said. "That'll give me time to look for her card." She had to prompt him. "My cousin, remember?"

"Oh, that's all right. Just tell her to get in touch."

"Yeah, okay," she said, turning to a customer. "She's good at that."

One of Gwendolyn's sisters, the one who had flown in

from Denver, took a look at the card and said, "Reilly. I'm not sure I know her, but I remember her husband. He's a dreamboat."

The next morning, Raymond drove him to the airport, first stopping by the store so that he could collect his purchases. Jimmy was on his way back to the car when Kathleen came running after him. "Mr. Gillespie," she called out, "I found her card."

He waited. She was in red again, something he could never seem to describe afterward but which appeared to gather her up like one of her cloud-shapes and hurl her toward him. In the morning sun, she was dazzling.

He took the card and said matter-of-factly, "You certainly are gorgeous."

She laughed, startled, and backed away. Hesitated, as though about to say something, then turned and went quickly up the sidewalk.

"Redheads," Raymond said as he got into the car. "You always hang out with redheads." He started the engine and headed back toward the highway.

"Well," Jimmy said, "it seems to run in my part of the family," by which he meant that his sister Patricia had red hair so luxurious it had been compared to their mother's, which he had never seen except in photographs, she having died when he was born. Emily and Hope, the other two girls, and then Raymond, had come along after Dutch remarried. None of them had had red hair. "Anyway, this one's happily married and a thousand miles from home. Besides, I just said something stupid."

He glanced down at the card. Karen Kohl, it said. Not Irish. German, like the former chancellor. A transplanted fräulein, probably pudgy and heavy-hammed. Who looked out at her viewers and said, "You will watch the news." Or would she be like her cousin, fiery, with a smile that lit her up and left you wondering whether it was sunrise or sunset?

Raymond said, "Do you require my legal services?"

"No. All I did was tell her she looked great. I think I embarrassed her."

"Oho!" Raymond said. "You ought to know better than that. Wilkes-Barre girls are pretty uptight about compliments from strangers, especially if they're married. It's the old Catholic impasse: Don't do it, and don't even think it."

Jimmy looked at him. "You think she thought it?"

"Looked like it to me."

Back in Chicago, he wrote Kathleen a brief note. Liked the painting, liked the leaf. Liked meeting her. "Hope the bookstores prosper, hope to see you again," he wrote, and added, "sometime." Wouldn't want her to get the wrong idea, make her feel guilty. Then, to make sure she didn't, he added a postscript. "Hope you weren't offended by my remark on the sidewalk. I guess it was dumb. But it was well-intended, and it was true."

He didn't expect a reply. But a few weeks later, a package arrived in the mail. Another leaf, and a note saying, "I don't think what you said was dumb. I thought about it, and I thought, Well, maybe I am after all! Anyway, thanks. There aren't that many nice people in the world any more." Somehow that sounded a little sad.

He sent a thank-you postcard, and that was it. But he thought about her whenever he looked at the painting. It glowed, like her skin, like her hair.

When Karen Kohl arrived with her new husband late in the summer, he was somewhat disappointed. This fräulein was well-groomed and lithe and movie-star beautiful, and she said all the right things, so she would probably do well in the interviews he had lined up. She was also half-Irish. But her long coal-black hair seemed to underscore a cool detachment, toward him and toward her husband as well. Very determined, very professional. Cases like this, he told himself, you have to watch yourself. You have to know what's really there before you start wondering how far they can go.

11

Not far, the detective was muttering to himself. "As my old man used to say, 'About as far as time, God, stupid mistakes, and ambition will allow.' "

That's how far Kirkpatrick saw himself moving up in the department. This time, for instance, he seemed to have bitten off more than God was going to let him chew. The medical examiner had turned cagey, yielding only as much as he figured the commander in charge of Violent Crimes was going to need just to keep him safely out on a limb. Murder? No problem. But serial murder? Good luck, Art. As far as the first two victims were concerned, the examiner had balked, adding to his findings of suicide only the Machiavellian disclaimer that the evidence permitted argument. Which might have been enough had the captain been less nervous. The trouble with Art was that he'd spent most of his career in Property Crimes and truly didn't feel comfortable with deadly violence.

The other problem, Kirkpatrick thought as he sat in a spare office going over his notes, was that he had no richly endowed suspects. He had his eye on two possibles. The doorman, who didn't look like the type, and an old boyfriend of the victim's who didn't have a discernible motive. No, the wounds that had cried out were now strangely silent, and there were no other witnesses. What he needed was another kind of miracle.

Still, he had been fortunate, running into the boyfriend. It had happened at a hockey game about a year ago, back when he hardly knew who Marlee Roberts was.

The sergeant had been at the Stadium with his wife, waiting for the game to start, when all at once the stands around them had gone silent. He had glanced up higher to see a spectacular looking woman, great gobs of auburn hair trailing over her broad shoulders, attired in soft colorful layers of this and that, fine woolens and strands of silk. With a certain look of amusement in her warm brown eyes, she was watching the man moving along the aisle toward her, a big guy dressed—you should pardon the expression—to kill. Sports coat, turtleneck with gold chains, and riding boots. His sleek dark hair and arrogant, steely eyes made him look Latin to Kirkpatrick, kind of a king of the pampas. At least he looked far out of town.

His wife had whispered, "That's Marlee Roberts."

He'd had to think for a minute. "Oh, the newscaster. Who's that with her?"

"Where?" She'd had to crane her neck. "Oh, him! I don't know, but aren't they something? I just never pictured her going out with somebody like that."

"Like what?"

"So elegant. They look like real celebrities."

She did. He looked like either an elegant stud or a standard-issue nickel-and-dime con artist. The sergeant was curious, so he asked around later. It turned out the man was a wealthy boat dealer from Miami. Kirkpatrick had put his name and numbers into the hopper for Narcotics to surveil, but nothing ever came of it.

After the murder he had asked some detectives he knew in the Metro-Dade homicide bureau in Miami to look him up. The guy spent half his time in Chicago but apparently was on home turf when Roberts was killed. He said he was out in his boat, which as an alibi struck Kirkpatrick as the Miami version of going to the movies. In any case, nobody looked any better as the deceased's mystery guest than Florida's most eligible bachelor, which he could have been if he didn't have a wife and kids squirreled away on Key Largo.

Nothing at all came up when friends and neighbors and relatives—Roberts had a brother in the northwest suburbs—were asked about a possible motive. Unless a woman who allowed footloose, wealthy family men to pursue her was also into concealing illegal drugs for them, Marlee Roberts lived just the way she looked, and the adjectives that came to mind were wholesome, active, and hardworking. She certainly knew lots of sporting types, though, skiers mostly, and saw them in and out of season. Her friends mentioned weekends in Vail or workouts at the health club they all frequented, down by the river.

Most of her colleagues at Channel 2 either didn't work out much or else went swimming at the Y or jogging in the park. Three of those who did belong to Roberts's health club interested Kirkpatrick vaguely. They all seemed tied into the matter of finding or becoming Roberts's successor on the nightly news, and like her, they all lived roughly Near North. None of them had much of an alibi for the time of death, either, which the examiner had graciously put at around five o'clock. Not that they were likely suspects. They were just interesting.

The female reporter—let's see, the name was Karen Kohl—was temporarily taking Roberts's place, probably because she had whacked the chief in the televised interview that should never have happened. Monday had been her day off, and she'd been working out at the club when it happened. She went there a lot, and looked it.

Her boss, the news director, didn't. He said he had gone home early in the afternoon to fix dinner for his wife and kids, who were at an after-school Christmas pageant. But, just like a guy with a III after his name, he had dozed off, waking up with only enough time to take a hike down the block for a pizza and come home and whip up a salad. He looked harmless, but the way he wiggled his eyes when he smiled was kind of scary.

The other one Kirkpatrick knew. Jimmy Gillespie, a sad case on account of his family history, the big murder case in the suburbs. When he wasn't working or sleeping, he was either at the health club or up along North Avenue at a journalists' hangout, which is where he had gone about 6:30 on the night Roberts was killed, he said, when he couldn't stand watching the early news bulletins. But it was his day off, too, and so he had still been home at the time of the murder. So he said.

Not that any of this mattered. But wasn't it interesting that they all lived up around there, Kohl right across the street, Gillespie a few blocks away on Lake Shore Drive and the news director not far from the tavern Gillespie wound up at, and all of them off-duty with no one to corroborate their stories except the girl. Kohl was observed at the club at about that time.

Not much by way of alibis in the first two killings either. The one on Clark Street, Gillespie was supposedly at work. The other one on Pine Grove, the girl reporter said she had called in sick and wasn't answering her phone, so she was returning the taped calls around the time of death. A couple of her callers confirmed that. The news director said just put it down that he worked all the time, he really didn't recall. So far that seemed to check out. Kirkpatrick could care less, the guy was such a pain in the butt.

The detective got up and strolled out into the nearly empty work area, where his current partner, a sallow-faced young fellow of forty called Ginko instead of his almost unpronouncable Polish name was catching up on paperwork. "The lieutenant wants you," Ginko said, looking up.

"Why didn't you tell me?"

"No, I mean it looks like he does." Ginko nodded down the room past Kirkpatrick, who swung around and saw the lieutenant cha-chaing toward them, one finger beckoning.

"The commander got a call," the lieutenant said in his best *Beverly Hills Cop* manner, "from the medical examiner. It looks like Eddie don't want to get caught bothering you with his suspicions." Yeah, Kirkpatrick thought, why should the examiner talk to me? I'm just saving his ass for him. "Come on," the lieutenant said, "we'll talk about it."

The sergeant and his partner followed him into the captain's office, which was only a little bigger than the lieutenant's but had three windows, two behind the desk and one on the side. The lieutenant shut the door and the captain stood up.

"How's it going?" he said, hitching up his pants, his idea of an indirect approach to a sticky subject. The red suspenders over his sparkling white shirt emphasized the barrel chest. He had just had a haircut, but that hadn't made what was left of his hair behave.

"So-so," Kirkpatrick said. "How's the examiner?"

The captain frowned. "Now, listen. He called me because

you're giving him fits. I don't want any more pressure."

"No pressure, Art," the sergeant said calmly. "I just want him to do the right thing."

"Right." The commander looked down at the notes of his conversation with the examiner, already typed up on a single sheet. "Now the good news. He found contusions to the back of the head in all three cases."

"That's it, then!" Ginko exclaimed.

The lieutenant nodded. "Same MO. That gets us off the hook on the serial part of it."

"The important thing, it gets the chief off the hook." The captain narrowed his eyes at Kirkpatrick. "He could have been screwed by that dame and almost was. Why didn't you tell me the examiner wasn't up with you yet?"

"He was there. He just didn't know it."

"Bullshit. You didn't know either, not for sure. He's upset, and I can't say I blame him."

Kirkpatrick shrugged. "Once he agreed to look back at the first two, there was no problem."

"That's what you thought? You really believe that?"

"No question."

The captain looked at something out the window. "Next time, you don't tell me you've got it worked out until it's got blisters."

"Yes, sir."

The three of them waited as the captain picked up his notes and studied them. Finally, rubbing his forehead, he said, "The bruises were almost identical, lower part of the skull. Would have shown up eventually as heavy bruises. Two of them with moderate hemorrhaging under the skin, but all similar in severity, except for Miss Roberts. She showed an occipital fracture." He glanced at Kirkpatrick.

"Drugs. You know about that, the drugs the first two victims took?"

The sergeant nodded. "From the labels on the bottles."

"Prescription drugs in the bloodstream, both victims, heavy stuff. Thorazine—"

"Major tranquilizer," Kirkpatrick said. "Antidepressants, Prozac and Zoloft. The usual anticonvulsants for the Thorazine. Typical daily intake for your everyday disturbed personality."

"Same Michigan Avenue psychiatrist prescribed for both victims." The captain looked up. "You talk to him?"

Ginko said, "He's out of town until after Christmas. In China. From what his associates say, both women had been seeing him for years. One of them, four times a week. Both of them were on government assistance. I was told he's one of the few shrinks in town who takes Medicaid patients."

"They know each other, these two women?"

"Probably," Kirkpatrick said. "We're looking into that. By the way, there's no indication Roberts had a history of psychiatric treatment."

The captain put his notes aside and sat down. "And no pills? Roberts, I mean."

"Just Valium. Lots of Valium. That's it for now?"

Ginko opened the door. "For sure, she wasn't on Medicaid."

The captain said, "Get to it then. The pressure's still on."

"I thought you'd ruled out pressure, Art," the sergeant said.

The captain looked up and said softly, "Kirk, you big dumb flatfoot, you almost cost me my job. Get your eyes out of here." He blinked as Kirkpatrick gave him a stony look. "Sorry. I mean your ass."

The other two, at the door, were standing there transfixed, staring at the captain.

"All right," he said angrily, "all of you get the hell out of here, and don't come back till you bring me a killer."

"Good, Art, I like that," Kirkpatrick said. "I may use it some time."

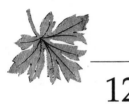

12

Christmas day. Somehow, Patricia thought, I've gotten the family together for dinner. Well, most of them.

With only three months before the wedding, Raymond was spending the holidays in Pennsylvania, and Emily was still traipsing around London. Good lord, she'd been there six months! But Frank and his family were in town from D.C. since Congress wasn't in session. With a new Democratic president, it should have been a good time for him, but Frank was being his usual fretful self, and he had caught a bad cold. He worked for a second-term Congressman whose political sponsor, the senior Illinois representative from Chicago, was in hot water over the House bank, the overdrafts and all that, plus irregularities in campaign financing. Frank was worried that if the sponsor fell from grace, his boss would be the next Big Domino. He had come downstairs complaining that he felt as if he was in a collapsed oxygen tent and that his eyeballs weighed ten pounds. But he had volunteered to collect Dutch in Skokie, the next suburb west, and Don, Frank's brother-in-law, had gone along. Jimmy was driving out from the city and would be here shortly.

Meanwhile Wilmette looked heavenly in the snow, and there was more than enough help in the kitchen, Frank's wife and her sister from Winnetka. The high schoolers were someplace in the big house, and so was Mike, lord of the manor. Pat and Mike, that would be her father's sly joke again this year, beyond a doubt. Well, she and Mike were right on schedule. He had just turned forty and in a few months so would she. Wouldn't Dutch have a fit when the time came to tell him they were thinking of splitting? Just like the last time, he'd say, and he'd be right. Only now she was fifteen years older and the children were almost ready for college. That was one good thing. Before, the kids hadn't even been old enough to start school. And at least Mike was being halfway adult about it, trying to work out their differences in therapy.

And what would Dutch say when she announced she was looking for a nursing home because he was too much for her, living alone miles away? One thing he'd say for certain: As long as you won't have anything else to do after the divorce, what's your complaint? Anyway, he'd say, I'm no trouble. If I were, I'd get to see you more than twice a year. He had absolutely no sense of time, and sometimes no sense at all.

Oh God, she thought, I'm beginning to sound like a crabby old maid.

And Jimmy, all he had needed to occupy his mind was another death in the family—his working family this time. Three years ago he had changed jobs and started drinking a bit more, and these days she seldom saw him. But at least he'd had a few good reasons, which was more than she could say for Mike's daffy lurch toward freedom. What was it, an early climacteric? Dreading the loss of his powers, seeing the end of his life when he was no more than halfway through it? Mike had no excuse, none. When they met, he had already sown his wild oats. What did he think he was doing, reaping the whirlwind?

Oh God, Mike's right, she thought, I'm a confused bitch. And Dutch is right, I'm going for my doctorate in marital failure. Well, might as well be a nag. Nobody loves you when you're sweet and sassy and pushing forty.

Jimmy arrived before the rest of the men got back. He looks haggard, she thought, giving him a hug. "Do me a favor, hon," she said. "Let's you and I go easy on the Christmas grog. My diet."

But he took his time following her into the dining room, and when he finally did he had a pool-size Scotch in his hand. He stood watching her put last-minute touches on the Christmas table, great clumps of carnations and holly, and twelve tall candles. The holly and the candles would stay on the table, one less candle each day, until the last of them was snuffed. He said, "I don't know why you're on a diet. You look a little skinny to me. Younger, too. I'll bet you haven't even started coloring your hair."

"Bless you, but you don't know a thing about me." She thought, He's right. I'm still one of the three greatest looking redheads on the North Shore. She changed the subject. "That young woman who's been sitting on the anchor desk, she's the one you were telling me about, isn't she?"

He stared at her as if he hadn't heard. Probably wishes he had a cigarette after all these years, she thought. I know I do. Or is it the girl? Could they be romantically involved?

No, surely not, she's not his type. Why do I keep thinking she's some kind of vampire, like that slinky low-cut character who introduces the monster movies?

Jimmy seemed to awaken. "Oh, you mean Karen. She's just there to give all of you the feeling the Channel Two family is sharing the holidays with you."

The Addams family, that's the one, she thought. "I don't like her. Something's lacking. Maybe just experience." She wanted to be fair.

"It's only for a few weeks. They're looking for a permanent replacement."

Pat shivered. "It's horrible, right there on the Gold Coast. Who could do a thing like that?"

"Some psychopath who'll never be caught. It's over." He sipped his Scotch.

"You really think so?"

"Sure. He's got everybody's attention, so now he can stop."

She looked up at him. "Easy for you to say. He could be out there right now. Whenever I go outside, I find myself looking for strange footprints at the windows."

Jimmy grinned. "Trust me. It's Christmas."

The other three came stamping in from the cold. Frank sneezed, and Don went off to the kitchen to see how dinner was doing. Patricia was folding her father's threadbare woolen shawl, a red plaid relic he had taken to wearing instead of a muffler, when she heard him clear his throat and say huskily, "Jimmy!" Another harrumph. "So when are you getting married?"

She turned, exasperated. "It's Raymond, Father! Raymond's the one who's getting married."

"I know that," Dutch snapped. "Don't you think I know that? I'm talking to Jimmy."

He's bluffing, she thought. It was worrisome, how forgetful he had become. Of course, he saw even less of Jimmy than she did, and he hadn't seen Raymond since—when? Two years ago? Maybe she ought to start writing things down for him: "Raymond is the one who's still in college. You can see Jimmy on the news, on weekends. And Emily—" He'd probably look blank and say, "Emily? Who's Emily?" No, that was a cruel exaggeration. Was she rehearsing being single and stony-hearted again?

Dutch was saying to Frank as they all went toward the living room, "I just want to know when he's going to settle down," and Frank laughed.

"Sure, Dad, everybody wants to know that." He turned to Jimmy. "It's time you came east for another visit. Hearts are breaking all over Washington."

Dutch said, "You see, Jimmy? See what it'll be like as you get older? Just wait till you start getting invited as the extra man. It's hell, being stared at all through dinner."

Jimmy sat down heavily in the big chair, and Patricia said, "Oh, Father, give it a rest. Do you want a glass of wine or would it upset your stomach?"

Dutch whirled on her angrily. "That's the kind of thing they ask you, looking you over, all the matchmakers." He said to Jimmy, "They have this damned little smile, and they poke you and prod you with questions. What they really want to know is the state of your health and the size of your bankroll. They say, 'Are you interested in being on an invitation list?' They say they know some very lovely people. Then they nudge you and say, 'Single women aren't all hanging from chandeliers.' "

Frank, at the window, seemed to be feeling better, maybe just glad to be back home. He said, "I always liked this house. It goes on for miles." He giggled. "Jimmy, remember the old place? You and I used to hide out in the back bedroom whenever Dutch wanted us to do something?"

"I always found you, too," Dutch groused.

Jimmy said, "That was Bryan." The lost brother. An uncomfortable silence fell and he moved to fill it. "I always got found because I was youngest and hadn't learned to hide very well. I always wound up doing it."

"Damn right," Dutch said. "Damn right."

If they had needed a Santa for Christmas, Patricia thought, Frank would be the one to play him. He looked jollier now, and dapper as ever. At forty-five, a bit heavier but more distinguished. It was the pink cheeks that made her think of Santa. Maybe Dutch was right. Getting married was the only way to go, and staying that way, if you could.

Frank took Dutch upstairs to see the children, and she said to Jimmy, "Well, nothing much has changed. I hope Frank remembers to run Father past the bathroom before he comes to the table."

Jimmy grinned and got up, heading for the stairs. "I'll take care of it."

"And remind Father that the children don't need to have their meat cut into tiny bites any more. It would help if he made a better impression on them this year, so they'll have nicer memories of him." She sighed, watching Jimmy go up, taking two steps at a time, like Mike. She had always been grateful that she had found Michael Daughterty. So bright, so strong, so . . . well, say it. Successful. The toast of the LaSalle Street financial district.

Success wasn't everything, she thought, but when you gathered around the Christmas table it made all the difference. It made you feel that Santa was real, whether he was or not, and that if you found footprints of somebody skulking around the house they were probably his. She shivered and crossed the room to look at the thermostat, thinking, I know what it was, about that young woman on the news. Vampirish. Vampira, that was it! She's like all those spiderish types who'll be going after Mike if he makes his move. It's time I calmed down. I don't want to lose him by becoming hysterical.

Then she thought, Why *am* I losing him? She couldn't think of a thing, but when she knocked the cover off the thermostat and saw it rolling across the floor, she knew she must be hurting, and angry as hell.

13

Karen Kohl. That was her one playful joke, served up with a rare little giggle to people who wondered how to spell the name. "K-O-H-L," she would say, and then, as Jimmy winced, hearing it again, "I'm just a simple coal miner's daughter."

Kohl and coal. This perfect pun (like a perfect rhyme, as he had learned in Lit class, because it rhymed exactly) was passed along with a certain stubborn pride as part of a long-established family tradition. A Kentucky-born country music star had titled her autobiography *Coal Miner's Daughter*. But though Karen's hair was a glossy bituminous, her long legs, silky skin, and coolly efficient smile didn't figure in people's picture of the coal patches, hillbilly poverty, black lung, and all that. Karen didn't strum a guitar, and her eyes were not go-yonder but come-hither, or else keep-your-Goddamn-distance. So the pun was disconcerting.

Well, she didn't come right from the mines. Karen's father headed a big printing house in Scranton, Pennsylvania, where she had grown up in an urban household.

Nevertheless, she did have a legitimate claim to the title. It went all the way back to the discovery of "black gold," when some forebear or other had gone to work in the anthracite fields that lay north of Philadelphia, in Schuylkill County, the home, half a century later, of the Molly Maguires.

The Maguires, a secret society of coal workers, were said by some to have killed a number of mine bosses who had frustrated their attempts to unionize. This was in the late 1870s, when it was still Irish against Welsh and English, and Catholics against Protestants, the age-old story. Twenty Maguires were hanged after the owners brought in the dreaded Pinkertons.

Kohls, up to and including Karen's grandfather, may have worked the mines but they weren't Irish, so none of them could have been a Maguire. The Germans were resented by the Irish because, like the English and Welsh, they held the skilled jobs.

"Oh, that's right, you're Irish," Karen had said to Jimmy once, "like my mother." They were having lunch in a German restaurant-bar on Clark Street, one frequented by cops from the nearby eighteenth district police station. "One of my great-great-grandfathers is rumored to have sent an Irishman to the gallows. My mother will never forgive my father for that." She didn't know whether her forebear had been a Pinkerton detective or just a hired company cop.

In any case, the conversation had cast Karen in a whole new light. In his pre-television days, Jimmy had done a series of articles for the *Tribune* on the coal fields of West Virginia and Illinois. He had gone down into the mines, watching the huge, ear-splitting machines gouge out the overhead seams and picturing tired miners of yore with blackened faces moving bent-over through the dark, yelling, "Fire! Fire in the hole!" as the coal face blew, filling the air with stifling black dust. On the surface, he'd been awed by the sprawling breaker-boys' sheds where, in the old days, kids as young as seven or eight sat for hours, grimy and sweating or freezing, discarding chunks of slate from the lumps of coal that flowed endlessly off the conveyors. The big dark ungainly breaker buildings, some said, looked like huge praying mantises.

If Karen's genes came through this blackened hell, Jimmy thought, they had to be shot through with brimstone and sulphurous tears.

Last summer, three days after Jimmy had gotten Kathleen's package, Karen called, asking if he could possibly set up some interviews for three days in late August, when she and her husband would be in Chicago.

Pretty cheeky, he thought. But as a favor to Kathleen, he arranged for Karen to see key people at all three network-owned stations and the major independent, and invited her to lunch on the first day. She and her husband seemed to be well matched, ideal embodiments of traditional American values. He had been captain of the football team, student body president, and class salutatorian. She had been a prizewinning gymnast, one of the leads in the senior play, and a top interscholastic debater. Naturally they had been high school sweethearts. Same college, same story. Then both had gone off to Philadelphia, he into insurance and she into television news, starting as a sports reporter. So on to the storybook climax: the wedding, and only a matter of time until the family came along. Attractive people, both of them, really nice folks. After lunch, while her husband went to look out the top of Sears Tower, Jimmy put Karen in a cab for her first interview, and it was absolutely true that he had been as impressed by her seriousness and independence as by her great legs.

So what juggernaut had crushed this promising union, and so quickly, even before her first month on the job was out? How did it happen that the picture began to darken, or to put it another way, when did their marriage go down into the mines? Maybe, he surmised, the picture never really got painted. Maybe it was just an album of random but very pretty snapshots they had started believing in when they were kids.

And of course the news had to come from Howard. Hands in his pockets and grinning sublimely, he stood in the doorway of his office as Jimmy came by and said, "Well, she did it!"

"Who?" Jimmy said. "What, when, why?" He had been in a bad mood.

Howard looked to see if Dorothy was there. She wasn't. "Karen. She's filed for divorce."

"No kidding. She didn't breathe a word. Too bad. No vine-covered cottage, no picket fence."

Howard, suddenly solemn, put a hand on his shoulder and walked him down the hall, his head wagging back and forth as it did when he was in denial. "Actually *he* filed, can you believe it? Kissing off a package like that? You've got to love her following you around on the police beat. Is she picking up on things as fast as I think she is?"

"Sure. Fast is the only way she knows to go." Jimmy stopped and looked at him. "How's your marriage, Howard?"

Undaunted, though he must have known how rumors

about him and Karen were flying, Howard said, "Fine, just fine! Funny you should ask. Beth and I are thinking of having another child."

"Congratulations. Boy or girl?"

Howard smiled. "We want a girl this time. Girls are wonderful."

"Yeah, I know. Too bad about Karen."

The other man flinched, apprehension on his face. "What do you mean?"

Jimmy stared at him. "The divorce, what else?"

"Oh, yeah." Smiling again, Howard backed away toward his office. "But don't worry, she's going to be fine, Jimmy. I knew it the first time I saw her. She's going to be just great!"

Later, after their innocent hand-holding and their half-consummated falling into bed, neither of which Karen seemed to recall, Jimmy remembered the metal plaque he had seen on the wall of the history museum in Wilkes-Barre, the day Kathleen Reilly had told him she had a cousin. The plaque had memorialized the nineteenth-century disappearance of a little girl who, decades later, was found someplace in Indiana. She had been stolen away by the Indians. Jimmy had read firsthand reports which maintained that, by and large, native Americans had treated the prisoners they took with kindness and consideration, as one of themselves, and that captives who had lived among them for years seldom wished to return to the white man's civilization.

Karen could play that part, he decided. For years, it seemed to Jimmy, she had been hidden away in some dark wilderness in which she had made a secret life among strange companions, not all of whom had been kind, and at some point she had chosen not to return to the light. He or

Howard might play little games with her and it might be exciting, but they would never be able to reach down into that unknown country she inhabited without being lost, too.

He told himself he was overdramatizing. He really knew nothing about her. She was basically just an ordinary human being especially well endowed with beauty and brains. And drive, don't forget drive. And don't, most of all, forget to be wary.

Howard was probably right, she was going to be a star. But there were all kinds of stars, shooting stars and fading novae and dark stars. Stars twinkling in the forests where Indians once dwelled, stars glittering deep in mines. Stars, if you held them trustingly in the palm of your hand, that would sizzle and burn right through. You could wish on the light of them and swear by their placements in the sky, but when the universe collapsed they would all be just nothing, right along with you.

14

Ginko and the sergeant were eating cacciatore over on Broadway, not far from the lake, just north of Diversey. It was an Italian place Ginko favored because he knew one of the waitresses. Kirkpatrick didn't much care where they stopped for lunch, or sometimes whether they ate at all. He had a slight interest in German food, and once in a while he found an excuse to stop off in the South Loop near the Federal Building, at the Berghoff, which still retained some of the feel of old Chicago and made its own beer.

"You know what I think?" Kirk told his partner between bites. "I think you've got a crush on her. The waitress."

"Crush?"

"You know what I mean."

"Oh." Ginko smiled. "Well, she's different. She's improving my English."

"Why? You speak it properly. She doesn't always, although she pronounces it well."

"Yes, but she's very educated, and I think I can learn something. English is like love. You may know it well enough, but you like to practice it all the same."

"Like love? Do you ever practice that with her?"

"No." Ginko laughed self-consciously. "She doesn't screw around."

Kirkpatrick stared at him, chewing. When he had swallowed, he said, "Do you know the difference between literal and figurative?"

"No, I don't think I'm clear on that."

"Well, if you want somebody to stop bullshitting you, or hurry up or something, you say, 'Stop screwing around.' If you're talking about sex, it's better to say, 'She doesn't sleep around.' "

"Oh. Sure, I know about that."

"That's if you know she doesn't sleep around. But we have it on good authority that you never know."

"So I should stop screwing around."

"Well, you can stop bullshitting me. That's more specific."

Ginko glanced around for the waitress he knew, probably to make sure she hadn't overheard them, but she was on the other side of the restaurant. Kirk guessed his partner knew her pretty well, but he doubted that she either slept or screwed around. She was pretty but she was Polish, working only briefly in this country, to earn some money to take home. She seemed to be all diligence. Ginko said, "Specifically, how am I bullshitting you?"

Kirk cut a chunk of veal and rotated it in the sauce with his fork. "I've been wanting to talk to you about this for some time. You've got to stop telling people what I think."

"Specifically?"

Kirk chewed. "You're responsible for what happened to the chief last week. Karel Kohl heard it from you, about the serial murders. She heard it from you last fall, that I thought they weren't suicides, and that night you told her I was thinking serial. If she hadn't heard that from you, she wouldn't have been able to bring it up on TV. You see how loose lips can sink ships?"

"Sink ships?"

"That's right, you were born after the war. It's an old military saying. You should watch what you say."

"I will. I'm sorry."

"Because if you ever do that again, I'll cut your heart out."

"I'm really sorry. I thought we were teaching her. She's learning the ropes."

"You bet she is. She doesn't need any more help."

The waitress came over and picked up Ginko's plate. He smiled up at her. "You weren't in Wednesday," he said.

She seemed somewhat flustered. "Yes. No. My friend came over and we went out." She had a decided accent, unlike Ginko. "Did you stop by?"

"Yes, I drove by but I didn't see any lights. You going to be home next Wednesday?"

"I don't know. Why don't you bring your wife?" she was smiling, and Ginko laughed. She looked at Kirkpatrick, who had just put down his knife and fork. "Are you finished, Sergeant?" He nodded, and she picked up his plate, then began gathering up the other dishes, stacking them.

Ginko said, "I told you, that's my night out. We could go bowling."

"Why don't you take your wife bowling?" She was obviously teasing him. It must be an old joke with them, Kirk thought.

"Come on!" Ginko said. "I mean get some of your friends and we could all go." She walked away, and the busboy arrived with coffee for Ginko. He said to Kirkpatrick, "It's my wife's bridge night, so I go out. Maria has lots of friends from Poland. Sometimes we go to dinner or the movies. She's a good kid."

Kirk patted his mouth with his napkin. "You heard what I said."

"You mean about keeping my mouth shut? Sure. Like a clam."

"I mean it. I'm serious."

"Does anyone else have to know?"

"No, it's between us. So far."

"Okay. You don't have to worry."

Kirk looked at his watch. "We see Clara Turner at two o'clock. Drink your coffee."

Ginko picked up his cup and sipped. "I don't know about this. It could be delicate. She's a screwball, huh?"

Kirk was picking his teeth with the toothpick Maria had brought. He drank coffee only at breakfast, to get himself going. "She's not a screwball. Not crazy, not a psychopath. She's sick."

"Only in the mind." Ginko nodded and drank some more. "But it must be serious. She's paranoid. Well, I don't mean technically. But she's afraid of this guy. She thinks he's after her."

"She may be right."

"But her friends died months ago, and she's never seen him, not for years. Isn't that a little paranoid?"

Kirk shrugged. "Somebody killed them. Why not him? It's pretty logical. It's far from crazy."

"Yeah, but the guy may be dead himself now. He moved out of his office and took everything. Just disappeared. He was probably afraid of getting sued, the things he did."

"He's a good suspect as long as he's a fugitive."

"But what about Marlee Roberts? She wasn't one of his patients. He didn't even know her."

"Everybody knew Marlee Roberts. They saw her every night. Now, the doctor, if he did it, is your certifiable psychopath, your screwball." Kirk looked around. "You ever see anybody you knew back in Poland?"

Ginko finished his coffee and shook his head. "No."

"No old acquaintances? Relatives?"

"No. I married an American woman and I'm an American. I only hang around with Maria and her friends because sometimes I miss hearing the language. But they're younger and they stay only a short time and then go home, most of them. I don't want any old attachments. I'm an American, and that's what I want to be. Fuck Poland." He grinned, as if it delighted him to say something shocking.

"When you left, it was part of the Soviet Bloc. Don't you feel better about it now that it's back in the fold?"

"Sure. But I'm here now. This is my country."

"How'd you get out? You were just a kid, weren't you?"

"You been looking me up? No, I was in my twenties. I worked in a shipyard."

Maria brought over the check and put it down on the table. "More coffee?"

"No, thanks," Kirkpatrick said. "You ever hear of Mr. Gruszczynski here, back in your country? He was a refugee from behind the Iron Curtain when you were just a teenager. He's probably a hero over there."

She laughed politely, probably thought he was joking, and Ginko, looking disconcerted, smiled and said something to her in Polish. She nodded, blushing, and walked away.

"What did you say to her?"

"I said you were screwing around. You know, bullshitting."

"I hope you gave it the accurate translation. Not that she'd have to worry about me."

They sorted out the check and put on their overcoats and walked out to the car. There was snow on the ground and a biting wind.

"Now, remember," Kirkpatrick said, shutting his door, "this Turner woman may be skittish. I'm going to be very patient and fatherly. We want to find out all we can about this doctor she's afraid of, and we need to find out fast. But if she's greatly upset it may take a while. So if you want to leave, feel free. Hopefully, it won't take long."

Ginko nodded and started the engine. "Fucking heater," he said.

"That's the first word you learned when you came over, I'll bet."

Ginko grinned and blew on his fingers. "I learned that word when I was four years old," he said. "Right after 'okay.' I learned it from a Russian soldier."

"How did you come over?"

The other man shrugged and pulled out into the traffic. "At night. There were ships in the harbor. I sneaked aboard. It went to Panama."

Kirk yawned. "The commander is very anxious to have the doctor brought in."

"I know. We'll find him. I plan to help check the neighborhood Wednesday if it's okay with you."

"Your day off? Okay, but don't expect to find anything. It's highly transient, and he moved out a long time ago."

"I know. I might find out something. This Clara Turner, maybe she knew some of his other patients. If she does, I'll talk to them."

"How did you know I thought it was a serial killing?" Kirk said.

"I heard you. I don't know, talking to somebody."

"The examiner."

"Maybe."

"I didn't talk to anybody else, not about that."

"Maybe the commander, earlier."

"Right, maybe the commander." Ginko hadn't been there when he had phoned the captain, but he could have been there when the captain came in. He was a smart SOB. He could have put two and two together, and maybe he did overhear something. "You know where it is. Just south of Division."

"Got it."

"There's only one thing that troubles me about you, Ginko." His partner said nothing, kept his eyes on the road. "You never look at me, I mean directly."

Ginko laughed, embarrassed. "I don't?"

"No, you don't. Never right in the eyes. Why is that?"

"Well, you know."

"What?"

The man shifted uneasily in his seat. "Well, you know."

"Tell me."

"All right. You got one eye doing this and the other doing that. I don't like to call attention."

Kirkpatrick laughed. "Don't worry about it. I have the same reaction when I look in the mirror, when I'm shaving." After a while he said, "Refugees are remarkable people. They work harder than anybody. Is that the way you are, Ginko?"

Ginko grinned. "All my life I worked my balls off. Is that good enough for you?"

Kirk put his head back. "Good enough for me, Ginko." He looked over, watching him drive. "That should be good enough for anybody."

15

In Chicago, one lives life by degrees. February, the cold dark month of president's birthdays, blood-red Valentines, pewter skies and leaden slush, had the town by the throat. It didn't help at all that somewhere out there an unreconstructed killer might be planning to kill again. People on the street had a weird look in their eyes that said, He could be any one of us, he could be you or me.

Of course there was a bright side. The murders were a bonanza to television news, which was already a bonanza. This was especially true of the new Channel 2 News. All fall and winter it had struggled to catch up in the ratings, but the latest sweep figures showed it neck and neck with the other major stations, with most of the gain coming from viewers who didn't usually watch newscasts. In death, Marlee had caught the public's imagination, and apparently Howard's slam-bam minicam format seemed to have sustained it. Lord knows, the new staccato billboard delivery style Stanford had finally mastered was made for glorifying serial murder. Wherever the killer was, Jimmy thought, he must be as slam-bam gratified as Howard.

Everybody else, though, seemed immobilized by the dark, the ice, the economy and the regulation winter blahs, except for a few people in authority who were mad as hell over the lack of police action. The commander in charge of Violent Crimes was starting to buckle under the pressure. He was getting a reputation as a whiner, for nothing seemed to be going right.

First, Clara Turner's legitimate Michigan Avenue shrink, back from China, appeared to have forgotten his native tongue, except for that old song and dance about conversations with clients being privileged. Then when Marlee's Florida gigolo had been brought in, he was packing along several Miami attorneys with sworn affidavits stating that he had been nowhere near Chicago on the day in question. The special investigative unit under Detective Kirkpatrick had no suspects other than Clara's rogue therapist, who they were starting to think existed only in her haunted dreams.

Now the medical examiner, to protect his reputation, was publicly accusing the police of foot-dragging, of ignoring his early findings of murderous intent, and on that basis the second victim's father, a North Shore electronics manufacturer who had abandoned his daughter to the predators of the city, was threatening to sue the department. The police chief was steamed, the mayor was livid and the governor, who was a member of the opposing political party, was being as smugly indignant as only a downstate born-again Christian could be.

Jimmy Gillespie wasn't much happier. Howard had decided that Karen would remain on the anchor desk indefinitely. Jimmy could see why. She and Stanford were good together. They balanced each other: her exaggerated whiteness of skin against his unmistakable blackness, and youth against age. She appeared to trust Stanford and followed his lead. If she lacked Marlee's experience and warmth, her occasional lapses into youthful confusion only seemed to give Stanford confidence, enhancing his air of mature understanding.

So, fine. It was okay. Jimmy was happy for her. Besides, it was preordained.

Still, he was uneasy. She and her husband had seemed good together, but look at what happened. How long would Karen be content to play second fiddle, Goody Two-Shoes to Stanford's Wise Old Owl? Jimmy took it for granted that she was deliberately stifling her natural sophistication, lest too big a jolt of it alarm her fellow anchor and turn him against her. She was too shrewd to sabotage herself in this way, especially with Howard in there coaching.

Now that the job and the divorce had come through, she seemed quietly exuberant, and why not? Nothing so reassures a woman who becomes single again as having a powerful friend and ally like Howard, especially if, when she pats him on the head, he pants eagerly and wags his tail. She was free, she was still a prizewinner and she was in control. You could see all this on the home screen if you knew what to look for in that lovely, somewhat arrogant ingenue's face.

It was true that her smile was more fixed than spontaneous, and that every so often the artfully outlined, carefully innocent eyes burned into the camera with more intensity than news of icy streets or choked homeless shelters warranted. But she was still learning, and waiting. For now it was enough to be seen as aware and sensible and subordinate. When she finally decided to pull out the stops, Jimmy decided, she would be formidable, and that would be something to see.

Dorothy took him aside one evening as he was on his way home and delivered herself of a "Ten O'Clock News" critique. "She's mocking Stanford up there," she groused. "She's putting on airs by letting him think she respects him. She doesn't. You can see how impatient she is to see him gone by how she holds herself in. She's the explosive type, and she's been holding herself in too long. Someday she's going to bust out and scream, and then it'll be either her or him. You wait and see. I'd like to get her alone in a broom closet for ten minutes and pound some sense into her. It doesn't worry me that she began fooling around with the boss as soon as she walked in the door, but you don't mess with a man's entire career just to get what you want. It ain't natural." She sighed.

"Oh, I know what's going to happen. She and Stanford are polar opposites. Irreconcilable differences, that's what it's called. She couldn't be any different if she tried, and there's no reason for him to. Oh my, and Howard Damen Custer, the third, just waiting around for it to happen. He knows. He's crazy about her, but he's using her, too, to get what he wants. And when the big blowup comes, he's going to say to you, 'Get up there, Jimmy. Stanford ain't coming in no more.' What will you do then, luv, just get up beside her like nothing happened? Like there was never any age of the dinosaurs, the Greeks and the Romans never killed each other off, and history started the day you were born? Nothing matters, does it, honey? Except what you want and I want and she wants and he wants, and everybody's got to have it now, devil take the hindmost. Whewee."

Jimmy was somewhat staggered by this lengthy lecture, but he managed to say, "Truer words were never spoken, Dorothy."

"True, my very pretty young juicy ass! We don't know any more what's true or not, we're just in it for the leavings. You think he cares what happens to this place? He's in there, day after day, bent over his computer, and you think he's giving his all for the company? You should see what he writes when he thinks no one's looking. My, my, how he does fancy himself! You think he's all business, but you should see all the poetic rambles and personal letters—hah! You don't know half of what he's up to, thinks he's another Bernard Shaw. All the correspondence with that agent in Hollywood, asking about this producer and that director, and stars' names galore! You'd think he was on his way to the Academy Awards in his limo. Well, why doesn't he go back out there then, close to the action? Chicago's not the land of dreams.

"And you think his wife doesn't know how he is? You think that family's home free? You think they don't have problems, her working her butt off with some advertising agency, and looking after those two spoiled-rotten kids? Having to get him out of bed after he's been up half the night working on some project he wants her to take out to Steven Spielberg because she knows him, yes she does! He didn't marry any coal miner's daughter. She had her own career, and how he talked her into coming with him to Chicago—why, she knows now it was the second worst mistake she ever made. Hooking up with him in the first place, God save her!

"You should hear how she babies him, picks him up when he's down. Oh, I hear them talking on the phone. He says, 'I have this idea, it isn't any good, is it? What do you think, help me work it out.' And she says, 'No, honey, it's all right, it's good. But maybe it could be a little more this way or that way,' and he says, 'Oh, thank you, sweetie, you did it, you're my brain!' And she says, quiet-like, 'I'm not your brain, you got a perfectly good brain, you just have to remember to relax a little, have confidence in yourself,' and she sounds so sad, trying to get through to him. And he says, 'You're right, I know you're right, but you're still my brain,' and who wouldn't feel sorry for herself, giving up the good life for somebody like him?"

She shook her head. "Oh, my Lord, I'll be glad when he's gone. Only trouble is, there'll be another one along just like him, only different. Somebody just as full of himself as Howard Damen Three."

"Oh, come on, it's not that bad," Jimmy told her. "Things change."

"Yeah, you get changed, I get changed, everybody gets changed. We all get it, whether we deserve it or not." Then she brightened. "Thanks for listening, honey. I know you got to go."

"Good night, Dorothy. Take care."

It bothered Jimmy a little to hear her talk this way. Not so much what she revealed about Howard's inner turmoil and after-hours pursuits, but the fact that she had access to such personal details of his life. What did she do, listen in on his private phone conversations? Go through his computer records? Was there anything about Howard she didn't know or couldn't find out? What was she up to, anyway?

Polar opposites, she had said, speaking of Stanford and Karen. Irreconcilable differences. He was convinced that Howard was able and that Dorothy was a force for good, but were they on a collision course, too? One that was taking them all rapidly in the direction of that other cliché, the point of no return?

16

Jimmy's phone was ringing when he reached home after stopping off at the tavern and then for Chinese. It was Karen, calling from the newsroom, where the "Ten O'clock News" telecast was only an hour away. She was getting the hang of things and sounded like it. "Where've you been, for God's sake? Clara needs help, can you go? I told her you would. She's at the eighteenth district police station, scared to death, and nobody will listen. She's been there for two hours."

"What's her problem?"

"She spotted the man she told Kirk about. You know, the doctor she had when she was first in treatment? He followed her home after dark and wouldn't go away, so instead of going in she went on to the station hoping the cops would pick him up. Nobody would listen, so she got desperate and called me."

"Why didn't she call Kirkpatrick?"

Karen huffed in exasperation. "Oh, she had his card and she lost it! She gets so rattled, you know how she is."

"No, I don't. Why don't you call Kirk?"

She was losing patience fast. "Look, just get over there and take care of it, will you, Jimmy? I've got a show to do. Call me if there's anything newsworthy, anything at all."

"Okay, but it sounds like something the assignment desk should handle."

"No! It has to be somebody Clara trusts. I've told her she can trust you, okay?"

"Karen—" But she had hung up.

He was tempted to call the assignment manager himself, but decided he might as well go. He phoned Sergeant Kirkpatrick, who wasn't in, and wound up talking to a detective named Scharf, whom he knew slightly. "I'm told she's over there waiting for me. It's possible the guy's still in the neighborhood. That's all I know."

"I guess we could send somebody." Scharf, the lethargic.

"And let Kirk know, will you?"

"Yeah, we can do that."

"I should be there in ten, fifteen minutes."

Jimmy threw his hat and coat back on and went looking for a taxi in the wintry dark. It was snowing again and there were no cabs, not even at the hotel across from Marlee's building where they usually were stacked up waiting for trips to the airport. He finally found one a block south, disgorging partygoers in front of a Division Street singles bar. He told the driver to hurry, but with the snow and icy slush and the singles-bar traffic the trip seemed to take forever.

At the 18th district police station, an attractive blonde sat alone on the only bench in the place. The bench faced a chest-high counter behind which two or three uniformed cops were casually answering phones and doing paperwork. Several other officers, some in plainclothes, sauntered in and out of the enclosure, conducting their business and trading friendly insults. Doorways at the rear of the enclosure led to the cramped offices of the captain and his aides. At the far end of the hallway, back by the holding cells, a stairway led up to a dingy dayroom, detectives' offices, and small rooms for interviewing prisoners.

It was plain that the woman on the bench saw none of this. She sat within a world of her own, looking down at the scruffy tiled floor. Her lap held a large black leather handbag, and beside her was an overflowing shopping bag. Had she not been the only customer, Jimmy would never have taken her for Clara Turner. Forty, was that what Karen had said? She looked younger. Aside from her padded winter coat, she seemed to be fashionably dressed. She had long, slim calves and taffy-colored hair that fell almost to her shoulders. The hair was a bit tousled, but it had the look of a salon.

Still, as he came up the steps, stamping snow from his shoes, and she abruptly looked up, Jimmy was unprepared for her fine-boned Nordic beauty, especially the large, pale, almond-shaped eyes and what he saw in them: some combination of fear and hope and hopelessness. They looked away, sadly dismissing him, as he headed for the counter. He recalled that she had come here to find someone who would listen.

He said to the desk sergeant, "You get a call from Scharf, over at Violent Crimes?"

"Yeah. He said he was coming by."

"That the Turner woman?"

"That's her. Nutty as a fruitcake. Some looker, though." The sergeant grinned salaciously, as if fruitcake filled his dreams.

"Thanks." Jimmy went over to the bench and Clara Turner stood up, the eyes full of apprehension. "Karen sent me," he told her. "I'm Jimmy Gillespie."

The shopping bag had tipped over, some of its contents spilling out onto the bench, but she seemed not to notice. "Oh, thank you for coming, Mr. Gillespie," she said. Tentatively, she held out a gloved hand, then quickly withdrew it. "I hope it wasn't too much trouble. I wouldn't have called, but I didn't know what else to do." She was tall, with an aristocratic bearing, but her voice had an impulsive, jerky quality, as if she was having trouble getting it in gear.

"Karen said—"

"Yes, and every time I turned around there he was, staring at me." She nodded vigorously to underscore this. "And listen to this: I even said to him once, 'Oh, hello, doctor,' but he just looked away, as if he'd never seen me before." She added confidentially, "He's a doctor, but he's not a psychiatrist or anything. But he was my therapist." She nodded emphatically. "I was petrified, if you want to know. What if he's planning to do to me what he did to them?" Her lip trembled, as if she might break into tears.

"This is the same guy whose office used to be across the street from where you live?"

"Yes, except he hasn't been there for years. It was horrible, going there. You had to go down this long, dark passageway to get into the building, and it nearly scared me to death. Can you imagine going to a therapist in a place like that?" She stepped closer and narrowed her eyes. "I don't think he was really interested in his patients. Something about him made me ver-r-ry uneasy. What do you think of this: He'd sit down beside me on the couch and unbutton his shirt all the way down, and he had me take off my blouse." She squealed with sudden embarrassed laughter she tried to suppress. "And you want to know something? Once when I couldn't function because of the pills he gave me, he said I should stay over. He was always telling me I had to loosen up, don't be such a prude, or I'd never get any better—"

Jimmy put up a hand, interrupting. "Clara, what makes you think this guy killed your friends?"

"Because, back before we knew each other, they went to see him, too. We used to talk about him, how he had this way of getting your confidence, but he had only one thing in mind. And like, he'd say it was better to be dead than go on living the way we were. I thought he was just being sympathetic, but now it scares me just to think of it. He wasn't just saying it either."

"You're positive it's the same person?"

"Oh, I couldn't forget him! He had more of a beard then, and he was younger, of course, but it's the eyes. The eyes!" She gave a little sob. "And listen to this: My doctor, the one I have now, said he wasn't a real therapist and I'm lucky I stopped going there. I've seen dozens of therapists, and none of them have ever helped me, not one. Not until now."

"Where'd you see him last? Right outside?"

"Outside, yes, and he was standing on the corner, watching." She shook her head, swallowing hard. "The officers looked out and said no one was there, but he's there, all right."

"Clara, why don't you take it easy for a while? A couple of detectives will be here soon, and they'll want to talk to you. You can trust them. They're from Detective Kirkpatrick's office."

"Oh, good! Do you think it would be too much trouble

for them to take me home? It's dark, and I don't want him following me, and I'm feeling kind of sick. I don't have anything in my stomach." She sat down, spotting the overturned shopping bag and beginning to restore its contents. "I have to shop in the Loop, where it's cheaper. Don't you think they'd have some stores like that around here? But it's so expensive, except the shoe store, and their boots leak, did you know that?"

"You want some coffee, Clara?"

She looked up, smiling, her face almost in repose. "Oh, that'd be nice! Artificial sweetener, though. I've gained so much weight nothing fits any more."

The detectives showed up ten minutes later, and while his partner took Clara in tow Scharf walked Jimmy down the hall. "Kirk wants us to ride around for a while. You think she knows what she's doing?" Like Jimmy, he was tall and sandy-haired, a little younger but twenty pounds heavier even without his gun.

"I think so. I think she saw him, all right."

"Well, he's not still hanging around unless he's a loony. You want to come along? Maybe you can be, you know, a calming influence."

"Maybe we can stop for something to eat. She hasn't eaten all day."

"First let's see how it goes."

They toured the slush-filled streets of the Near North Side for twenty minutes or so without tracking on anything except a career drunk urinating in an apartment house doorway. The detectives turned him over to a passing uniform car, and when they set out again Clara had the giggles, explosive outbursts that rocked her back and forth and ricocheted around the car. She wouldn't look up when Jimmy, behind her, touched her shoulder, hoping she wasn't becoming hysterical.

"Oh, it's too embarrassing!" she wailed, overcome with hilarity. "It's so funny! I thought you'd found the doctor, and instead—oh, you must think I'm terrible! You'll think I'm crude, or a prude." She looked around, clowning, sharing the moment. "Hey, that's a rhyme. I'm a poet and don't know it!"

Jimmy said, "Clara, what do you see out there? We don't want to miss him."

Sobering, she began taking quick, deep breaths, with little humming cries in between. "I'm sorry. I feel kind of sick. Do you think it would be all right to stop for a minute? I have to, you know, use the bathroom." She looked quickly around at each face. "Oh, not on the sidewalk!" Her sudden laughter ended in a whimper. "I'm sorry. I usually start taking my pills about now."

Scharf braked in front of a decent looking ham-and-egger, saying, "You can go in here. It's okay, they know us." He looked back at his partner. "Maybe you should go with her."

The partner said, "How much longer we going to ride around?"

"Not long."

Jimmy said, "I'll go. I need to get her something to eat."

"Sure," Scharf said. "Pick up a sandwich. She can eat it in the car."

"Maybe we ought to just eat," the partner said.

Scharf said, "I thought we were going to wait. The guys will be expecting us."

The partner shrugged. Jimmy opened the rear door and Clara said softly, "There he is!"

Two more doors clicked open. "Where?" Scharf said. "Inside?"

"No." A sob. "He's over there by the donuts."

Nobody stirred. A shadowy figure moved into the doorway of a donut shop two stores away, lounging back out of the Halloween-orange street lighting.

"How can you tell it's him?" Scharf said.

Clara swallowed, as if trying not to throw up. "He was right there, under the light. It's his eyes."

"All right, get him," Scharf said, throwing his door wide and scrambling out. Looking frightened out of her wits, Clara screamed sharply, and the man in the doorway jerked upright and ran into the street.

"The El!" Scharf yelled. "Don't let him get down the stairs!"

Jimmy went through the traffic after them, seeing the man disappear down the subway entrance built into the opposite curb, with the partner in hot pursuit. Following Scharf downward, he reached the ticket area in time to see the detective one-arm himself over the turnstile and head for the lower level. The rattling noise he heard grew and then suddenly stopped, but he was halfway down the second set of stairs before he realized what it was. A train had pulled in, and now it was leaving, probably right on schedule.

17

The doctor had made his train all right. Unbelievable, because Scharf's partner had been right behind him, close enough to see the finger the guy gave him as the doors closed and the train pulled out. And the yellow smile that broke apart his crust of beard.

It was now midmorning, and Howard was sitting at his computer as Jimmy walked into the office and flung himself down on the couch. The words on the screen suddenly vanished. A private memo? Jimmy wondered. It hadn't looked like a memo. A full screen with no paragraphs. Not poetry. A movie outline?

Howard swung around. "How's it going, buddy? You look beat." He was smiling, but his eyes said he had just returned from some point deep in his brain. He was the one who looked tired. He had complained recently about lack of sleep, of going home and falling on the couch, dead to the world for hours.

"Nothing happening. No trace of the doctor. Kirk's in a lousy mood."

"Well, at least we've got a manhunt. And a killer."

"Is he?"

"Doesn't matter. It leads into Karen's idea, remember? Chicago's lost women. Hopeless, sick, poverty-ridden, defiled. Nobody to help, and somebody's killing them off."

"I don't remember 'defiled.' "

"Strike it then. It would make a good film. Sounds like the kind of thing Karen should go after for the next sweeps. How does it strike you?"

Howard rarely asked Jimmy's opinion. He seemed to be making an effort to be courteous. He looked unusually uptight. Jimmy said, "I'm going to a wedding sweeps week. Besides, Karen doesn't need my help."

"Oh, she can handle it. I just thought you'd be interested, since you'd met one of them." Howard got up and started shuffling a stack of papers on his desk, pausing to read one, then another. He looked through them for quite a while, and then he said without looking up, "Ever thought of getting out of this business, Jimmy?"

"Never crossed my mind."

Howard gave him a sudden, brilliant grin. "Just get out? Leave it all behind?"

"And do what?"

The smile faded. "There must be lots of things you'd rather do. Don't you just want to chuck all this, get out from under?" He looked back at the sheaf of papers. "Think about it."

Jimmy sat up. "This isn't just idle chitchat, is it?"

Howard made a face, as if something disagreeable could no longer be avoided. He came around the desk and sat down. "Let's face it, Jimmy. You're not going anywhere here."

"I'm not?"

"Your contract runs out in August. That should give you

enough time to relocate. And Stanford, of course."

"I thought—"

Howard was shaking his head. "I'm bringing in someone from the coast to do the show with Karen, starting in July. Perfect match. It's somebody I met a long time ago in Beirut. Just a kid then, but an ace reporter, nobody better. Somebody I could really talk to. You'd like him." Howard looked him in the eye and blinked. "Look, there's just no painless way to do these things. We've known each other a long time. I want to be straight with you, buddy."

Straight's the word for it, buddy, Jimmy thought, straight and hard. He got to his feet, and so did Howard. "I'll be out by the end of the week, okay?"

"I want you out today. Don't forget, your salary's covered until the end of summer."

"I want it by the end of the week. Six months' worth, that's what I get."

Howard managed a feeble smile. "I see you've read your contract."

Something in his face made Jimmy start figuring. March to September, that was six months, too. What a coincidence. He and Stanford would be out of the way in plenty of time for Howard to ready his new anchors for the fall season. "Perfect timing, Howard. That's always been the key to your success, hasn't it? Beirut when the Marines blew up. In L.A. for the riots. In Chicago when the killer strikes. Good luck with Karen. How's the wife?"

He walked out without waiting for an answer. Dorothy was hovering just outside the door. She backed away, fluttering like a flushed bird. "You get all that?" Jimmy said. "You get that about the six months' pay?"

"Yeah, I got it. We'll make out the check," she said, trailing him down the hall. She had short legs and he was walking fast. "I got it because I'm the head spy. That's about all I'm head of so far, but I've been promised more authority, luv, and when I get it that'll be the end of *him*. He can't do this to people. You don't treat people like this. What's this about Stanford? When does he go?"

"He's got a few months, maybe a lot less."

"And you're leaving now?"

"Soon as I get my head together."

"That's terrible, Jimmy. That's awful." When she said nothing more, he turned around, walking backward. She was waiting, her bright Asian eyes watching him. He waved and kept going.

Karen's door was open, so he stopped and looked in. She was standing at a long work table, her back to him.

"You're here early," he said.

She turned, and it was clear that she had been crying. For an instant he wondered if the tears had been for him. Then she said dispiritedly, "Oh, it's you. Yes, I have to tape an interview. I have to leave in a few minutes. I was looking forward to it, since it's sports and I started in sports back home. But something's come up." She opened a closet and took out a fur that looked taller than she was. "Jimmy, now that you're here . . ." She got into the coat in one smooth wrapping motion that included closing the door. "What the hell, at least I know with you I can come right out and say it. I need a loan."

"Everybody I know seems to have perfect timing. It happens I've just come into some money."

She brightened and said breathlessly, "Have you? I don't need it long, and I can give you a post-dated check right now."

"How much?"

"Three thousand dollars."

He took that in. "I don't have it on me."

She didn't laugh. The fingers moving here and there as she fastened the coat about her were nervous. "I need it badly and I need it today, or I wouldn't ask. If you don't have it, just say so. With the divorce lawyers and the new apartment, it just *goes*. And I *had* to get a car! You can cash my check in six weeks, no sweat. Please, Jimmy. I'd ask my father, but I haven't spoken to my father since the divorce, and my mother won't stand up to him, and my sister . . . my sister's a troubled person. A very troubled person." She shrugged. "It's all right, I can probably get it someplace else. I don't want to put you on the spot."

Jimmy held up his hands. "Don't have my checkbook either."

"You don't understand. I need it in cash."

"You're in some kind of trouble."

"No, no, it's just that I've had a flock of overdrafts and I'm changing banks and I need it right away."

"Maybe the company . . ." Meaning, why not Howard?

"I don't want anyone to know about it. Not anyone at all, you understand?" She looked at her watch. "I've got to be out at the stadium in half an hour or His Bullness will be very angry and speed off in his Ferrari." She was talking about the biggest basketball star of all time, that's all. "Please, Jimmy, just to tide me over. There's no one else I can turn to. No one."

He thought about it. "All right, I'm taking the rest of the day off anyway. I'll have it for you by three o'clock when you come in for the staff meeting. You can give me the check then."

She brushed past him, pulling on her gloves and opening the door. "I'll be back by two. Small bills." She whirled and kissed him on the cheek. "I've got to run. You'll never know how relieved I am."

Stanford wasn't in. Jimmy called him at home.

"Jimmy? What's up?"

"I don't know, just feeling restless." He doesn't know either, Jimmy thought. Howard must be saving it for three o'clock. "I wanted you to hear it from me, Stanford. I've been bounced."

"Bounced? As in 'let go'?"

"Exactly. You haven't heard about anyone else, have you? There's kind of an undercurrent here about more to follow."

"No. No. Haven't heard a thing." There was a pause. "Jimmy, I'm next, is that what you're saying to me?"

"Give Dorothy a call. She may know something."

"All right." Another pause. "It's not as if it's a complete surprise. I mean, it is, about you. As for myself, I guess I knew it was coming. Still, one hopes. I had the impression he was behind me at least ninety-five percent. What are you going to do?"

"I'm going to my brother's wedding. Then maybe I'll go along on the honeymoon."

Stanford chuckled. "You'll wind up somewhere. At your age, a man's quick on his feet. I'm a little slower, but I can still do a pretty good buck and wing. I might go into his office that way this afternoon, how would that be? Shuffle off to Buffalo. Say, what's next on his agenda, anyway? Where's he heading with all this, do you know?"

"Aw, Stanford, it's new blood, new excitement, new thrills. No standing still or the past will catch up with you. Marlee had it right. Why lead when you can panic?"

"Oh, Marlee." Yet another pause. "Things just haven't

gone right since she left us, that dear woman. Well, he's right about one thing. I'm too old for this shit."

As far as Jimmy could recall, that was Stanford's first truly abandoned lapse into the vernacular of the city.

That afternoon, he collected three thousand dollars in small bills and Karen's post-dated check, then cleaned out his files and packed them in boxes and kissed Dorothy good-bye, driving by later, after the newsroom had cleared out, to pick up everything. As far as he could tell, Karen still didn't know he was leaving, only Dorothy and Stanford, the only people in the place he really cared about. Having heard nothing more from Stanford, he assumed his dismissal was on hold.

He sat around the house for ten days or so, leaving it only for food and drink and an occasional movie, and one more trip to the bank to deposit the check from Channel 2. He didn't watch the news. Then, the first week of March, he went to the wedding.

18

The plane taking the four of them to Wilkes-Barre was crowded, but Jimmy had gotten them into first class— Dutch, looking a bit peaked but nearly as big as life (the oversize vigor she remembered in him) and Patricia and her son, Billy, who at eighteen was nearly as tall as his dad. Mike was busy at the options exchange, and their seventeen-year-old daughter had stayed behind to look after him, really to keep an eye on her boyfriend. Frank and his family were driving up from D.C., and Emily was flying in from London, so the Gillespies, though considerably outnumbered by the bride's family, would be adequately represented.

Jimmy, as always when he was on vacation, wouldn't talk about his work. He sat across the aisle with Dutch, who had insisted on being able to look out the window even though he knew he'd be getting up frequently to go to the john. Watching him rise creakily and peer down the aisle, getting his bearings, then shove off, a bit wobbly but ramrod straight, Patricia recalled her father as he used to be, a size larger and craggier, ham-handed and abrupt, a great lover, she was sure, and a great scuffler, always grabbing you by the shoulders, challenging you not to like him but to *be* like him, even if you were female.

Patricia knew what life was and what death was, but where, she asked herself, do people go when they begin to die? Do they know? Do they know where they are, or are they just lost in all the confusion? Robust enough to assert themselves but too frail to do anything about it? Their gnarled hands reach out and then withdraw, as if they know it's no use, as if they're in training for another kind of life altogether, where it's all in the mind, and then all in the memories of those they leave behind.

What am I *doing?* she asked herself, beginning to mourn him already? Christ Jesus, I'm going to a wedding, not a funeral!

Beside her, Billy cried, "Ow, that smarts!" He was grinning up at Jimmy, who was standing in the aisle and had his nephew's bicep in a death grip, just like Dutch. Jimmy winked at Pat and said, "So what's this I hear about Princeton in the fall?"

Taking his arm back, Billy said, "Yeah. Well, that's where Dad went, back in the Dark Ages."

Patricia said, "Your father was quite a hit at Princeton. They remember him there." At least they seemed to, at the last reunion.

Billy asked his uncle, "Did Uncle Frank go to Princeton?"

"Shame on you. You don't remember his Notre Dame soccer stories?"

"Oh, yeah." Billy nodded. "Big man with Our Lady."

Pat, picking a thread off her skirt, gave a short laugh. "Your grandfather would dispute that. He never quite got over Frank not playing football."

"Soccer's just as rough."

She glanced up at Jimmy. "Try telling that to Dutch."

Dutch worried her, though. When her limo had stopped by that morning to take him to the airport, he hadn't answered her ring, so she had used her key and found him still dozing. He had looked up bleary-eyed when she shook him and said softly, "When did you die?" She had almost cried out, thinking he'd had a stroke. But it was only a dream he'd been having, and once she and Billy had gotten him into his brown woolen suit and tie, he was himself again, chin up and jaw set firmly, grumpy the way he had always looked in an argument. The browns set off his white hair, which held traces of the red that had always characterized him, like his temper. He had never been one to suffer fools gladly, not in his years as a crusty banker nor now. He probably didn't even understand the sense of that.

Hearing him yelling in the rear of the plane didn't particularly surprise her. There he was in the aisle, blocked by a serving cart and not about to put up with it. He actually *liked* upsetting people. That's why he had chosen a window seat. It wasn't the frosted brown fields, the sparkling icy waterways, the crisscross coagulations of towns and cities. It was so that he could be sure to bother somebody when he went to the bathroom. It gave him a feeling of power.

He was arguing with the flight attendant now. He cried, "Why do I have to cross the entire state of Ohio just to get to the can?"

Jimmy went back to extricate him, and after a while Dutch returned complaining about having to be rescued but giving Pat quick little leering grins. She hated the grins, but they weren't leering really, just his way of saying, Gotcha! while denying any embarrassment. Oh well, my God, this might be his last long trip. Surely he could be forgiven one more time.

That first night after the wedding rehearsal, so many people were crammed into the little twin living rooms that Dutch couldn't seem to get over it. Who could? But for him, Pat thought, it must be like coming suddenly into bright sunlight. Dazzling, and a little scary, all those old family feelings crowding back.

Raymond had chosen well. The bride was lovely and came well equipped with relatives: besides her mother and her uncles and aunts—one a priest, one a nun—eight strapping siblings, most of them married with offspring of every age. Not to mention all of their friends, some of them members of the wedding party. Dutch wandered around as if he knew everybody, somehow remembered them out of his long and variegated past. Actually dumbstruck, but looking terribly pleased, and apparently quite taken by Emily's new British accent, the way her sentences now ended in question marks.

Dutch had been in London during his old war. He had come away with profound respect for British proficiency in banking and governing. He listened, aghast, as Frank explained how the Democrats in Congress were forestalling national disaster by keeping the new president in line. Hogwash, Dutch said. Washington was so inept that it was turning the country back to the Indians by default. Frank giggled. His most endearing quality, Pat thought, was his unbounded appreciation of his father's most outrageous behavior. The giggle was only partly nerves. Dutch drove him wild sometimes. But Frank had the patience of a saint. Got it, she thought, from their mother, the first Mrs. Gillespie, surely as long-suffering and obliging as she was beautiful. Dutch had always picked women he thought he could manage like a bank.

At 11:30, most of the Gillespies went back to their hotel,

leaving Jimmy, the best man, and Dutch to share a room on the second floor of the crowded Beckham homestead. Jimmy had blinked when he heard that. Sleep with the old man?

Pat was overcome by mindless hilarity on the way downtown with Emily and her son. One of the elder Beckhams— an uncle, the one not a priest—was driving them, a friendly but taciturn man.

Billy, up in front, said, "What's wrong with that? I've slept with Dad lots of times."

"Well, you've never slept with Dutch," she said, tittering helplessly. "I can't imagine how either of his wives—" She fell suddenly silent.

"His wives what?" Emily said.

"Oh, nothing, dear." But neither of his wives had shared his bed for long. Ten years, no more. Both had died, Emily's mother horribly. "I was just thinking, he's slept alone so much of his life."

"So have I," Emily said. She was nearly thirty, and exquisitely small and dark. "But it's still not worth getting married for, just for that."

Billy, getting interested, swung around to look back at them. "Sure, I agree with that. Besides, look at all those women he hangs with down in Arizona."

"Billy!" Pat put a finger to her lips. The uncle was keeping awfully quiet.

"Well, you and Dad talk about it."

"He's old, Billy. It's not as if he sleeps with them. He goes down there to see your Uncle Eric—"

"The billionaire."

"Millionaire, and there are lots of friendly, very nice elderly widows—"

Emily said, "You think he might get married again?"

Pat stayed relaxed. "Arizona's exactly why he wouldn't."

"What do you mean by that?"

"Well, it's just what you were saying, all right? With all those widows at his beck and call, why should he?" Now how had she gotten trapped into saying that? Her son looked back in stern surprise. "Well," she said defensively, "that's what he says, I'm only quoting." She sighed. "Anyway, I've told you repeatedly, listen to me, not to your grandfather." That hadn't come out quite right either. But her son turned away and began talking to the uncle.

So she and Mike talked about it, did they? What else did Billy hear them talking about, ending a perfectly good marriage?

She said to Emily, "You must be exhausted after your flight," but she was only dimly aware of what anybody was saying after that. She wanted to go home. More than anything else at that moment, she wanted Mike.

19

Jimmy and his younger brother ran downtown the next morning, the Saturday of the wedding, which was scheduled for four o'clock. The sun was bright, but it was in the forties and they were zipped up tight. A bachelor's last fling, up Hazel Street and down past the YMCA, through town around the central traffic circle, then across the bridge over the river and into the park.

They cut past a small pond on which several mallards sat motionless, then across a wide expanse of grass to a high embankment, where Raymond pointed out twin culverts barricaded by heavy grillwork, long cylinders large enough to walk through. It was the local custom, he explained, to shout into them and wait for an echo. But the echo never came, so they charged up the slope and ran along the levee for half a mile, until it ended near a shopping center on the highway.

Starting back, Jimmy said he couldn't remember when he had felt so unfettered and free. "Loose as a goose" was what he said.

Raymond rolled his eyes. "You trying to tell me something on my wedding day?"

"No, I just feel lucky. Some days you feel lucky, you know?" So at a drug store near the traffic circle he bought two instant lottery tickets, not at all surprised when both of them paid off. He gave the bridegroom his twenty-five dollar winnings with the admonition not to spend it all in one place.

"I may have to," Raymond said, going out the door, "if that damn Buick breaks down in the Poconos."

"I thought you'd decided to get rid of it. You won't need it in Brooklyn."

"There's still lots of miles between here and Boston, then back again. Just pray it lasts through the honeymoon."

"Well, as long as the rest of your equipment is working. Bachelor party joke."

They were walking in the general direction of the downtown railyards, the sun in their eyes. Raymond yawned. "You sleep all right?"

Jimmy laughed. "Dutch has the most Godawful snore. He doesn't just snore, he groans and flings himself around like he's fighting somebody."

"Comes of sleeping alone."

"What's that supposed to mean? I'm a quiet sleeper."

"How do you know?"

"Aw, come on. Nobody's ever complained."

"She ever wake you up in the middle of the night?"

"Who?"

"Whoever's not complaining. Maybe it's not your irresistible body she wants when she wakes you up. Maybe it's a little sleep."

"How do you know all this?"

"I'm a lawyer. Lawyers have to know."

A red Corolla pulled alongside and a female voice said, "Hi, Mr. Gillespie! I hope you're enjoying your painting."

Something leaped in his chest, and Jimmy bent down to look in the window. "Kathleen?" What was the rest of it, O'Reilly? No, just Reilly. "Hi. Where you off to?"

"I'm going to work." Her smile seemed somewhat mocking, but he couldn't be sure because she looked all charged up, red lips and blue eyes and rust-red hair, and a rust-brown coat buttoned tight around her throat.

"This is my brother, my running partner. He's getting married today. Raymond, Kathleen."

"Oh, how wonderful! Congratulations!"

Raymond stuck his head in the window beside Jimmy's. "One of my fiancée's sisters thinks she knows you from high school. Julie Beckham."

She looked puzzled. "Time's gone by. I don't think I remember. What are you doing, out running on your wedding day?"

Raymond did his Groucho Marx bit, the cigar and the flickering fingers. "Nothing compared to the running I'll be doing after my wedding day."

She laughed. "Are you done? Can I give you a lift?"

Jimmy looked at his brother. "Ride?"

"Why not? It's my lucky day." Raymond got into the backseat. "I just won a small fortune in the lottery. What'll you take for this Corolla?"

At the gold-domed church, as directed, Kathleen turned down toward the house. She said to Jimmy, "I was going to write you about Karen."

"What about her?"

"I can't talk about it now." She braked, slowing down, and glanced at Jimmy. "Which house?"

"Right here," Raymond said, and the car drew to a stop. "Don't mind me, I've got a busy day planned." He got out. "Try to be back by two. I need guidance and counsel." He waved and went toward the house.

"You want to drive somewhere?" Jimmy said. "You have time?"

She nodded. "Afterward I'll just go to the mall store, as long as I'm out this way. Mother can handle things downtown. Have you seen all of Wilkes-Barre you want to see?"

"Everything except the mines, I guess. Somebody said there were still some old breaker sheds around."

She thought. "I'll show you one. It's right outside of town." She took off, making a left and pointing the car toward the mountains. He watched her as they entered the main highway and she accelerated, taking them up a long rise. Steady hands, he thought. Slow hands, like the country song.

"You're beautiful. You have strong, beautiful hands."

She gave him a swift, unsmiling look. "Hold it. You already told me that, and it's lucky I wasn't driving because I don't get told that every day. But you'd better stop saying it because I'm married. Very married. With two kids and a mortgage and a business to run." She glanced at him again and shook her head. "Oh, you're impossible! That's because you're Irish. But I really do need to talk to you, that's the only reason we're doing this. I have to apologize."

"For what? Karen's doing fine."

She shook her head again. "I can't think and drive. We're almost there."

They topped the crest of the hill and there it was, a brooding black rectangular building poking into the sky, reminding him sharply of the other mine fields he had seen, with their vibrations of the past: dripping water in the underground dark, the blown coal face, black clouds rising, the same gritty stuff that also filled the moaning cavern of the breaker shed, that dusted the floors of the houses and was ground forever into the miners' faces. She pulled off the highway and they sat looking at it, all its clanking frenzy stopped, though in his mind Jimmy heard it still yaw and rattle, its blackened and rusted old plates ready to collapse the way most of its windows had.

She said, "We used to ride our bikes out here and sit looking at it, from this very spot. Karen said she knew a way to get inside, but I never believed her, not at first. Later I found out lots of kids knew how to get in. They used to scare me with goblin stories."

"Have you been inside?"

"Just once. That was enough for me." The sun was bright, and her squinted eyes gave her face a pinched look. She seemed to shake it off, whatever had gone through her mind. "About Karen. I can't forgive myself, pushing her on you. I thought it would be so great, her getting married and moving to Chicago, and there you were, asking about the leaf, and I just couldn't help myself."

"So what's the problem?"

She stared grimly at him. "You don't know what I'm talking about, do you? Well, it's all over Wilkes-Barre, the divorce."

Jimmy smiled. "Well, sure, I know about that."

She looked away. "I don't mean just the divorce. I mean the rumors." She sounded angry.

He waited. When she didn't continue, he said, "Why do I think it's something ugly?"

"Don't laugh." Her hands gripped the steering wheel tight, but her voice had faltered. She looked as if she was holding a wheel of fortune she was too afraid to spin. "It's not as if it's a totally different chapter in her life. She's always been . . . free with men. Her sister was the same way. And her parents fought all the time because her father thought her mother was. Free with men." She leaned back and her hands fell to her lap. "Last summer, a few weeks before the wedding, there was some kind of high school reunion. A hotel in Scranton. Karen went. Dave couldn't, some last-minute thing at work. It turned out to be pretty wild. The story is she made out with half the football team."

"Huh. What does she say?"

"Wait. This all started coming out after the news about the divorce. The other story was, the night before the wedding, Dave found her in bed with the best man. She told him they'd been having an affair for months and were saying good-bye. It was over, she told him, all this kind of activity was over, and he forgave her. I don't know how, but he did. Dave has a lot of faith in people. Or he did."

"What about the football team?"

"I don't know. I guess she convinced him it didn't happen. But it did."

"So then why the divorce?"

"Your boss, you know him? I hear he's a very glamorous figure, a big war correspondent, very macho. Just Karen's type."

"Oh. I see."

"When Dave found out about that, he just went crazy. He packed and left, and that was it. Anyway, what I'm trying to say is, I'm just so—" She shut her eyes. "I'm just so sorry for her, and so angry at her, and I'm just so sorry I got you into this." She put one hand over her eyes, trying to hold herself in. "I really thought she'd changed, but right now . . . right now, she's down in Mexico!" She banged her fists on the steering wheel and then looked away, out at the highway, wiping her eyes and calming down. "I'm just so mad at her for pulling this, I could just die. Forgive me, I'm all right now." She sat back, found a tissue. "She called and said she needed some money to go down to Acapulco, somebody had invited her down there. Some married guy, right? She just laughed, she doesn't care what anybody thinks. I know she's hurting, but she won't let anybody see."

"Did you send her the money?"

"I sent her some. She said she'd get the rest."

"How long's she been gone?"

"Oh, just this weekend." She looked at him. "You didn't know she was gone?"

"I've been on vacation."

"Well, I hope none of this reflects on you, for getting her the job." She sighed. "That's what I had to say."

"So who's she down there with? Not the boss."

"No, it's a whole new thing. I don't know, I don't care. That's enough about Karen." She straightened her coat beneath her and reached for the key in the ignition.

"Kathleen."

"What?" She looked at him.

"I know I'm not supposed to say it—"

"Then don't say it." A slight frown clicked into her eyes. "Did you and Karen ever talk about me?"

"No, I don't think we ever did."

She started to say something more. Stopped and tried again, somewhat shyly. "Did she ever come on to you?"

He hesitated. "Not really. Briefly. I thought we might have something going, but it stopped as soon as it began."

"That's because you're not married. Married men turn her on." She colored, then made herself say it. "Maybe you're the same way. Maybe that's why you keep—"

"What?"

"Coming on to me."

Well, there she was, this married woman with kids and a career and lightly freckled skin infused with a glow from inside, like her paintings, and hair a hot russet color that reminded him of prairie grass, rich autumn browns that turned red at sunset and even in the early winter rains. And Raymond was about to plight his troth and there were faint signs of spring across the rounded mountains, so he leaned over and kissed her, young Mrs. Reilly. She moaned, "I can't do this, somebody will see," but let him kiss her again and then hold her, his lips to her ear, repeating over and over, like a mantra, "Kathleen. Kathleen."

20

Looking frightened nearly out of her mind by her feelings, Kathleen let him out on Hazel, a block or so from the Beckham place. It was around noon and she was very late for work. "Dinner," he said, leaning in the window. "I leave tomorrow."

"Impossible. You don't know what you're asking. This is a small town compared to Chicago."

"Out of town then."

She stared at him, looking as if she wanted to flee. "I don't know. Call me. I'll be at the downtown store until late. Call after five." She took her foot off the brake and Jimmy stepped back as the Corolla bounded away. He watched it turn at the light, and then he crossed the street, heading up the slope toward the house.

Half a block along he looked up, hearing the distant clank and rattle of tin cans on pavement. Far up the long hill that led to the church where the ceremony would take place, Raymond's old Buick was coming down toward him. It was trailing tin cans and a couple of dozen people, little kids among them.

Most of this festive crowd appeared to be Beckhams, or Beckham friends, and most were casually dressed in jeans and ski togs. But the young men running alongside the car wore various items of formal wear—black trousers and stiff white shirts, with an occasional black tie, or a tie undone and flying, with several black jackets among them. For a moment, Jimmy was afraid he had missed the wedding.

But the bright yellow head in the crowd belonged to Gwen, and as the Buick approached the turnoff to the house he saw that the driver in the red sweater was Raymond, and that the car was coasting silently downward, engineless. Raymond braked, making the turn, and Jimmy fell in beside Gwen, noting the sign in the rear window that spelled out JUST MARRIED.

"What's up?" he asked, and she said gaily, "Oh, they took the car up to the church to decorate, and Raymond went up after them because he was afraid it wouldn't start, and of course it wouldn't. He's fit to be tied!"

As the car rolled to a stop in front of the house, a round of applause came from the porch. It was led by the uncle who was a priest, a genial man whose eyes seemed to have seen everything.

"Hey, Father, where were you?" someone shouted. "We coulda used some Hail Marys."

"I don't do miracles," the priest called back. "My job stops at the altar."

The hood of the Buick went up, and as one of her brothers leaned down to inspect the engine Gwendolyn cried, "Oh, look at Joe, he's going to fix it!"

"He much of a mechanic?"

She laughed. "The worst!" She joined the others drifting up the front stairs, and Jimmy went over to the car.

"It's the water pump," Joe said, coming up for air.

"Hey, Raymond, it's the water pump," another brother said, and bent down for a look.

"Water pump!" Raymond muttered to Jimmy. "The frigging garageman ordered one three days ago and I'm still waiting." He looked around as Patricia called down from the porch, "Your father wants to help. Is it all right?"

Dutch, standing beside her, said, "Of course it's all right." His hair was in disarray, and he wore a heavy dark topcoat buttoned over his pajamas.

Jimmy went over and watched him come down the stairs, one step at a time. Two down, several more to go. "Raymond's waiting for a part, Dad."

Dutch glowered, taking another step. "Does he know what's wrong?"

"He thinks so. He's got a water pump on order."

"Well, it could be the water pump." Another step, another glower. "Or it might not." He took the last steps to the sidewalk and looked around. "You were the only one who was good at cars. Is Raymond any good at cars?" There was a lot Dutch didn't know about his last-born.

"He does okay, Dad."

"Why aren't you out there?"

"Waiting for the expert."

Dutch grinned. "Well, he's arrived." He moved off toward the street.

Jimmy went up onto the porch, and Patricia said impatiently, "Let him think he's doing something. Let's go in. I'm cold."

They stood inside the storm door watching their father shoo the younger men away from the Buick, taking over. The large living room, interrupted midway by low, pillared dividers along two walls, was filled with kids playing board games and watching a video of *The Sleeping Beauty* as grownups came and went. Frank joined them at the door. "They've got soup and hoagies in the kitchen," he said. "Want some?" Pat shook her head. "I tried to get Dad into some clothes, but he was in a hurry. You think he's warm enough out there?"

Pat said, "Don't worry about him, he's in his element. Cars and boys."

"Ah," Frank said, "do I detect a note of rancor?"

"You bet." She sniffled, and Jimmy was surprised to see tears in her eyes.

"What's the matter?"

"Oh, God," she said, "don't let anyone see me like this." She found a handkerchief and blew her nose. "I told Frank, you might as well know. I called Mike last night. He wants to talk about a trial separation when I get back."

"How long has this been going on?"

"Months. I wanted to keep it quiet until after Christmas, then after the wedding, but I don't care anymore."

"Does Dad know?"

"Oh, God, no. Neither do the children."

One of Gwendolyn's sisters stopped by with a platter of sandwiches and asked, "Is everything okay?"

"Fine," Frank said with a smile. "Wedding jitters."

With a concerned look at Pat, the sister made herself scarce. Pat said, "Here he comes. Tell him I'm upstairs with Emily. If he asks." She turned away as Dutch began the long climb to the porch.

Jimmy said to his brother, "What can I do, anything? Take Mike to lunch?"

"They'll work it out. Mike's a good man."

"I thought she was a little hyper at Christmas."

"Actually she's been taking it well, considering. Divorce was never her favorite thing."

Breathing hard, Dutch made his way inside. "It's the water pump. You know your cars, Jimmy." He nodded emphatically. "Now, listen, here's how we handle it. You boys go downtown and rent a car. I don't care what kind it is, I'll pay for it, a wedding present. Now, when he gets back to Boston, Raymond's going to lease one until they get settled. He'll send me the bill."

"We can help, Dad," Frank said.

Dutch eyed him. "Like hell. This is my son, you leave it to me. Where's Patricia?"

"Upstairs. She and Emily are getting dressed."

Dutch snorted. "Humoring me." He took a couple of deep breaths. "Didn't think I'd find out what it was. The water pump, did I tell you that?" His bleary eyes tracked across the rug, past children at their games to the scattering of husbands and wives, parents, brothers and sisters, uncles and aunts, the lot of them, friends and family, extended, extruded, yet here, on this day, compressed and compact, each an original. To Jimmy, they had the look of a caravan come to rest.

All at once the old man cleared his throat and called out, "It's the water pump!" and everyone looked up, all but the youngest, attentive, acknowledging the information and seeming to estimate how far in years and accumulated wisdom it was from them to him, this prophet, this seer, this ancient of days. Pleased, Dutch made his way through them toward the kitchen.

Frank said softly, "It's the water pump," and Jimmy nodded. "You better believe it."

For Jimmy, as he dug the ring out of his pocket and handed it to Raymond that afternoon, the wedding was an occasion for wondering how his brother, a whole decade younger, had made it to the altar ahead of him. It was as if he had momentarily looked away and the world had jerked forward, leaving him in another country. At the reception in a downtown hotel, while the gleeful bride was being relieved of the obligatory red ruffled garter, he slipped out and called the bookstore.

Kathleen sounded worried and unapproachable. "Yes, all right. Dave's out of town, and I went home to change. And explain to the sitter I'll be working late. I hate doing this."

"Then don't do it." Jimmy waited. "No. Do it."

"I am. I want to. You know what I mean. I feel so guilty. I'm very happily married. I love my husband, I love my kids. Isn't that enough?"

"Well, why isn't it?"

"I don't know. I want to see you. I want something more than I've got. Maybe I'm just bored." When Jimmy made no comment, she said, "I've never done anything like this. I'm terrified of being seen."

"It's just dinner, Kathleen."

"Exactly. I know that. What about the bride and groom, will you be there to see them off?"

"They're leaving in the morning. They have a room in the hotel."

She laughed, sounding relieved. "I'll get you back early so you can bang on their door."

It was a small neighborhood restaurant ten miles or so toward Scranton. They had drinks at the bar and Kathleen ordered for both of them. Strombolis, ethnic and delicious, pastry baked around seafood. She wore an almost sleeveless sea-green dress that showed off her long slender arms. Her fingers sparkled with rings, gold and silver and deep amethyst and one large pale opal. Her wrists were bare of jewelry, and in the candlelight he noticed for the first time the tracery of pink lines running along the inside of one wrist halfway to the elbow. The lines were too faint to be called scars.

Putting down his wine, he took the wrist and drew it toward him. "What are those?"

She looked down at her arm without expression. "Oh, that. Youthful indiscretion. You see, I have been indiscreet before."

He frowned. "Meaning what exactly?"

Kathleen withdrew her arm and put her hands in her lap. "It happened a long time ago."

"What did?"

She sat looking down at her wine glass. Jimmy had the impression that the blood pulsing through her temples was coloring the roots of her hair and filling her up with fearsome memories, making her draw away. Not so much from him as into herself. He said, "You don't have to talk about it," and waited. Time went by, maybe a full minute.

Then she said, "No, I want to." She looked up but not at him, and gradually she seemed to come back. "It was a bad time, right after high school. I was supposed to go to college and then get married. It was all planned out, but I didn't want to. I took to brooding a lot. Crying jags. Once I left home for a week and didn't tell anyone where I was. I took the bus to Philadelphia and stayed in a rooming house downtown. It was awful. I cried a lot. I didn't even go out. I remember sitting at the window and staring down at this gas station next door, where this little boy rode his tricycle around and around and around. I don't remember how I got home. I wound up seeing a psychotherapist and spent some time in a hospital ward. I told him I wanted to die. I wanted to kill myself."

"Because of all the plans?"

"Because I hated my life. It was over. There were no more surprises." She shrugged. "Sometimes you just can't do it, what's expected."

"Go on."

"So I did. I mean I tried, but I couldn't do it. I even had some help, can you believe it? That knocked me out. I couldn't believe someone would go that far for another person. And so I went ahead to college. I don't know how I got through the first two years. Eventually, in my junior year, I moved in with the boy I was supposed to marry. He practically looked after me, like my mother, and that knocked me out, too. I began to see him differently, and marriage, and everything." She smiled. He liked the way the corners of her mouth turned up, like the rounded lips of a ceramic pitcher. "So you see, I don't ever want to hurt him."

"Who tried to help?"

She sipped her wine. "Just a friend."

"How?"

"What I was using. A razor blade. This person . . . this guy I knew saw the scratches and made me go home and get it. He took it and I thought he was going to lecture me, but what he said was, 'We can do better than that.' "

"My God."

"I know it sounds bad, but it wasn't like that. He wouldn't have done it, not really. But it shocked me, it woke me up. Really! I was touched. People—" She stopped, looking inward again. "That's the reason I couldn't go through with it. People like that, and like my husband. They cared. They were kind and supportive, and they let me make choices. Hard choices. I wouldn't have come tonight if I hadn't learned I could make my own mistakes. I'd have stayed home like a good little wife."

Jimmy said, "What's kind about helping you kill your-self?"

She stared back. "Maybe you have to be cruel sometimes, to be kind." She shook her head. "No, I don't mean cruel, I mean honest. He said if I'd made up my mind to kill myself, I had that right. I believe that, don't you? Is this making any sense to you? Anyway, I started getting better after that."

"Maybe you were already getting better."

"Maybe." She seemed doubtful. "Part of my trouble was I always used to envy girls who didn't take themselves too seriously, because I did." She laughed. "Like Karen, she was so bad! She had this terrible reputation. To tell you the truth, back then I found it kind of thrilling."

"When you were kids?"

She nodded. "We practically grew up together. Week-ends, her parents would drive down from Scranton and drop her off, and there were whole summers she'd stay at my house. Oh, it wasn't me she came for. She'd have done anything to get away from home. In high school, she'd go off on her own, dating Wilkes-Barre boys, but we saw a lot of each other. We were on the same track, college and marriage and a family, but with her it was different because she'd mapped it out all by herself. She didn't understand me, but that was okay because I didn't either. I envied her, but I didn't know how to be like that. Maybe she didn't understand herself as well as she thought she did."

Jimmy looked down at his empty glass. "This guy in Acapulco. You know anything about him, anything at all?"

She shook her head. "I didn't want to know. He could have been from down there. I think she said he was Latin."

"Try to think."

"Just Latin. I think she mentioned his accent or something. That's all I know."

Outside, it had turned colder, and in the darkness Jimmy felt the soft plops of snow on his face before he saw the big flakes coming down. He took Kathleen's arm, felt her shiver.

"Kathleen?"

"Don't say it."

He watched a car go by in the snow. "That's not what I was going to say."

"What then?"

"Don't ever do that again."

"What?"

"Cut yourself."

"I won't. Jimmy? Have they always called you that?"

"Yes."

"I used to be called Katie when I was little. Karen called me Kate. She thought we'd make a cute sister act. You know, Kate and Karen, Karen and Kate?"

"But you chose Kathleen."

"Yes, that's who I wanted to be."

In the light from the street, her nose made a perfect little swoop at the end, like a child's slide. He reached out and touched it. It was damp, from the snow. He leaned down and kissed her. "I could love you, Kathleen Reilly."

"Don't. It wouldn't be right."

"I may not have a choice."

"I mean it. You always have a choice. Besides, I might not be able to stand it."

"What?"

"I don't know if I could stay away from you."

He smiled, looking down at her. "I want you, Kathleen."

"I know. It's not possible."

"I'm flying out tomorrow."

"I know."

"I'll be back." She smiled and looked away. He said, "I will."

"I don't know if it's a good idea." Her eyes came up. "Even if I wanted to, Jimmy Gillespie, we could never do what you have in mind. You understand why?"

He nodded, then put his arm around her and walked her to the car. He started to look for his keys, to open the passenger door, when he remembered. "I forgot, it's your car."

She held up the key like a crucifix between them. "My car, and my life. Don't forget that."

He nodded. She kissed him lightly, like the snow, then went quickly around to the driver's side.

21

Sergeant Kirkpatrick looked the young woman sternly in the eye. Ginko had begged off, saying he needed to do some more legwork in the neighborhood, and this was the second interview. It was going better than the first, but she still couldn't seem to bring herself to look up at him. Though she was much calmer, her eyes still shifted this way and that. Didn't want him to think she noticed, was that it? His one eye going off to the right? Well, Clara Turner was obviously a sensitive soul. Trembling. Jumpy as hell. The important thing, though, was that she seemed to know what she was talking about.

"What's this about a cabin in the woods?"

She nodded vigorously. "Yes, and he wanted me to go there with him. He wanted me to spend several days there while he was working on the shack, and we'd have to sleep in a tent."

"Where was this? Some forest preserve?"

"I don't know. He didn't tell me that." She nodded. "Yes, and he said I could help him paint. He said it would be part of the treatment."

"Paint what? Paintings?"

"No." Suddenly she seemed irritated with him. Did she suspect he was a little slow? "The shack. He was building a shack in the woods, so he could take his patients out there for therapy."

"So you'd paint and that would be part of your therapy, is that it?"

"Occupational therapy, yes."

"But you didn't go."

"No! When I told my boss at work, he got all upset. He said, 'Don't you go out there with him, Clara. Don't you go out there in the woods.' "

"You told your boss about this?"

"Yes, and you want to know something?" She glanced up, but not quite at him. "That was the last place I ever worked because then I got real sick from the drugs and was hospitalized, and the nurses said, 'Tell us his name,' and I wouldn't. I was too scared. Then I was transferred to the psychiatric ward and that's where I met the doctor I have now. He asked me if I wanted him to call this man and I said no, I was afraid of what he might do to me."

She almost looked up again. "The first thing I remember was waking up in bed, and there was Dr. Loomis. That's my doctor, the one I have now. He was bending over me, and the first thing he said to me was, 'Is there something you want to tell me?' And I said, 'Yes, I've just been sexually abused.' And then he said, 'Do you want me to call him?' and I said no. I was too scared. I've never told anybody his name but you."

"And you never saw him again? Until the other day?"

"No. I thought I was going to faint, seeing him again. He looked just the same, only much older."

"When you were in treatment with him, you said he gave you drugs. Thorazine?"

"Yes, and listen to this. He nearly killed me then. Once he gave me a really powerful sleeping pill, I'll think of the name in a minute. He could prescribe these things so he was a doctor, but he couldn't have been a psychiatrist. I'd get the prescriptions filled at the drugstore, and one day the druggist said to me, 'Clara, do you know what you're taking here? Some of these could kill you if you took a drink.' You know, alcohol. And I said, 'I don't drink,' and he said, 'Good. But be careful. We've got our eye on Doctor So-and-so.' "

"Okay, Clara, we have the name, but we still have to find him. Any idea where he went when he moved out of his office?" She shook her head. "No idea where the woods were?"

She glanced up as if she thought Kirk might be off his rocker. "He wouldn't be there. It's too cold."

Well, he thought, she's right there, on both counts. "Clara, I wonder if you'd do something for me. Now that we know he's around someplace, I'd like you to have some protection for a few days, just while you're on the street. You wouldn't see the officers, but if the doctor showed up you could let them know. Give them a pre-arranged signal. The two detectives who were with you the other night got a peek at him. I'd like to assign them. What do you say?"

"It's so cold out. Would I have to walk very far?"

"No, we'll keep it short, maybe half a mile from your place. And you can stop in a restaurant for coffee when you feel like you've walked too far. Sit in the window where we can see you every minute. We'll buy."

She smiled. "Oh, that'd be nice! I'd like that. What do I do if I see him?"

"Well, maybe you'd be wearing a scarf. Then when you see him, you could take it off."

"Oh, I see! Yes, that'd be good."

"Chances are we'll see him before you do. And don't worry, we'll be right with you every step of the way. Now, do you think you can do that?"

She nodded. She wasn't trembling, and she was looking him right in the eye.

Scharf and his partner were lounging in their car near a Mexican restaurant on Dearborn, waiting for Clara to come out. The entrance was across Dearborn, on the corner. They could see her in the window, second table back, wearing a bright blue scarf. This was the third day of the watch, and though it was only for a few hours each time, they'd had enough.

"At least the weather's holding out," the partner said. The morning had started out almost balmy for March, but now the wind had changed and it was turning cold again.

"That must be her fourth cup of coffee. Don't you think she'd have to go to the can? I never see her use the can."

"She says she wants to keep visible, even if she doesn't know where we are."

"Where the hell is he? Where is he, anyway?" Scharf slumped farther down in the seat and tipped his hat over his eyes. "Wake me when it's over. If I don't respond, you'll know I've been bored to death."

After a while the partner said, "You think the guy will show up?"

"I don't know him that well. Do you?"

"He gave me the finger. Maybe he thinks he's impervious."

"Impervious. Is that like pervert?"

"If it fits, use it. She says he only took good-looking dolls at his clinic. But he's more screwbally than that. She says he was always breaking into tears, afraid his girlfriend was leaving him. Says he smelled. Didn't believe in washing up."

"Yeah. That didn't stop him from tossing her into cold showers. What I don't get, why would she let him do that stuff to her?"

"She was sick. He had her doped up."

"If you ask me, she enjoyed it."

"How could somebody enjoy cold showers? Anyway, she says he was the first guy ever touched her. Hard to believe she was that inexperienced, but he was a doctor. She thought she didn't have a choice but to trust him."

"It's like a cult. What was the name of that clinic? Transcendental something?"

"Something like that."

"Something more French. International something."

"International House of Fruitcakes."

"Yeah, amour, amour. All those French are sick. Mention something dirty, they did it first. French kiss."

"Yeah, but good things too. French fries, French doors, French wine. . . ."

Scharf said, "Okay, who lost two world wars? Who lost Indochina and Algiers? Have they ever won a war? Napoleon got beat at Waterloo. He lost Russia."

"They lost Indochina? Wasn't that Vietnam, before?"

"They put a curse on the place."

The partner took hold of the steering wheel. "How did we get onto the French?"

"The doctor."

"Is he French?"

"Only that he's flaky." Scharf tipped his hat back. "Look, she's going to pay the check." He waited, "Now where's she going?"

"Maybe to the bathroom."

Scharf sat upright. "Did she have the scarf on?"

"How do I know? She just ducked back there."

"I didn't notice either. God damn it, where'd she go?"

The partner put his hand on the gear shift. "She'll be back."

Scharf settled lower again. "Let me know when she shows."

"Look, there he is." Scharf raised up a little. "He's coming out. It's him! He's looking around."

"I can see. Cruise!"

The partner jammed the car in gear and it roared away from the curb, slicing into the opposite lane toward the intersection. Cars coming from the opposite direction screeched and swerved out of the way. "He's back inside."

"Get me to the corner and cover the rear. Where the hell is she, anyway?"

Ginko came on the phone. "Scharf? How could you lose them? Both of them? Never mind. Take it easy, I'll tell you how. She panicked and ran out the back, the way he came in. I don't know, maybe he thought she went to the restroom. She called from the Chicago Avenue subway. Kirk told her to stay there, but she was too scared. So he told her to take the next train and we'd meet her at the end of the line. Get there as soon as you can. By the way, she won't be wearing the scarf. She lost it on the way to the subway. Yeah, what's so odd about that? Didn't you ever mis-

place a personal item, Scharf? Put it in the wrong place?
Your dick, for instance?"

Howard Street, the dividing line between Chicago and the
northern suburbs, always sounded like a parade. Just one
marching band after another, the bass drums coming along
every sixty seconds. Only what it was was the sound of cars
stereophonically wired, and the pounding was so loud you
expected to see the car inflating rhythmically, like a Disney
cartoon. It wasn't a pretty street to look at either, at least not
where the elevated ran. Down at street level, on a light pole,
a faded banner read, HOWARD STREET, NEIGHBORHOOD SHOP-
PING IN CHICAGO, WELCOME, the only sign the street might
have higher aspirations.

Kirkpatrick stood on the platform with Scharf's partner,
staring down at what he could see of it. Howard Street was
the end of the line for the Chicago El. The trains were
stopped, cleared of all passengers and then sent on a run
around the yards, which were actually in Evanston across
the street, returning empty along the other platform for the
trip back downtown. A few people over there stood waiting for trains, and once in a while an empty came along.
Scharf and Ginko were down below in the station, among
the fruit vendors and dealers of stale donuts and filthy
magazines.

"They think they figured out which train, but we can't be
sure," the sergeant said to the partner. "We can't even be
sure she got on one, much less where he is." The wind was
cold up here, blowing pretty good off the lake. He pulled
his coat up around his throat and glanced at the waiting
passengers, finding the plainclothes transit cop who was
supposed to point out the right train. The transit cop was an
offduty Chicago police officer, but he looked like he'd just

gotten out of bed. There were only a few people on this platform, maybe waiting for the Skokie Swift. He hoped it wouldn't be too difficult, finding Clara or the doctor when the train unloaded. "I hate to think what she's thinking right now," he told Scharf's partner. "Probably wondering if this will put her back in the psycho ward."

"Or the cemetery."

A northbound train was stopped at a signal a hundred feet away. The transit cop shook his head: Not this one, not yet. After a while it came on, disgorged its passengers and then moved off toward the turnaround tracks, vanishing among the surrounding buildings.

It wasn't the rush hour, so trains were fewer and farther between. They could figure out which train was due when she hung up the phone, and they could surmise she had taken it because she wasn't in the subway when they got there and the one after that came along. But that's the best they could do. There was no way to tell, for instance, if she might have hung up the phone and returned to the street.

"Next one," the transit cop said, suddenly beside him.

"How long?"

"Five, ten minutes."

"Well, you have their descriptions." The cop nodded and moved off. He said to the partner, "I'll be around the corner," and eased around to the other side of the covered stairwell, leaning back against the wall, glad to be out of the wind. He was facing the empty platform fifteen feet away and at the top of the four-story building beyond it. There were no people on the other platform because Scharf and Ginko, downstairs, weren't letting them go up. The bank nearby had Art Deco designs grooved into its cement wall. Across Howard Street, to his right, a two-story building's intricate terra cotta facade ran for half a block. He was reminded of his youth, when such decorated structures were signs of growth, not tarnished decay.

The train was on time. It paused, then came ahead, rolling along the platform. It stopped and the doors opened. "Everybody out," came the scratchy amplified voice from inside. "All passengers must leave the train at Howard Street." He watched as those disembarking headed toward him for the stairs or straggled up the platform to wait for a train that would take them into Evanston or Wilmette or Skokie. None of the passengers was Clara, but more than one resembled the doctor. The train doors closed and it moved off.

Kirkpatrick had just leaned back again when suddenly there came a sharp little scream and people began backing away in alarm. He pushed his way into the crowd. A man was spreadeagled against the opposite wall of the stairwell, the other two cops standing over him.

"No sweat, sergeant," the partner said. "He's clean, except for these." He held out his hand. In his palm was a plastic razor along with several single-edge razor blades in cardboard protectors.

Kirkpatrick took one of the sheathed blades and held it in front of the doctor's face. "What are these?" The man's old woolen coat flapped unbuttoned in the wind. He was ridiculously thin, with a four-day-old scabrous-looking beard and red, rheumy eyes. "Is this what you use when you get the urge?"

"I have to shave like everybody else," the man replied. There was a flash of yellow teeth.

"What, with this?" The sergeant held up the razor. "Sure, once a week. But look, these blades don't fit. What do you do with them?" He grasped the doctor's shoulder and spun him around. "Look at me! Where's the girl?"

"I don't know what you mean."

"Was she on the train? Where is she?" The doctor shook his head, not so arrogant now. In fact, he looked oddly abject, as if he might cry. Kirkpatrick turned to the transit cop. "Couldn't you hold the train, for Christ's sake?"

"What for?" the cop said. "Everybody got off."

"Not if one of them was a body. Where's the train now?"

"It'll be back in a minute, on the other platform."

Kirkpatrick said to the partner, "Read him his rights and cuff him," and told the transit cop to go downstairs and send the other two detectives up. "But stay down there and keep the other platform empty. No passengers, you hear me?" To the curious, as he pushed his way through, he said, "Keep going, vamoose. Get lost, it's all over," and then he started to run.

At the end of the platform, a stairwell led up to a railed walkway over the tracks. He ran up, crossed over, and made the other platform just as an empty train pulled in. He ran alongside it, stopping to peer into the moving cars through the narrow windows of doors that wouldn't open, no matter how hard his fists banged on them. The train came to a stop, and he shouted, "Open up, for Christ's sake! Open the fucking doors!"

Midway along the train, he heard Scharf's partner shouting from the other track. "That's not it! The next one. The one after that!" The sergeant turned and nodded, seeing the doctor sitting with his back to the wall of the stairwell. Several other transit workers were clearing that platform of arriving passengers. Scharf, he saw, was on the pay phone, probably filling in the captain.

Then he saw Ginko far up the same platform, heading for

the stairs that led over the tracks. He turned back to the empty train, which had started again. It stopped as soon as it had cleared the platform, leaving room for the next. He stood looking at the bank building across the way, waiting.

Ginko came puffing up, and the sergeant said, "Go all the way down. When it gets here, start working your way toward me. We'll meet in the middle." His partner nodded and went on past. Kirkpatrick turned and walked the other way.

Any minute the train would return, and then he would have to walk through it, hoping not to find her. He tried not to picture her, tried not to imagine whether it would be the wrists or the throat, tried hard not to think of her at all. He wished he played golf, then he would have something else to think about. He wished the bank over there were brand new, that this was then, not now. Then years would have to go by before he would have to be here, in the wind, wondering where the hell she was and hoping not to find out.

He heard the train before he saw it coming, and as it ground to a halt, sounding eerily empty, he began moving down the platform, peering in and pounding on the doors. "Clara! You in there?" Why the fuck didn't they open up?

When the doors finally slid apart and Clara fell out, it was far down the platform and into Ginko's arms.

"She's okay," Ginko shouted, but it looked as if he was supporting her full weight because she couldn't seem to stand.

Running toward them, Kirkpatrick called out, "You sure?" Her head was on Ginko's shoulder and her long flaxen hair hid her face.

"Yeah, she told me," his partner said as he reached them. But her breath was coming in gasps, and she shook uncontrollably.

Together, they walked her to a bench, where she collapsed in a heap, drawing her legs up, her eyes shut tight. They bent over her, and when she opened her eyes she said three words, getting them between spasmodic sobs: "What's your name?" She was staring up at Ginko.

"Gruszczynski," he said with a grin, pronouncing it for her: Gruth-trinth-ski. "Okay?"

She nodded and closed her eyes again. Kirkpatrick straightened up and called out to Scharf on the other platform. "She's all right. Take him downtown." Then he leaned down and said to Clara, "He's gone. We have him in custody. What happened on the train?"

She opened her eyes and swallowed. "Nothing."

He stared down at her. He thought he had never seen a countenance so guileless, so innocent, so pure. "Nothing?"

She nodded. "I knew he was there, I could feel it. But I never saw him, not once. I went through the cars until I was nearly at the end of the train, and then I had to sit down. It was so cold I had to put on my hat. I guess that's why he didn't recognize me."

"You had a hat?"

She nodded, getting a little into the spirit of it. "I keep it in my purse, for when it gets really cold. I pulled it down over my ears and put my head down, and I pretended to be asleep. I was too scared to move. I could hardly breathe."

Ginko looked up at him in amusement. "The guy was looking for somebody in a scarf. He didn't know she'd be wearing this." He dug into the pocket of his coat, producing a red stocking cap.

"You put that on, huh," Kirkpatrick said. "A ski hat."

She nodded. "I think I'd better sit up now. I feel kind of sick." They helped her do so, and Ginko sat down beside her, one arm gripping her shoulders. "Yes, and listen to this. When the train stopped I was too terrified to get off with the others. I knew he'd be out there, so I just stayed on. I didn't know where it was going, but I said a little prayer that when it stopped he'd be gone." She looked over at Ginko. "I was so happy it was you and not him. I hope I didn't embarrass you, falling all over you like that. Could you say your name for me one more time?"

"Gruszczynski. It's Polish."

She nodded. "Yes, and the pope is Polish."

Ginko smiled and looked up at Kirkpatrick. "See, the pope is Polish. Now will you believe me?"

22

The morning of the doctor's bond hearing, Jimmy called Dorothy to check on Stanford. She sounded different. He was used to hearing her voice at full throttle, and now she was trying not to be overheard.

"No, Stanford didn't get his walking papers yet," she said, "but Mr. Big's gone off like a flash to New York. He's been promoted out of here to the network. I don't think he liked you, honey. I don't think he thought you were too bright, or maybe a radical."

"He was right. I could never take him seriously."

"Un-huh, bad attitude. Anyway, with him gone, Howard's lost his best friend around here. They're bringing in a new general manager in a week or so, I think from New Orleans. Too bad Howard moved on you so soon. I don't think he wants to make any more moves until the new boss gets here. Oh, and he's changed his mind about the California dude."

"Karen get back all right?"

"Oh, was she gone? He's been awful jumpy, maybe that's why. One thing he did do, he made me special assistant to the executive producer. From what I can see, so far I'm still just his secretary. I think he wanted to butter me up a little."

"Congratulations."

"Un-huh. Thank you, honey. You all right?"

"Fine."

"That's good. He's been working overtime on that computer of his, writing down all kinds of trash. I finally figured out the poetry. It's not poetry, it's love letters! I can't always make out who it's to. You know it's got to be Karen when he spells out her name in the shape of a heart, but that other stuff—"

"Dorothy, does he give you these things to send out?" She made no reply. "Are you going into his computer?"

She gave out a hushed but gleeful chuckle, then shushed herself. "Honey, how you think I got my new title?"

"That's blackmail, Dorothy."

"You call it what you like. I call it whitemail, and that's spelled m-a-l-e. You innocent Caucasian boys got a way of digging yourselves in deeper and deeper, like a sticky fly in the ointment."

"You have printouts?"

"Honey, I got better than that. I made a copy of his disk. You think he wants his wife to know about those letters? Sugar this and sugar that, I think it must be half a dozen different women, one of them in sales. You think she wouldn't do a slow burn? And how about company time? Stay tuned, honey."

"That's why Stanford's still there, isn't it?"

She hesitated. "He's coming. I got to go. Remember, Jimmy honey, next time you mail me a postcard, make it out 'special assistant.' "

"How about 'Ms. Big?' "

He had spent most of his time since the wedding sorting

out his job options. They looked slim. Now that the serial killer had been caught, Channel 7 wasn't buying into his special connections to the case, and although he knew a lot of people at Channel 5, he wasn't sure he was ready to go back to so many bad memories, all those upturned faces. Nobody had a real anchor problem except maybe the independent station. He'd had a feeler from the Fox outlet, but neither of these places seemed to regard him as more than an extra body, so he decided to let things lie. Maybe it was time to try something different. Get back into print. Maybe carpentry. Frank had always wanted him to try public relations, but he thought he could do better than that. PR was a last resort. In that regard, Jimmy was a purist.

Meanwhile, he had no immediate money problems except the unsecured loan to Karen, which all of a sudden had begun to look like a bad debt, and his morale was okay except when he thought of Kathleen.

It made no sense to him that he hadn't simply been able to walk off with her. Maybe he had been spoiled by too many women who hadn't hesitated to get down on their knees, some of them literally, and beg for his undivided attention. But he had never wanted to tie himself to one woman. Marriage, for now, was out of the question. He found it impossible to imagine being as married as Frank, or as passionately wedded as Patricia had seemed to be until now. Or as Raymond was, off in the Poconos. But then he had never felt as certain of his feelings toward anyone as he did toward Kathleen. So where was she? Why wasn't she here? He knew what her answer would be, but her absence troubled him all the same.

The fact that she had once tried to slit her wrists weighed on him, too. That, and the sheer synchronicity of it, wrists cut all over the place, and guys who went in and finished the job, or offered to. Completely meaningless in Kathleen's case except a hazy dread in his mind for her. What if she had succeeded? The dread was just part of his longing, the fear of losing someone who wasn't even his to lose.

And maybe the dread tied into the other thing that bothered him, what she had told him about Karen. Not the gossip so much, he found that mostly amusing. So Acapulco, why did that stick in his head like a buzzer? It was just more of the same, another raunchy weekend with a married man on the loose. Maybe it was his growing irritation over the three thousand dollars. Because if that's where it had gone, along with whatever she had gotten from Kathleen and who knows how many others, what did she spend it on? Parasailing wasn't that expensive. Was it what she said it was, down payments on a condo and a car? Possibly. A divorce alone might cost that much, although there had been no contest as far as he knew, and no big settlement since both parties had good jobs.

But say it was all those things and you had a big nut to pay off, why would you call on your friends, cash in all your markers? Why not the usual channels, a company loan or the bank? Did it have something to do with the guy with the Spanish accent? What had Acapulco been for anyway, business or pleasure?

He drove over to Belmont and Western to see Sgt. Kirkpatrick. "With all the excitement," the sergeant said, "I wondered where you'd been. Enjoying your vacation?"

"Wintering in Wilkes-Barre is pure pleasure. You get a confession yet?" He knew the doctor had a sharp lawyer provided by his family and wasn't talking.

"No, but we will."

"You can put him there, at the scene?"

"We can't put him anywhere for certain, except where he is right now. We'll just work on him a little while every day."

"He won't get out this afternoon?"

Kirk shook his head. "No bond, the state's attorney will insist on that."

"Can I see the file?"

"What for? We have the killer."

"I have to do a wrap-up. Actually it's more like, what if you're wrong?" The sergeant's left eye was looking back at him, but the right one drew a bead on his left shoulder. Jimmy concentrated, trying to will them together. Refocus. "You know, other possibilities. The guy from Miami, who is he? Who's the doctor, really? Who has an alibi, who doesn't? Me, for instance. Karen." For an instant, the eyes seemed to lock in. "What's the story on her?"

The eyes drifted off. "You wouldn't do her on TV. She's on the home team."

"What if I didn't work there?"

"You switching channels?"

"I might."

"Well, the Miamian is clean as far as we can tell. The doctor won't tell us anything, so we don't know, do we? You and Miss Kohl are not suspects. Maybe you should look for a different angle. All this sounds pretty vapid."

"Let me see the file."

"All right, first Kohl was out of town, then she was home making phone calls, and when Marlee Roberts got it she was toning up her bod at her health club. Who else?"

"Howard Damen Custer the Third."

"Nothing. Anybody else?"

"Who else is in the file?"

Kirkpatrick winced and shifted in his chair. "What are you really interested in, Gillespie?"

"Karen went out of town ten days ago while the doctor was trying to nail Clara Turner. I wonder with who. She suddenly needs a lot of money. I'd like to know why."

"How much?"

"Thousands. Could be a few, could be many many. Of course, she has lots of bills."

"Who was she with, out of town?"

"I'm told the guy doesn't speak much English. Married. Fun to be with."

Kirk snapped, "You're wasting my time. Why?"

"I can see your guy killing the first two, the ones he knew, and going after Clara. By why Marlee?"

"Our doorman thinks he recognized the voice. He thinks it was the doctor on the phone."

Jimmy gave him gaze for gaze, and the sergeant sighed. "You won't find any answers in the file."

"Nevertheless."

The eyes went skyward. Kirk rose to his feet. "Wait here."

Jimmy jotted down two names, people who said, yes, Karen had returned their calls at the times she said she had. He made a note of the dates she was out of town last fall, and the times she had gone to and from the club. He wrote down the phone numbers of the man from Miami. There didn't seem to be very much recent information, hardly anything on the doctor and of course nothing about Acapulco. Kirk hadn't given him all of it and wasn't about to. Why not? Leaving the file where it was, on his way out he stopped by the desk where Ginko was concentrating on a printout of street names and house numbers, most of them checked off.

"Hear from Karen lately?"

The detective looked up, puzzled. Then he said, "Oh, *that* Karen. Hi, Jimmy, how's it going? No, I haven't run into her lately. What's new?" He looked different. Something about him.

"She and I went out of town, weekend before last."

Ginko squinted up. "You what?"

"Different directions, Pennsylvania and Acapulco. Guess which one I got."

"Un-huh." He looked down at his list.

"Congratulations on the doctor. Say, Ginko, I hope you didn't get into any trouble, tipping her to the serial murders."

The detective put down his pencil and leaned back in his chair, looking somewhat annoyed. "Oh, yeah, well, Kirk chewed me up pretty good. Sometimes I talk too much." His eyes narrowed, making him look a little like one of Genghis Khan's troopers, right out of the Urals. "Don't worry. I figured it was you that passed the word. I forgave you already."

"You got to be good buddies."

"Me and Karen?" He picked up the pencil. "Yeah, we hit it off. She's a smart one. I like a woman like that."

"Polish women, those I've met, strike me as very bright."

Ginko laughed. "Geese! Always busy, one step ahead. They don't go, 'Take it easy.' They go, 'Honk! Honk!' "

"Karen goes, 'Acapulco! Acapulco!' "

The other man nodded, to show he understood. "That's what I like about American women. They want the fine things in life. Cars, jewels, a big house, and winters in Mexico or the Caribbean. A Polish woman, she'll settle for an old car, or a tiny apartment with one window, a few pots of flowers. Maybe a healthy cow." He laughed.

"She has expensive tastes, all right. She ever borrow money?"

"From me? Where would she get money from me? Anyway, we aren't that kind of friendly." Ginko turned back to his work.

"You just exchange information. A wise man. How's the doctor?"

"Keeping mum."

"Interesting that she knew the same women the doctor did. I don't suppose they ever ran into each other, though."

Ginko looked up. "Who, the doctor?" He laughed. "If they did, she'd run so fast! The smell alone, whew! Well, keep him away from me."

Jimmy dropped into the old metal chair beside the desk. "Yeah, what did he say? Never wash away the natural body oils?"

The detective was still chuckling. "What a creep!" His eyes seemed to go blank. "Smart, though. Smart as hell. He could've done it. Most criminals are naturally stupid, but he could manage a thing like that." He turned away, bent down and began looking through a heavy briefcase resting on the floor.

"You checked out the health club. Any way she could have left there without being seen?"

One hand in the briefcase, Ginko looked up impatiently. "Many ways. There are always ways it could happen, a thing like that. But she was seen coming and going. You could slip out or in without someone noticing you, but not both. Even once might be too much. What are you asking that for?"

"Just curious."

Ginko brought up a thick manila folder and put it on the desk. "You're a strange guy, Jimmy. I don't understand, you asking about something like that."

"How'd you get onto the first two killings? That they were murder."

"Hey, remember? That was the sergeant. He's the one with the experience. I always go with him."

"How did he know?"

"Well, it wasn't for sure until the last one. Marlee Roberts, that made him sure."

"That surprise you?"

Ginko shrugged and smiled. "That's me. I tag along and get surprised. How many Polish detectives does it take to screw in a light bulb?"

"How many?"

"None. We don't do light bulbs."

Jimmy got up. "So many things, so much to do." He stretched mightily, trying to get a look at the folder. "How many Polish detectives does it take to screw Karen Kohl?"

Ginko stood up. It always surprised Jimmy, his looking unexpectedly taller than he remembered. "Hey," he said evenly, "don't talk like that. Aren't you friends? I thought you were friends with her."

"I am. I just thought you might. She seldom turns down an acquaintance, especially if he's married."

The other man shook his head sorrowfully. "Ah, Jimmy, Jimmy, she must have done something real bad to you, huh? Something that made you mad?"

Jimmy picked up his coat. "No. I'm sorry, Ginko, I'm just off my feed." He backed away. "Take it easy."

Ginko nodded, watching him go. As Jimmy reached the doorway, he yelled, "How was Pennsylvania?" Jimmy waved and went down the stairs.

23

There was a letter from Kathleen when he got home. He had written her twice, at the downtown store. She wrote in part, "Your hopes for us are what make me write you. I keep trying to tell myself it never happened, but I can't because I keep hearing your voice insisting. You can be very persuasive, but I keep telling myself you're from Chicago and you do this all the time. I know you don't, so don't bother to argue the point. It's just me, trying to keep my life in perspective." She also wrote, "I've been trying to remember about Mexico. Karen said foreigner, I know that. She was laughing about it, like their only common language was in bed."

The next day he worked out at the health club. He had been coming there for ten years. Afterward he looked around the place, wondering how he could get out and back without being noticed. In the glass-enclosed lobby, everyone was required to sign in and out. The only other exits were emergency ones that promised to trip an alarm. He gave up and had lunch there.

At two o'clock he stopped off to see Clara Turner. She

lived in a HUD apartment in a relatively new building on Clark Street, north of the Loop, a place she had somehow lucked into after two decades of crumbling walkups in Uptown. Someone was always on the premises, she said, a doorman or management, and although they treated everyone on public aid like dirt, it was nice to feel safe. The one-bedroom apartment had new carpeting and large windows, but it was dusky because the day was overcast and she hadn't turned her one living room lamp on. She owned an old dining table and several straight-backed chairs, and one nondescript armchair he was invited to occupy. She brought him a Coke and one for herself, and made sure he noticed the two low shelves of books, the statuette of the Madonna and the crucifix on the wall. There were no paintings or family photographs. She had broken only recently with her parents, whom she said she loved even though they were torturers.

"I couldn't sleep last night," she said. "I watched him on TV. I'm afraid to go out for fear he might be there, and I'm worried about the trial. I'm afraid if I have to testify, I'll get real sick again and have to go back to the hospital. My doctor says that's what will happen if I do. He says the lawyers will do everything they can to make me look like I'm out of my mind."

"They will."

"Yes, and they're trying to think of some way so I won't have to appear in court. I don't know what it would be. They have what they call a deposition, don't they? Or maybe a video, without him sitting there."

He sipped from the can, looking past her at the tarred rooftop across the street, a four-story office block from the 1920s, the kind Capone assassins holed up in to await their prey. "Karen Kohl got to know your friends, the ones who were killed."

"Yes, but they weren't really friends any more. One was being real hostile, and the other one had gone back into herself, she had no time for me. I hadn't talked to them for months except when we'd meet at the doctor's office. That's how we got to know each other, but after a while all they talked about were their own problems. Karen was different."

"Where did you meet?"

"There, in the waiting room."

"Your current doctor's waiting room?"

She nodded. "Yes, but we didn't have the same doctor. Karen had Dr. Goodman. Dr. Goodman's really a psychologist, and she's always real nice. She always smiles and says hello. Karen said she was getting a divorce, and that's why she was there. She wasn't there very long."

"She ever talk about her marital problems?"

"No, and see, that's the thing. She was the only one I could talk to, you know, like a personal friend. Everybody else was so busy. The only ones that would listen were my doctor and my priest. You won't tell anyone about this, will you?"

"No, I won't."

"Well, with Karen, we could discuss things back and forth, like adults. Once in a while we'd go out for coffee, and sometimes, like at the end of the month when my check runs out, she'd give me something, otherwise I wouldn't eat. She knew I couldn't pay her back. Every month I work out a budget with my doctor, for food and dental, and the electric and the phone, but it's never enough. I have lots of dental bills, from so many years of taking the Thorazine, and public aid doesn't cover that any more. I'm probably going to lose most of my teeth."

"So you'd go out for coffee?"

"Yes, and sometimes she'd come over and bring things. Once she brought me lots of dresses, things she couldn't use any more. She has a good sense of humor, a really sharp wit. She should write a book. She knows about literature so we could talk about that. Not to brag, but that was my best subject in college, before I got sick. She said some famous writer lived where she did, in Pennsylvania, and wrote about it. What was his name? O'Hara. He was Irish."

"Pottsville?"

"Yes, that's what he called it. John O'Hara. It was near where she grew up, lots of coal mines."

"Did she mention the documentary she was thinking of doing?"

"About women on public aid, yes. That's why she wanted to meet my friends."

"Did you talk about your past? Your problems?"

"She knew about my mother because one time Karen called and I couldn't talk to her because I'd just gotten off the phone. My mother broke my brother's leg once, pushing him down the basement stairs, and I can't discuss what else she did because it's too sickening. I was the oldest, and I was never tortured physically, but my doctor says that was the worst torture of all, being made to watch. I've stopped talking to my parents. My doctor says I should cut off all communication, they're so sick. Only I keep wanting to talk to my grandmother. She's nearly ninety, and I try to talk to her but my parents won't let me. They say I'll upset her and kill her, the way I made my mother have high blood pressure. I don't know what I'll do when my grandmother dies. The worst thing is, when she does they might not tell me. That's what they do, they keep you guessing." She jumped up. "Would you like some coffee? I can make some fresh."

He said no, thanks, and she sat down, staring at the red can in her hands. "I shouldn't have caffeine, but otherwise I'd be too tired to talk." She grinned, her face lighting up. "I'd be like a zombie."

"Did you ever tell Karen about the doctor? The man they arrested?"

"Yes, and listen to this. She told me how depraved he was. That was the word she used, depraved."

"Did you tell her his name?"

She sat up and looked about, her blonde hair flying. Then she relaxed. "The only one I told was Sergeant Kirkpatrick. I said I didn't want to talk about the doctor in the documentary."

"You still see Karen these days?"

She shook her head. "Not for a long time. She's gotten very busy, on TV."

"Do you watch?"

"Sometimes the early news. I go to sleep early because of the medication."

"What do you think of Karen?"

She stared blankly and seemed to sag a little. "Well, she's highly intelligent and very beautiful. I thought we were really good friends, and I don't see why she can't find time to talk once in a while. She was very nice to me, not like some of the others, especially in this building." Her eyes took on the look of tunnels. "Some people here you wouldn't want to meet."

He stopped by the buildings where her friends had lived and died, first renewing his acquaintance with the landlady on Clark Street. "No, I told the police there's no way anybody could get in," she said, huffing and puffing, her broad hips flattening the pillows of her couch. "He'd of had to get past me, and I'm always here. Always. Of course, there are visitors coming and going, but I always know who they are. I run a clean, quiet place. No loud music after eleven, no cooking in the rooms." She pushed back a lock of wild graying hair. "Sometimes one of them might sneak by, but they better be careful, I raise hell. She'd been acting kind of funny lately. Snippy, rolling her eyes. Always flying up and down stairs, like being chased by the devil. I said she'd have to find another place if she couldn't calm down. Rock 'n' roll, that was all she played. No job, she was on disability. I've been getting rid of them when I can, trying to upgrade. It's a clean, decent place, as you can see. I won't have it, not at my time of life. I can't stand it. Could you?"

The resident caretaker at the apartment building on Pine Grove was lean and hard, genial but abrupt. You could see him smiling and lifting a stein in some German rathskellar.

"Oh yeah, the killer. You want to know why they let him out?"

Jimmy stared. "He's out?" He had been so certain Kirk was right, he hadn't bothered to watch TV or read the papers, and no one else had mentioned it. No wonder Clara had been fearful.

"You didn't know that, hah? A newsman, they don't tell you?"

"He's out on bail?"

"A million dollars, how's that? A lot of money, even today. He's home, his parents' house in Flossmoor. He can't leave, but a house in Flossmoor, who'd want to go out anyway? Far south, richest suburb in Chicago, more income than Kenilworth or Lake Forest or anywhere, at least it used to be. Lots of bankers and professional people. He was a doctor, the killer. To me that's the same thing. Go to the doctor, nine times out of ten he's going to kill you. Now why would they let somebody who killed three women out on the street? Flossmoor, that's why. His family's rich, that's why. And his father being a retired judge, that doesn't hurt.

"How'd he get in here? I never saw that face around here. I don't like strangers hanging around. I tell them, Take a hike. It's a nice place. Yellow brick, you like it? The cops been all over here, and they never saw anyplace so good. Look at that grass, already, in March. Ever see grass better than that? In the spring, it's green as a billiard table.

"How would you get in? You wouldn't unless they knew you and buzzed you up. That's the only way, the buzzer and the voice box. She'd have to say, 'Okay, come on up,' and buzz you in. She'd have to know the voice.

"She was raised on the North Shore, did you know that? Expensive stereo, nice clothes. I knew she was a little crazy and her family didn't want her back, but believe me, she was no trouble. I don't like trouble.

"Say, don't I see you on the weekends? On the news?"

That night, there was the doctor on TV, just a glimpse of him getting into a shiny black sedan, and then his lawyer, a little guy, very quick, very sharp, and a suit to match. "I have nothing to say. The press has already convicted my client. If I talk to you, I talk to his persecutors. He didn't do it. There's no proof he did. He's an eccentric, but he's not a murderer. It's wrong, it's unjust to assume he is. He's a doctor, a physician. There may be questions about his ethical conduct in the past, but there can be no question of his innocence in this case. He didn't kill anybody, and I'll prove that in court. Then I'll talk to the press and try to explain to you the rules of justice."

Jimmy flew to Miami the following week and had lunch with a college acquaintance who now worked as news editor for the *Herald.* "Ernesto Escobar, yes. I'll tell you what it's like down here, Jimmy. It's a play, more of a melodrama, and all the players are villains. Mystery men. A mustache. Flinty eyes. Big money. Fine cars. Protection. Complete insulation, just like 'Miami Vice.' It's not so much the Spanish or the Columbians anymore, though. What's really got everybody worried now are the Jamaican gangs. They're fierce, and they're all up and down the East Coast.

"Escobar is a mystery man with an unsavory public life. He doesn't care if you know about it, and I guess he doesn't care if his family knows about it. He likes being seen in public places, which is kind of unusual, but that's what he goes for—fine women and faultless service—so he just goes ahead and flaunts it. It's drugs, sure, no question about that, but so what? That he can hide, and of course he washes the money clean. Even if he couldn't, he has several legitimate businesses, yachts and laundromats and cleaning shops and currency exchanges and so on, and they're successful so he doesn't have to hide the money he spends in public. He likes celebrities, so I'm not surprised he went after Marlee. Knowing her, I'm surprised she'd allow it, but what the hell, a girl has to have some fun. I mean who are we to say? You don't suppose she was onto something, do you? I mean, working up a story or fronting for the feds? What brings you down here after all this time? You're not going after him, are you?"

"No. I want to meet him, though."

"If you've got any kind of claim to celebrity, you shouldn't have a problem, although it would be better if you were a good-looking female. I thought you had the killings cleared up."

"How?"

"You want a list of his favorite places? I can get that for you. Then just hang out for a week or so—but you know all about that. Or I can make a few calls, maybe give you an idea of where he might show up when. Where are you staying?"

Jimmy talked to several Miami detectives who added little to what his friend had told him, and then, three days later, he was at the appointed place, the palm-laden bar of a sleek Coconut Grove restaurant, when Ernesto Escobar walked in, a tropical plant of a woman at his elbow and assorted thugs hovering like cacti at the door. He saw the manager speak to him and Escobar shake his head and move on. But an instant before he did so, their eyes met. Just an instant, but it was enough. There were other ways to investigate without tangling with pure menace.

Jimmy spent the rest of the week on the beach, and then he went home.

He had lunch in Winnetka with Patricia the next day. A bit wistfully, she told him how nice he looked. "Mike and I are still talking and he still sleeps in the blue bedroom. I should chuck everything while he makes up his mind what to do with the rest of my life. Go get some sun. Get brown and lovely all over, like you."

Lovely and brown. What Karen looked like on the news these days, like Acapulco.

24

The check bounced, or would have if Karen hadn't called three days before it was dated and asked him not to cash it. "What a month!" she exclaimed brightly. "I've got all these bills! My house, my car, my lawyer, and now my mother's surgery, and there was a special condo assessment, and somebody borrowed my car and smashed in the door—oh, Jimmy, I don't believe it. Can you wait a few more weeks, till the end of April? One thing I've always done is pay my way. You know I'm good for it."

"How's Howard?"

"You should hear him go on about the new g.m. He tells me everything. He won't shut up! Charlie's making changes. Charlie's playing rough. Charlie hates me. God! You'd think Howard never made any changes. I say to Howard, 'Look, what do you expect? Charlie's got a mind of his own. He just doesn't go for the sirens and bells you do.' He's a really good news guy, I mean before he got into management. Kind of cerebral. It started out with a short, very heavy lunch. I mean shouting—at the Standard Club! Now they have long, quiet talks in Howard's office.

Nobody can hear what they're saying, but poor Howard. He's still worried about his digestive tract from that first lunch."

"Who said what at the Standard Club?"

"Well, the way Howard described it, Charlie said, 'You've put a lot of thought into the news format,' and Howard was beaming, and then Charlie said, 'So why don't I like it?' Howard was starting on his salad, and he excused himself and went to the bathroom! He stayed there as long as he could, and then he came back and said, 'Which news show do you like?' and the g.m. said, 'I don't think I've seen one I liked lately, but CBS used to do a good one with Edward R. Murrow.' Edward R. Murrow! Howard nearly spit up! He was thinking, How do I find one of *those?* He was in a panic!"

"A new experience for Howard."

"I haven't seen much of him lately, just glimpses on the run. Jimmy, I think his wife is asking for a divorce, do you know anything about that?"

"I thought you'd be the first to know."

"Don't be cruel. I know I was out of line, getting overinvolved, but I've learned a lot in the last few months. I learned a lot from you, Jimmy."

"Apparently."

"I said don't be cruel. There was something there, I mean between you and me. That night you put aside your own pleasure for me, I just realized. That was love, wasn't it?"

"Or lust."

"Yes, of course, there was that, obviously. But you put your feelings aside because I asked you to."

"Karen, I've always helped old ladies across the street."

"No! Stop being clever. There was more to it."

"Well, if you must know, Karen, I was pretty teed off."

"You were angry? I didn't know you were angry!"

"I thought, If this woman values her writing assignments—well, hell, they weren't even assignments, they were queries! But, above me, if she values— If taking her pleasure with me ranks so low on her list of things to do—"

"Oh, Jimmy, you're funny!" She was laughing! "I guess I just get so overwhelmed by deadlines—"

"It was your own deadline. You could have changed it!"

"No, that's just the point! I'm a deadline person. I set personal goals, and once I've set them it drives me wild not to accomplish what I've set out to do. I know it's not good to be so compulsive, but it just drives me out of my mind!" Jimmy said nothing. "Are you there?"

"It isn't that big a deal, Karen." He was no longer shouting. "I mean what happened. I'd forgotten about it."

"Oh, sure! You pulled out and you were pissed, and you forgot about it. I'll believe that when I believe angels are jet propelled."

"I'll talk to you sometime, Karen."

"That's right, walk away from it. I thought you might be different. Howard said you were no different. He said—"

"Howard?"

"Yes, you dumbbell! Why do you think he fired you?"

"Tell me."

"He found out about us."

"What about us?"

"Never mind!"

"Oh, but I do. You told him we'd been in the sack?"

"Yes! And he didn't give me a clue he was firing you, and neither did you, come to think of it. And then you'd gone, and I told him I quit, and he said—the bastard said, 'Go ahead'! He called me on it and I didn't have the nerve. I'm too hungry, Jimmy, you'll find that out sooner or later. I'm not a very good poker player."

"Not even strip poker?"

"Well, I tried!" It was a wail, and then he couldn't tell if she had fainted away or what.

"Karen, why would you do that? Tell him about me?"

"I was angry about something. Him, not you." She had a case of the sniffles. "I'm sorry."

"Karen, I'm coming over."

"No. I have to go to work."

"I won't stay."

"All right, come if you want to, but I haven't got a stitch on. Give me half an hour."

Jimmy walked the half dozen blocks to her apartment, three down the lake shore where the waves were lashing the concrete embankment, then three inland. He saw Marlee's building first—the back of it, tons of red brick and solid creamy windows, and then Karen's across the street, virtually all glass, with stacks of balcony railings and intermittent strips of pale brick and colorful plastic.

At the door she was barefoot and brown and smiling, trying to look pleasant. She had washed her hair and wore a fuzzy white bathrobe that looked as if it might have come from a hotel in Acapulco.

"Hi, Jimmy, long time no see."

"Hi, Karen, long time between paychecks."

She sat down on her couch and stared at an ashtray full of cigarette butts, then deliberately covered it with a copy of *Vogue*. Tucking her feet under her, she looked up with the expression of someone who has been in a fierce argument and is determined to be open and nonjudgmental.

Jimmy could see Marlee's building out Karen's window,

though her apartment was out of sight, far above them. He noticed an older woman walk up the drive to the garage, open a pedestrian door, and disappear.

Jimmy said, "Where do you park your car?"

"In the building. Why?"

He sat down facing her. "Six, seven years ago, some guy tried to help Kathleen Reilly kill herself."

She blinked, and he thought he could see innocent wonderment shuttle through her eyes. "I see," she said. "I didn't know you two were that well acquainted."

"You knew about it?"

"Yes, of course. Everybody did."

He leaned toward her, elbows on his knees. "Karen, it bothers me, the razor, the wrists. It's so much like Marlee."

Her jaw clenched, the first glimmer of impatience. "Well, I can see the obvious similarities, but what bothers you exactly?"

"Maybe that's it." He sat back. "A similarity without a connection. Just my own emotional wraparound."

The glimmer became open amusement. "You think I killed them all, just because I know about Kathleen?"

"No, of course not." He looked away. "I just want to know what happened to her. Maybe then I can begin to think straight."

"My, my, you *are* uptight. Well, let's see. She was very depressed and threatened to harm herself, and her parents were very concerned about it. So was I. My sister had tried it and nearly succeeded."

"You were around that summer?"

"I was up in Scranton, getting ready for college. I'll be honest, I behaved badly. I wrote her off, just the way I'd written off my sister. I did go to see her once, in the hospital, and I wished I hadn't. It was so awful, seeing kids my age locked up like that. I had to leave. I couldn't stand it."

"Like Clara. Like her friends."

"Clara's different. She's trying to better herself. Hell, she's trying to survive. But she's fully aware most of the time, and she's highly intelligent. I really had very little to do with her friends."

"You ever meet the doctor?"

She glared. "Clara told me about him, but he was long gone. I probably would have tried to look him up if I'd done the documentary. Tried to get him incarcerated."

"So what happened to Kathleen? Did you know the guy?"

"I may have, but I doubt it. She had her own friends." She looked down at her nails. "Jimmy, that's really all I know. I've got to get ready, and I don't like talking about this."

"Wrists and razors."

Her eyes flashed. "Yes, I hate it! My sister has ugly, ugly scars, and I sat and watched Kathleen try to keep steady in a ward full of sickos. There was the smell of death in that place." She stared at him, a dark shadow on that tanned, freshly scrubbed face. "But there *is* no connection, and I'm sorry you had to bring it up. That was a long time ago and there's not even much similarity. That was kid stuff. This is murder. Anyway, it doesn't matter how they died. They're dead, and I hate it." She got off the couch and went quickly toward her bedroom.

He said, "Who was with you in Acapulco?"

Without breaking stride, she said, "Jimmy, get out of here, please. I don't like the way this conversation is going," and slammed the bedroom door behind her.

Getting off the elevator at garage level, he asked the attendant, "You keep a record of cars going in and out? You know, on the residents?"

The man grinned. "Now, why would we do that? We got enough to do, just keeping busy. You want your car?"

"No car. I just wondered."

"Naw, we couldn't keep track of that, not unless they drove into a wall. Then we'd remember." The door to the street went up, making a racket, and the man turned to the car coming down the ramp.

No one was in the garage across the street. To his left, between the ramps, was an empty office with a glass front. To his right, past several rows of sleek, glossy cars, was a glass exit door to State Parkway. Straight ahead was another door, this one painted black. It was locked.

Behind him, a uniformed car-park said, "Yes, may I help you?"

"Where does this door go?"

"Freight elevator. Receiving. You a guest, sir?"

Jimmy shook his head. "I'm buying in the building. Do residents have keys to this door?"

The man nodded. "They use that, yeah, those with packages or a cart." On the wall, the pay phone rang. "Excuse me. I think we got a few openings. If you'll come back after three, you can talk to the manager."

So that's all the killer would have needed, a key. Just walk across the garage, maybe carrying a bag of groceries, go up the freight elevator and knock on Marlee's door. Maybe two keys. Just let himself in and go right to work.

But where would the doctor get a key? And why would he bother with Marlee?

25

On April Fool's Day, Dutch sat on a bench in the park where his wife and one daughter had been found dead. He didn't mind that this was the place. Years had gone by. At the moment, he couldn't remember how many, but it was more than a dozen. And since Hope, the prairie had risen every year, and he liked the life that was in it. He no longer minded the leaves in the fall reminding him of death, theirs and his own impending one. The astonishing vigor of the high grasses each spring canceled that out, made death seem secondary, even necessary. Well, with plants. He didn't know how it applied to people, but with plants it was unavoidable and essential.

This year, as before, the new grass was flourishing green in among the dried stems, and here and there were clusters of trillium—what did they call it in London, wake robin? The Canada geese were back. A few days ago they had built two nests on a spit of land by the pond, about a dozen of them, so they were here to stay for a while. When the young ones were grown, they'd be on their own. Not like Americans. In America, the kids hung around forever.

Jimmy was coming up the path, rounding the curve. Dutch could see his head and shoulders some distance away. Jimmy didn't take the expressway, said he didn't like it. He took the Outer Drive along the lake, then Howard Street three or four miles west to Skokie. He did that what, once a month? In decent weather Dutch met him in the park. It was a better place to talk, and when it got boring they could walk.

He watched his son taking in the view. It was always a surprise to enter the park, a wide stretch of high brown grass and other plants left from last year, and the big oaks, still bare, towering knotted branches at the sky. Not so much the view as the feeling of it. Something wild. Uncut, untrimmed. Birds. Squirrels and chipmunks and rabbits, probably snakes. Lots of little spiders. Raccoons. Some said a fox. Geese, now, ducks now and then. Transluscent little bluegill in the pond. But most of the wildness lay quiet right there in the fields of grass, and it would grow as the grass grew. When they were ready, the tall green stems would shoot up overnight like fireworks. The ends would tassel, heavy tassels of seeds like grain, the next thing to bread. And over all the prairie the tall grass would bear its seeds skyward well into the summer, and the whole place would flourish, all wild. What was it? You could come upon a scene like that and feel the wildness in your bones and know that you were wild, too, that someplace inside you bore the seeds of a vast wilderness that made you one with this, and at home.

"What is it, Jimmy?" he called out, seeing his son approach. "What's this wildness? Tell me what it is."

Challenge him, keep him off balance. Teach him to keep his guard up, all this wildness.

"Hi, Dad." Jimmy sat down beside him, making the bench creak. "Not too chilly for you out here?"

"Ask the geese. They're back. Geese walk around looking like they're walking on their hands. Look, the grass is ready to spring. Buds coming soon on the trees. In a month or so, the week of the green mist." He slapped his son's thigh, not getting what he had meant to say quite right, feeling ineffectual. "So how are you?"

"Fine. You?"

"Fine." That was all they ever said about that. Damned if he was going to reel off a litany of current deterioration. Be glad you were still going. Be glad you were alive. "This murder, what do you think of it?"

Jimmy sighed. "Gee, I don't know, Dad."

"They got the killer. Why did he do it?"

"He's crazy."

"Crazy to pick young women who were vulnerable? Crazy to pick a celebrity, stand the town on its ear? The only thing he did that was crazy was to kill and then hang around where they could catch him. He got away with it, don't forget. He let himself get caught, he did society that favor. Now he's a celebrity. You're a celebrity of sorts. Is that crazy?"

Jimmy laughed. "It's not the same—"

"I know, he's an eccentric. Even his lawyer admitted that. He's brilliant. He killed three women and walked away, and got caught when he felt like it. Now he's enjoying the fruits of his labor out in Flossmoor with his parents putting him up. He's going to make society kill him. He has total control. Is that crazy?"

"Where are the geese?"

"They fly here, fly there. Sometimes to the lake, all but

the two parents. Right now they're all over by the pond, guarding the nests. The parents can't go anywhere until the eggs hatch. Then the others get out on bail, but not the parents. They have to serve several more months. By the time they get out, they've been punished enough."

"Goose prison."

"Well, they chose to be geese. He chose to be a celebrity. You enjoy being a celebrity?"

"What were you asking me about the wildness? Looks pretty tame to me."

"I was just watching the grass grow. It does a lot more work than I do these days. I read where a bunch of people were given a bunch of photographs to look at, of the outdoors. They all picked Africa. Kenya, I think it was. That was the one they liked. It was in their genes. They liked it because it looked like this place. Ancient. The place our first ancestors saw. Trees and water, and a good view of your enemies, except when they're hiding in the grass. A wildness in the blood."

They were silent. The clouds were moving fast. It might rain later.

Jimmy said, "I don't know if he did it. I mean, he almost certainly did, but something's missing."

"You're just feeling unsettled, because you're on vacation. Why don't you go someplace?"

"I'm not on vacation, Dad. I got fired."

"Fired?" Dutch picked up his cane and jammed it down on the blacktop as if he was driving a spear into the ground. Rising, he said, "Let's walk."

They headed up along the pond, where the willows were. Jimmy said, "It was a personal thing. It should never have happened. I haven't told anybody else."

"Tell everybody you know. Then head for New York or Hollywood. That's where the action is."

"Why should I have to live someplace else?"

"Doesn't matter. A few months, you won't know you moved." They walked a while, taking the narrow footpath the fishermen used, skirting the water's edge. Dutch said behind him, "See the geese?" They were gathered on a low-lying sort of peninsula, big, high-necked birds with black heads and skinny legs, looking as if they owned the place. "They're getting used to people. I think they may let us stay. Remember when we went to Virginia? You were out on a sandbar in the river and this mother goose came out there and laid her eggs, right in front of you. You were just a sprout and you couldn't believe it. Then this big old goose three times as big as these, he attacked you. There was a rowboat beached between you and him, so he started swimming around the boat to get at you, and you started yelling. I came running. Patricia came running, and Frank, I think." Dutch looked at him. "You don't remember, do you?"

Jimmy grinned. "Not very well."

"Well, you'll find a job."

"I don't want to think about that right now."

"You're angry. Stay angry. That's the best thing right now, gives you energy."

"Yes, but it's more like I owe it to Marlee, to find out why she died."

"I did the same thing with your stepmother. I did it with Hope. They wouldn't leave me alone. It's called mourning."

"No, there's something here I don't see. Something we've all missed. The doctor was always crazy, but as far as I know he didn't kill his patients. Why should he start doing it now, and for God's sake, why Marlee?"

"You don't know anything about him. He hasn't told anybody anything. Be a little patient. When he talks, you'll know."

They walked along a rail fence, upward into the trees at one end of the pond, past the visitors center, and then along the wider woodchip trail that went around the pond. When the trees and bushes leafed out and the cattails grew high, they wouldn't be able to see the pond except from a few vantage points. Now, however, they could see all the way across it. They could see the geese on the little peninsula, through the branches of the trees. Once around the pond, and around the farthest blacktop path, was half a mile. Dutch tried to make four trips around every day. That was two miles.

"When we were in Wilkes-Barre," Jimmy said, "I met someone I can't get out of my mind."

"What's wrong with that?"

"She's married."

"You go to bed with her?"

"That's none of your business, Dad."

"Well, you brought it up. How does she feel about you?"

"I'd say the same way."

Dutch said, "I met a nymphomaniac like that once. She was incorrigible. Don't take her too seriously."

"She's not like that, Dad. She loves her husband."

"This one had a couple of cats. You'd have thought they were part of her, like an arm or a leg. I'd reach out for her under the covers and there they'd be. This was in London, you understand, before I married your mother. In the war."

He stopped on the path, staring across the pond. The geese

were flapping about energetically in the water. "So what do you intend to do? Stay on vacation?"

"For a while."

"Well, let me tell you something. Don't disregard your feelings. I had a feeling when your stepmother was killed that somebody was out to get me. Turned out I was right, only it took sixteen years to find out." They stood looking at the geese for a while and then they walked on.

26

The call from Dorothy woke Jimmy up. "Hi, lover, I'm calling for Mr. Big, the new one. He wants to see you."

He groaned, feeling the effects of last night's overindulgence, whatever it was. He had the impression that if he moved anything other than his lips, his brain was going to fall off its pedestal and die. "Why? I mean—"

"I'm working for him now. The old Mr. Big took his secretary with him to New York, and I got the job. Only now it's called assistant to the general manager."

"That's real super, Dorothy. So then what does he want to see me for?"

"Why ask what, darlin'? He'd like you to meet him at his club tomorrow. Lunch. He wants to look you over."

"On Saturday? Things must be changing."

"They changed already, okay? Can you make it?"

"Sure. I guess." His mouth was very dry.

"You been off too long, Jimmy. Doesn't even sound like you."

"Same club?"

"Same club, new Mr. Big. Two o'clock. Reservation's

under Charles Acker, but be sure to call him Charlie, that's what he likes. Ta-ta!"

He remembered, putting down the phone. Some of the boys: Neville Freeman, the foreign news editor of the *Trib*, and his Argentine wife, one of the boys, too. Len O'Dwyer, a PR bigshot Frank had introduced him to years ago. Spanky Aronson, a reporter for the *Wall Street Journal*. They had tied one on at Riccardo's because it was bound to close one of these days, and if the best watering hole in Chicago shut down after seventy years, the town must be falling apart, like his head.

The new Mr. Big was taller than Jimmy but slight, a flexible wire of a man who looked as if there were all sorts of messages running through his body. He had a finely carved Roman nose and a very high forehead, and wore thick rimless glasses that looked as shatterproof as his smile. At least he smiled as if he enjoyed it. "So you're Jimmy Gillespie. I've seen you on tape. Tapes make you look heavier."

"I've got a pretty big butt, Charlie."

Charlie laughed. It was kind of a croak but he had fun with it. "You're very good, on the tapes. I'd like you to come to see me after your vacation. We're making some changes."

Vacation? Jimmy thought. What is this, Never-Never Land? "It would have to be anchor."

"That's what I had in mind. But not next week. I just got here myself, and there are some things I want to do first. But I want you to get back on the beat right away. We'll deal with the anchor bit when we revise your contract."

"I don't have a contract."

Charlie smiled. "There'll be more money, of course, all to be negotiated. You have an agent?"

"No." Jimmy looked out the window. They were a million stories up, and Lake Shore Drive looked like a thin noodle. "I'll go back on the beat, but not officially, okay? No taping, nothing on camera, not for a couple of weeks. But I'll stay close to everything. When do you want to do the contract?"

"Two weeks is fine. Work it out with Dorothy, the precise date. Do that on Tuesday. And as long as you're there, I want you to show yourself. Let them see you in the newsroom. Oh, and be sure to stop by the news director's office."

"Howard?"

"He'd like to explain what he's come to regard as a simple misunderstanding."

"Howard?"

For the first time, Charlie exhibited impatience. "Well, look, do him this one courtesy. You're old friends, aren't you?" Jimmy nodded. "Then nothing's changed, all right?" He picked up the menu card. "Let's order. Or would you like another drink?"

Charlie was trying not to look at him, but a flicker of his eyes said this was a test. Jimmy licked his lips and said no. He really didn't care, but this scrutiny was making him nervous.

"You sure?" Charlie said. "I wouldn't mind one myself." But he wasn't smiling.

"No, I don't think so."

"Jimmy," the g.m. said, "we need to talk about one other matter. It's important."

"What's that?" He waited tensely.

"Howard says you have a drinking problem."

"Howard said that?"

"Not quite. As a matter of fact, he said the reason he put

you on hold was that you were becoming a roaring drunk." Jimmy was so angry he couldn't speak. "I'm willing to believe that was an exaggeration. We'll have to see, won't we?"

They sat staring at each other, and then Jimmy said, "There's no problem."

"Fine. So let's order, and then we can talk about where you grew up and all that. I was raised on Puget Sound. Ever been out there?"

"Once." Jimmy cleared his throat, trying to unclench his jaw muscles. "My dad took us out there when I was in high school. We flew to someplace near Seattle and stayed in a house on the water. I remember the water lapping against the foundation when the tide was in. We fed the gulls from the porch."

"Hood Canal. I know the place." Charlie signalled to the waiter. "One gull out there is named Ralph, king of the gulls. He takes all the food. I only saw him chased once, when he was attacked by a mother mallard with nine ducklings. There are crows, too, and the odd starling. Do you happen to know how and why starlings were introduced to this country?"

Jimmy said he didn't. Charlie looked up, greeting the waiter. He didn't say whether he knew or not.

Howard swung his chair away from his computer, making what seemed to be a major adjustment in his life. His face was pallid. Hell, it was haggard. "Oh, come in, I was just . . ." With an effort, he got up and gestured toward the couch, then closed the door. "How are you, Jimmy?" He came over and sat down.

"Fine. You?"

Howard smiled. Cement, cracking. "Better, now that

you're back." He sobered, looking wary. "From vacation, right? So everything's wiped clean."

"You mean the firing?"

Howard winced and looked around to make sure the door was shut. He drew in his breath sharply. "That was a mistake. It never happened."

"Like whatever Karen told you about me, in anger."

Howard smiled wryly. "Karen. She's on the disk."

"What disk?"

"You don't know? You really don't?" Jimmy shook his head. "Beth's asking for a divorce."

"I'm getting confused, Howard."

"Sorry. I'm depressed, terribly depressed. I'm shook, Jimmy, it's awful. My two kids. Beth's the love of my life. I'm crushed."

"Well, you've got Karen."

"Don't say that! It's finished. I don't know her, she never existed. Only she does. It's on the disk."

"Howard—"

"From my computer. Somebody sent it to Beth. I know who."

"What was on it?"

"Everything. Notes, memos, my complete business file. Would you believe love letters?"

"Love letters."

"I knew you'd say that. What an idiot I am, Jimmy. I'll never forgive myself."

"You went crazy, Howard. You were carried away."

"But it was supposed to be private! Doesn't anyone know about privacy these days? I've been stabbed in the heart. It's like murder. She might as well have slit my wrists." He shook his head. "Forget I said that."

"Who?"

"No names! Never any more names." He glanced fiercely at Jimmy. "Charlie Acker, you like him?"

"He's okay."

"He's younger than I am by six months, and already a g.m. That's the way it is, but he's got a lot to learn. You don't get ahead by undercutting your executives, that's the old school of management."

"You'll survive, Howard."

"What about prevail, whatever happened to that? And what about my feelings? What about my *wife?*" If he'd had it in him to cry, Howard probably would have broken down at that point, but he'd done his crying. He had moved along to anger. "You won't find a disk in Charlie Acker's office. He's never gone crazy. He thinks love letters are what's deposited in his bank account every month. At least we had fun, didn't we, Jimmy? Creative ideas, action, lots of laughs?" No one had ever looked so joyless. "I mean, it's been kind of shitty lately, with Marlee and all." He brightened a bit. "Remember Dickens? Remember that? A little magic. Give them something extra at home." He choked slightly on the word "home." Suddenly he stood up. "So you're back." He smiled, hurting. "And better than ever."

"I hope so, Howard." He got up, and Howard put out his hand. Jimmy said, "How about a drink, to celebrate my return from vacation?"

"Sure," Howard said, "a little one." He went over to his credenza and came back with the usual glasses and a half empty bottle of bourbon. Howard held the glasses, and he poured enough to cover the bottom, looked up at Jimmy, and poured a little more.

Jimmy raised his glass. "To us, Howard. You'll forgive me if I don't join you. I've got a drinking problem."

Howard looked up, startled, and then watched as Jimmy poured the liquor on his shoes. It splattered onto the thick blue carpet.

Jimmy stepped away, put down his glass and went to the door. "See you, Howard," he said.

Dorothy was waiting for him in her glass-enclosed office off Charlie Acker's reception room, where two secretaries were working diligently. She looked crisp, absolutely crisp in a black business suit and little black tie. The little knot of hair at the apex of her skull had a white carnation pinned to it.

"You look sharp, very sharp," Jimmy told her, looking around. "We obviously can't talk in here."

"Why not?" She smiled. "What's there to hide?"

"Disks. Other things."

"Charlie knows about the disk. He's nonjudgmental, honey, when it comes to right and wrong. He even thought about letting Howard stay."

"He's not?"

She shook her head. "No way. Channel 2's ratings have dropped like an old shoe, and so have Howard's. That's when Charlie starts getting very picky."

"What about Stanford?"

"Still on hold. So's Karen."

"So why am I back?"

Her eyes lit up and the topknot seemed to vibrate. "I give good word of mouth, honey. Charlie was shocked you were out there where the competition could get at you. But he didn't just take it from me. He got up a dossier on you like the CIA. Maybe it was. He was in the State Department for a while, in Zimbabwe."

"He didn't tell me that."

"Look it up like I did. Oh, oh." On her desk, a little red light was blinking rapidly. "He's on the hot line, that means breakneck time. See you a week from Monday, ten o'clock sharp." She picked up a folder and headed for Charlie's office. Jimmy followed her out. The phones were ringing, and the two secretaries were busy putting calls on hold.

The newsroom was in a furor. It was like a big casino, everyone feeding the telephones and computers like slot machines. A few glanced up and said hello as if he had never been away. He heard Marlee's name, and Karen's. He saw the bespectacled writer get up and head for the washroom, a hand over her mouth.

He slid into a vacant chair beside the assignment manager and listened as he talked into his phone. "She's all right? She's hurt. She's on her way to Northwestern Memorial? Wait, repeat. Lacerations, contusions, trauma, sedatives. How did he get in? Un-huh. Any sign of him? No, we'll go live from the hospital when you get there. Call me." He turned to Jimmy. "The doctor got to her half an hour ago. She's all right except for loss of blood from a cut on the arm, and a fall downstairs."

"Karen?"

"They had a police car watching the place out in Flossmoor. Nobody saw him leave. There's a citywide alert. If you're working, we can use you at the hospital when she comes around."

Jimmy shook his head. "I'm not back yet." He got up. "Tell you what, I'll go over and see her and I'll stay in touch with the crew in case you run out of bodies. Why Karen, do you suppose?"

The assignment manager shrugged. "Why Marlee, or any

of them? Oh. They've got a guard around the other woman. What's her name? Clara Turner."

"If you send a crew over to her place, tell them to take along a case of Coke. Heavy on the caffeine."

27

Melvin G. Spanning, that was the doctor's name. M.D.
Jimmy caught Spanning's mother on the air while he was
waiting to see Karen. Channel 5. She was begging her son
to give himself up and stand trial. She knew he was innocent, and she and his father would stand behind him whatever came. It was a good spot. Mrs. Spanning had to be
seventy, but she was plump and vivacious, like an aging
cheerleader. Do it for good old Flossmoor. For the judge,
for the Gipper. Jimmy wondered how the old man was
really feeling now that his son had skipped out on a million
dollars' worth of bail.

He had talked to Ginko. Karen had been found on a land-
ing two floors below her apartment. The attack had taken
place upstairs, and how she got down there no one knew.
She was found bleeding from a slash that ran down her
inner left arm from the elbow to the base of the thumb,
deep enough to cause a significant loss of blood. She had
multiple bruises, most of which apparently had come from
the fall, and one on the back of her head where he must

have struck her, Ginko guessed with a metal pipe. It had been a glancing blow because she had tried to duck out of the way. She had been able to tell them that much, and also that he had fallen on her with a razor blade and she had started screaming. He must have run, and probably she had chased him. She said she hadn't known she'd been cut until they told her in the hospital when she woke up.

"How did he get in?"

"The doorman. He said he was a friend and she said come on up." Ginko had a funny smile. "He said he was you."

"Me?"

"Probably saw you on TV, wouldn't you say?"

"Why pick me?"

"I don't know. Anyway, she let him in."

"How did he get out of the house in Flossmoor?"

"Walked out the back way. His mother says he was gone for two days. They didn't tell anybody because they thought he'd be back any minute. Why not? He's a doctor. He makes house calls."

What was it? What was different about Ginko? As if he'd had a mustache and now it was gone.

The Channel 2 crew was permitted a brief interview, some sort of pool arrangement. Jimmy watched it on the waiting-room screen. Karen was only half awake, but she seemed brave, and more cheerful than not.

After another hour of waiting, he was allowed to see her. He took her right hand, which had no strength in it at all.

"I'm sedated, can you tell? They're sending me home in twenty-four hours, they think. It's so awful. It feels so bad."

"A lot of pain?"

She nodded. "It's not just the arm, it's everywhere. He's got to be caught, Jimmy. Didn't I say that on the tape?" He nodded. "Have you talked to Kirk?"

"No, he'll be here later. Ginko says the guy used my name to get in."

She smiled slightly. "I was looking forward to seeing you. I was typing and left the door open. Jimmy, he's completely changed. Clean shaven, all dolled up. He looked human, sort of."

"Yeah, you said that, too."

"Oh, did I? Did I do all right? I barely know what I'm talking about."

"You were fine."

"I talked to my parents. My mother's flying in. I don't think I want to see her." She was beginning to fade. "She's calling Kathleen. Kate will be worried."

"Relax. Everything's being taken care of."

She closed her eyes. "I'm so tired."

Despite the pounding she had taken, dozing off she looked surprisingly fit. It's the tan, he thought, the tan from Acapulco. And then it struck him, what looked so different about Ginko. Ginko's skin usually had an unhealthy pallor, like something from the swamps of Eastern Europe. But now Ginko had a lovely tan, too.

That night, Jimmy got home about eight o'clock, strangely restless, and soon he found himself thumbing through his address book, looking for Kathleen's number. Dialing the bookstore and hearing her voice, for a moment he couldn't remember why he had called. The voice had a strange effect on him, like falling through a trapdoor onto a warm water bed.

The conversation was brief. She was tired and about to go home. But it was very satisfying.

Karen went on the air the following afternoon, at five o'clock. She wasn't staying on for the late show. She seemed subdued but self-assured, and the bruises above her left eye and along her jaw were covered by makeup and her wound by the long-sleeved black silk blouse she wore.

"Police say they can't be sure exactly what they're looking for," she read from the prompter, "a shabbily dressed man with a day-old beard or one who's clean shaven and well dressed. But there's one thing Dr. Melvin Spanning cannot hide. His eyes. Seen up close, they are cruel and remorseless. Clara Turner saw them. So did I. So did Marlee Roberts and the first two victims. Maybe the eyes were the last thing they saw. I hope not, because when they look at you, you know you're no longer a human being but, to this marauder, this killer, easy prey. Well, not always so easy, as I learned the hard way. Stanford?"

Watching from the tavern on North Avenue, Jimmy guessed the doctor could hide his eyes behind dark glasses if he wanted to, but he couldn't change his shape. He was six feet two and skinny, only Clara recalled that with his shirt off he had an oddly protruding belly. Seeing him more recently in his baggy overcoat, she couldn't tell if he still had it. Sixteen years, a guy could slim down, work off something like that. But the doctor didn't seem the type to engage in vigorous exercise. Jimmy guessed he'd have to ask Kirk about it. He wondered if the cops were going around bumping tall guys accidentally, checking out their centers of gravity.

He was up early the next morning, twelve days before he had to be back at work. He flew to New York and checked into the New York Hilton at Rockefeller Center, the most anonymous place he knew, small enough to be squeezed into central Manhattan but large enough to get lost in, even on the way to the elevator. In his room, he made luncheon reservations at the Russian Tea Room and then lay back on the thick bedspread, waiting impatiently for twelve o'clock to arrive. When it did, he was standing at the window, staring down at a frenzied chunk of noonday traffic. At 12:15 he was staring at the phone. At 12:30 it rang.

"Are you there?"

"Yes. Where are you?"

"In the lobby." Because he couldn't quite believe this conversation was taking place, he was unable to speak. She added helpfully, "Downstairs."

"Come up to the forty-eighth floor. I'll meet you at the elevator. You can drop off what you're carrying and we'll go to lunch. We don't have much time to get there."

"I know. Sorry to be late."

"Never mind that. I've got the whole two days planned so you don't have to feel guilty about anything. Museums, things like that. Tonight, the theater. Get up here."

"All right."

Needlessly, he glanced at his watch. Then he put on his coat and checked his appearance in the mirror. Making sure he had his keycard, he closed the door and went down the hall. He stood at the elevators, checking the time, then the keycard, then the time again. He stared out the window, wondering what she would be wearing. By the time the elevator doors opened, he had forgotten what he had told her on the phone and started to get on.

"My bags," she said, her eyes brighter than he had ever seen them. She wasn't a woman, she was an astral experience. She wore blue and orange and pale green, but the colors kept blurring and rearranging themselves. He found it impossible to look directly at her so he didn't try. She was everywhere.

"Come on," he said, taking the bag that looked heavier while she carried the one that was like a huge slim black envelope with a handle, probably containing her paintings, and they went quickly down the hall, faster and faster, it seemed. Before they were halfway there, they were kissing and walking at the same time, as if that's what people's bodies were designed to do. At the door he kissed her while he unlocked it, not easy with a keycard, and when it opened he slowdanced her inside. Still kissing, he shut the door with one foot and dropped the bag, and they toppled onto the bed. Somehow they got out of their coats, and out of this and that, and there was a pause while he gaped in awe at her pale violet panties. She said, "No, we can't! I won't!" and he heard his own groan of protest, enormously aggrieved as if the Hilton had fallen to the ground. Then suddenly everything was as it should be, but happening too furiously to be recalled in detail. And afterward, holding her, hot and damp and breathing hard, he said, "We can still make it to lunch." They laughed all the way to the cab.

The entire two days were like that, too highly accelerated to make much of an impression on the memory bank. He tried to analyze it. If you broke awareness into three components, physical and intellectual and spiritual, they were experiencing each other on a plane too crowded with body and soul for the intellect to follow. Giddy heights something like that other song, where bodies merged like lemon drops and cries of love were bluebirds, and if there was a rainbow, they were somewhere on the other side of it, God knows where. It seemed unending.

But it ended. That was the hard part. He watched her carry a dozen very large red roses through the glass wall of the lobby—did she use a door?—and enter a cab. He knew then how it really felt, being lost at the Hilton. What would she do with the roses, give them to her friends on the other side of town? To the homeless? To the cab driver?

Kathleen had said no, it was impossible, she couldn't come to New York just like that. Then she said maybe she could, she had been waiting to show certain dealers her paintings. She had said, I won't come to your room. Then, Well, maybe just to meet, just to talk. But not overnight, are you crazy? I have to be at my friends' when my husband calls. Then, contrary to all she had said, she was there and she stayed. And then she was gone.

He flew back feeling his plane drop out of the sky in an arc that stretched all the way to Chicago. That was how you got back from over the rainbow, Mileage Plus. And then he realized that, incredibly, they hadn't mentioned Karen, though that's why he thought he had called. It was as if Karen didn't exist, just the way Howard had said.

28

A few days later, Dutch got Jimmy on the phone as he was having breakfast. "That girl was out. She's worried about you."

"What girl?"

"The one you brought out last fall. The anchorwoman on your station, the one who got slashed."

"Karen? What did she want?"

"Nothing. I guess she's recuperating from her wounds, getting some sun. It was a nice day. We walked around."

"She have any bodyguards?"

"I didn't see any. She was sitting all by herself on the bench across the street when I came out. This was yesterday, Sunday. She's not the one you meant, is she, the one from Wilkes-Barre? She's not married, you know."

"No, that's somebody else."

"Oh, well, anyway, she's a fine-looking woman. She went all around the pond with me, all four times. Then we sat and talked. I think she had a very unhappy childhood."

"That's what you talked about?"

"Yes. You know how it is. Someone who's looking for a father figure, there's nothing like an old man." He paused, maybe waiting for Jimmy to say he wasn't old. "I think maybe she was hoping you'd be out."

"No, she probably wanted to see you, Dad. I think you're right about her childhood. Her adulthood hasn't been all that great either."

"Why not? She's very successful."

"Yes, she is."

"She's divorced, you mean." He waited. "Well, what *do* you mean?"

"The divorce. The attack."

"Well, I don't approve of divorce, as you know. Is Patricia having some kind of trouble?"

"What do you mean?"

"Divorce trouble."

"I haven't talked to her in a while, Dad."

"I was talking to Billy. At the house. You know I go over there for dinner occasionally."

"Yes."

"I was talking to Billy, and he let a few things drop. But it's pretty obvious." Dutch harrumphed, clearing his throat. "They don't relate quite the way they used to. Patricia would go to pieces if anything happened."

"I haven't heard anything, Dad."

"I'm sure you haven't, or you would've told me. She certainly isn't going to tell me anything. Well, I just wondered."

"Mike's very busy."

"So I hear."

"Sometimes that's all it is."

"Sometimes."

"So that's all you and Karen talked about, her child-hood?"

"Well, as nearly as I can recall. She liked the geese. There were eight of them, the little newborn ones. Then there were seven. Yesterday there were six. A snapping turtle got one. One swallowed a fish hook. This morning they picked up a couple of strays. There were six ducks out here, too. No adults. One of the chicks was gone today. I tell you, Jimmy, people's lives are no different from the way things are in nature. One-parent families, kids in trouble. You can learn from nature."

"How tough it is, you mean."

There was a lapse in the conversation. Finally Dutch said, "You're not interested in that young woman, eh?"

"No, Dad. We work together."

"I haven't seen you on the air."

"I go back next Monday. You all right?"

"Fine."

"Don't worry about Pat."

"I won't. She said she might be out again, this Karen."

"I think she's setting her cap for you, Dad."

"If I didn't know you better, I'd say you were joking. But what I wanted to tell you, she asked me how you came to be so smart, which is the sincerest form of flattery. Flattering me by indirection. She's up to something. I told her you did it on your own, but she didn't believe me. She said it could be dangerous, that's what I wanted to tell you. She said, 'Look at what happened to me.' I said, 'Why did it happen, were you getting too close to the killer?' She said, 'Maybe I was.' She's smart. She said she should have taken precautions. She said you never know what can happen. We were talking about the geese."

Jimmy said, "Okay, Dad, thanks for calling. I'll try to get out before I go back to work."

"Good, but I wish you'd listen. She seemed to be telling me you ought to be more careful. Anything to that?"

"No, she's just skittish after her trip to the hospital. Maybe on Thursday."

"Thursday's good."

They hung up. He tried to picture the conversation in the prairie. Karen. What *was* she up to?

Somebody dialed 911 that night to report that they had seen the doctor near a bowling alley on Western Avenue. Jimmy found Ginko leaning against a uniform car, its blue Mars light flashing.

"False alarm?" he said, joining him.

"Well, we haven't found him." Ginko sounded somewhat testy.

"I've been wanting to ask you, where'd you get the tan?"

Ginko eyed him, in no mood to be friendly. "What's it to you?"

"I could guess, but I'd probably be wrong."

"Then don't guess."

"Acapulco?"

"See? Don't guess." A uniform returned to the car and tossed his riot helmet into the backseat. "Butt out," Ginko said. The cop looked at him, retrieved his uniform cap, and left. "I got your drift the other day, Jimmy. As far as I'm concerned, Acapulco is on the other side of the moon. I don't even know what the word means."

The moon was up, about half-size. Above the bowling alley, it looked like a football, hanging high. Jimmy said, "Karen was down there. The guy she was with had a language problem."

Ginko laughed. "I'd have a language problem, all right. You could put all the Spanish I know where the sun don't shine."

"No, I got the idea he was, you know, a foreigner."

The other man nodded. "I'm a naturalized citizen, my friend, but I read you all right. You know what? You're becoming a pest."

Jimmy laughed. "What the hell, Ginko, if you were down there with her, so what? I'd be filled with envy."

"Full of shit's more your style." He straightened up. "I gotta go."

"I could ask Kirk."

Ginko turned and stared. "Go ahead, ask him."

"I could ask your wife."

"You're making me mad, Jimmy. You could find yourself in big trouble." His eyes narrowed. "In Poland we have a saying: 'The one without the balls, that's no bull.' "

Jimmy grinned. "You speak the language, all right."

Ginko didn't change expression. "See?" He did an almost military about-face and walked away.

Next day, after three tries, he spoke to Kathleen by phone. "How are you? You get home all right?"

"Yes. I'm not exactly free to talk."

"I had a good time. I love you."

"Yes."

"Okay, we'll talk later. I'm going to give you a name. Tell me if you've heard it before. Ginko."

"It's a tree. Chinese, I think."

"It's a friend of Karen's. It might be the one who was with her in Mexico. She's never mentioned the name?"

"No. I'm sorry, I'd better go."

"You're sure you're all right?"

"I'm fine, really. Good-bye."

"I love you, Kathleen."

He sat with the phone to his ear long after she had hung up, listening for what he had wanted to hear. Her voice saying, "I love you, too," or at least, "Ginko, yes, that's the name." But there were nine hundred miles between them, and a lot more than that. A husband and two kids, a whole way of life with only scattered moments, scattered thoughts for him, splinters of light in the darkness. And what did it matter who Karen had gone to Mexico with? The doctor was out there on the prowl, a rat scuttling through the back alleys of the city. He had slain three women, slashed one and scared the bejesus out of another, not to mention a million others who feared they might be next. What am I doing, Jimmy asked himself, getting Ginko's back up, chasing shadows?

Slowly, he put the phone back in its cradle and sat looking down at his used airline ticket, wondering when, if ever, he would be able to see Kathleen again. Nine hundred miles had never seemed so far. Life had never seemed so empty, fate so cruel. Then he sat back and smiled, thinking about the two days at the Hilton.

He remembered his father shouting to him from out of the prairie, "Jimmy, what's all this wildness, do you know?" He could answer him now.

It was life, and fate, and whatever you did to shape them the way you wanted them to be. Except with the prairie, it was simple. It was growing, straight up. What was it with people? How could you tell if what you wanted was pure natural wildness, not bent and twisted? It wasn't just the law, because laws were often a matter of the majority's convenience. It was something inside. Something deep in the prairie that had struck Dutch as both fearsome and secure. Something inside a person, like love.

Jimmy got quickly to his feet, feeling a little embarrassed by such thoughts, and went down to get his mail. Christ, he thought, I'm beginning to sound like a priest.

29

On Thursday morning, as planned, Jimmy pulled on jeans, running shoes, and a light jacket and drove out to the prairie. He parked near the side entrance and went in, peering across the highgrass for Dutch. The main gate, two blocks away, was directly across the street from his father's apartment, but this one was closer to his bench.

The bench was empty so he sat down to wait. The day was cloudswept and on the cool side, the tall oaks and maples not yet starting to bud. Quiet except for the songbirds, one of which was calling very clearly, "Here, here, here." He expected to see Dutch any moment coming up the walkway from the visitors center, a small hexagon set on a man-made bluff at the other end of the pond, near the parking lot. Several recreation workers hung out there, Dutch said, between folksings and tentouts and cleanup chores.

Dutch was late. Unusual, because he still thought of himself as a banker who scorned bankers' hours.

After a while Jimmy got up and stretched. Then, leaving the blacktop, he wandered up along the woodchip trail that led around the far side of the pond, winding through tightly packed trees and thick undergrowth. He stopped and gazed across the water. The overhanging branches of the willows sweeping its unrippled surface were bare and the cattails just beginning to flourish, so he could see the distant ridge where the trail ran. If Dutch has taken the long way around, he thought, I ought to be able to spot him through the trees.

He heard the boys' voices before he saw the geese.

"Ribbet, ribbet," one voice said. "Ribbet, ribbet, ribbet."

The other kid laughed. "I hope a frog comes out and humps you." Clearly teenagers.

He saw the boys then, just past the willows. Two of them, about fourteen years old, crouched over fishing poles, the lines dangling into the water.

Go or stay? he wondered. Wait here or take the trail, maybe meet Dutch on the way?

He turned and started up the path, seeing the big goose a dozen feet away. It was staring fiercely at him, its head swiveled on an impossibly long neck. Black neck and head, snowy cheeks, brown plump football-shaped body. It was plainly on guard. Then he saw the others, another adult and half a dozen light-feathered little ones over by the timbered fence, nibbling new grass sprouting from among last year's leaves.

Steering clear of the geese so as not to upset them, he started past, and the sentry goose took a couple of steps toward him, opened its beak and hissed, revealing a vivid red gullet that looked to Jimmy like the gates of hell. He flinched but kept going as the toddlers followed their mother off into the high grass.

The two boys ignored him as he went past, rounding a bend and heading into a tunnel of overreaching branches filled with birds. They flew up, mostly robins, and then a number of red-winged blackbirds.

The trees thinned out a little up ahead, where there was more sunlight. The ice that had formed beneath the feet of winter hikers was gone, and stretches of the trail were strewn with fresh woodchips. Stray autumn leaves lay along it here and there.

With the melting snow and early spring rains, the pond had risen higher than he remembered it, covering the roots of the trees along the bank. Halfway along, two snapping turtles sat on a log jutting into the cattails, and across the water where the pond narrowed, he made out two scatterings of straw, the nests the geese had abandoned. Already he could hear the distant whine of traffic where Lincoln Avenue curved and dipped beneath the overpass where the commuter trains ran.

No sign of Dutch, no faint halloo. I probably should have stayed where I was, he thought.

At the break in the trees where the last leg of the trail began, he paused and looked back across the pond. The two boys had dropped their lines on the other side of the willows. He couldn't see the bench, or the geese.

He was about to move on when he saw them coming toward him along the trail thirty or forty yards away, Dutch and Karen. She was in black running togs. Jimmy waited, amused. He was about to call out something original, like "We've got to stop meeting like this," when behind him a twig snapped and a bird began furiously beating its wings.

The third sound was not really a sound at all but a reverberation in his skull as he was struck from behind. He fell, pitched forward like a sack of grain.

Karen screamed.

He landed face down, the ground driving the air from his body.

Dazed and gasping, he felt himself straddled. A hand clamped down on his left arm and twisted. He felt pain shoot through his wrist. Desperately, he tried to roll, and at the same time the weight on his back sprang free.

Someone was running away and someone else arriving, but he was asleep, his head resting on the bar of his favorite tavern. He had never been this drunk. He heard his name, felt someone trying to wake him. Opening one eye, he saw a dried leaf streaked with red, like a painted leaf in a window. Around it were reddening woodchips, and the red seemed to be coming from the cut on his wrist. It was smeared with his blood, which dripped on the countertop of the bar, among the woodchips.

High overhead, someplace his father was shouting and his mother was weeping. He lay on his back now, looking up, but he didn't recognize them. A young woman, blonde, her hair pulled back tight. Behind her the two boys, the fishermen.

A voice that didn't belong to any of the faces was asking how he was. He said, "I'm okay," but his lips didn't seem to move. He turned his head, trying to find the voice, but pain stabbed his neck and all he could see were the plastic-rimmed glasses and the white T-shirt bending over him. Some damn recreation worker, and the blonde, too. They were tying something around his upper arm, and around his wrist. On the wrist, a white handkerchief. He watched it slowly turn red.

Later, riding in the ambulance with Dutch beside him, Dutch gritting his teeth and grumbling to himself, Jimmy asked about the dead bird. A robin, Dutch said, a baby robin with its neck broken. Jimmy remembered it clearly then, lying a few feet up the path, one wing splayed out.

"Where's Karen?" He remembered her standing just beyond the bird. She was fitting a puzzle together in the palm of her hand. A razor blade she had picked up from the trail, and a cardboard sleeve she had taken from her jacket pocket.

"She found the sleeve where he dropped it," his father explained. "Then, a little farther along, the blade. I gave it to the police."

"The locals."

"The Skokie cops."

"What did they say?"

"What could they say? She said it was the doctor. I didn't get a good look at him. She said he came out here after her, and you got in the way. I guess you did."

"Where is she?"

"Went to find a phone. Said she was going back to the office."

"Dad, she took the sleeve out of her pocket."

"Sure, she found it first."

"You see her find it?"

"Dammit, Jimmy, don't talk."

"Why not?"

"There could be a concussion."

"Nothing else?"

"Well, the wrist. You'll get a tetanus shot for sure."

"Did you see her find the sleeve?"

Dutch sighed. "No, she came over and showed me what she'd found. It was already sheathed, the blade."

But it wasn't what she had found, or when, but the look in her eyes when she saw him watching her. The sudden fright. And he knew. Because the sleeve was the color of the woodchips and she wouldn't have been able to see it, would she? Find it that fast? But mostly because of what her eyes said.

Maybe the look had been fear of what might have resulted if the doctor had come across her first and been thorough in his work. But through the gently grinding throb in his head, Jimmy thought he knew what had happened; Karen giving the doctor the blade and putting the sleeve in her pocket, then crossing the street to see Dutch and keep him talking (that was easy) while the doctor followed Jimmy up the path, and who could reach out and strangle a bird about to fly up, or maybe it hadn't learned to fly? And so am I wrong? Am I crazy?

"Did she know I was coming out?" he asked Dutch.

The old man looked down at him, biting his lip. "Yeah, I told her yesterday you were coming. I said come on out, the more the merrier."

At the hospital, after the X ray and the needle and the stitches, they wanted to keep him for observation, but Jimmy wouldn't let them. Besides, Patricia was already there, waiting. So after he had talked with Sgt. Kirkpatrick by phone, she came to his room and collected him, angrier than she was upset, which was her way. She drove slowly, mainly because Dutch was following in Jimmy's car and hadn't driven in quite a while. Neither of them could recall whether he still had a license.

In Wilmette, wearing an old shirt of Mike's and pair of his Dockers that were too long, Jimmy lay on the couch and Pat was very solicitous, getting worried about him now. When he asked her how Mike was, she said, "Oh, fine," but as soon as their father looked away shook her head, meaning, Don't ask.

Sounding frail again, Dutch said, "When I die, I want you to toss my ashes on the prairie," and Pat said, "Oh, Father, stop it." She got up and left the room.

The assignment manager called at about one o'clock, and a Channel 2 camera crew came out and taped a ten-minute interview. He was feeling groggy but did the best he could. He forgot to ask them about Karen, how she was doing.

He was wondering when Kirk would be out for a face-to-face when, shortly after 3:00 P.M., he heard the news bulletin from the next room, saying that the doctor was holed up with a hostage in a Chicago apartment on North Ridge Boulevard. He made Pat call and get the exact address, then he was out of there, saying he would call her later. He had a little trouble staying on the road at first, steering mostly with one hand, but after a while it was no trouble at all.

30

The doctor was going to kill his hostage, that's what he kept yelling into the phone at the police. He had grabbed the girl, Vanessa Green, as she was coming home from high school and hustled her up the stairs to the third floor where she lived with her mother. Her mother was still at work. She was a nurse at Evanston Hospital, two miles north. A retired sixth-grade teacher who lived on the first floor had heard the ruckus outside her door and called the police.

So now the doctor was saying he was armed, and he was threatening to kill the girl unless the cops went away.

The apartment complex was about a mile from the lake, half a dozen or so three-story red-brick buildings grouped around a grassy courtyard. Each building contained six units, two on each floor, separated by the stairs. The doctor and the girl were in the third building back, in the unit facing east. The building was surrounded by police, firemen, and the press, and the police had told him they had no intention of leaving.

In the siege, now more than an hour old, the cops had commandeered all the best vantage points, third-floor apartments on three sides and a second-floor bedroom across the driveway in back. These gave them a view of every room, or would have if the doctor had not drawn the blinds. The media had paid their way into what space was left and available. Television cameras were stationed at second-story windows on two sides of the building and others were trained on the driveway. Along with curious citizens, the firemen waited behind the other buildings, staying out of sight until their equipment might be needed.

At 4:30 P.M. various reporters and one camera crew crowded into a third-floor living room across the hall from the police command post, which faced the bedroom windows of the Green apartment, a dozen feet away. Though not assigned to the story, Jimmy managed to squeeze in along the windows overlooking the courtyard. He sat awkwardly on the narrow sill, feeling weak. The other reporters left him alone, partly out of human regard, partly because this was a bigger story than what had happened in the park.

Sgt. Kirkpatrick made a brief appearance. "The offender has been in the apartment across the way for almost two hours," he said, not looking up from his notes. "As you know, we've established telephone communication and of course he's been watching television, so he knows what's going on."

"What's he watching?" someone asked. "Oprah?"

That got mild laughter. Someone else pointed out that Oprah was on in the morning and maybe it was Donahue or Geraldo.

"Knock it off, assholes," Kirkpatrick said. "The hostage isn't laughing." And then he said to the camera, "Wipe that off the tape or I'll take your press cards." There was general laughter at this, and even Kirk seemed to understand why.

"The apartment," he continued, slogging ahead, "is just like this one, same location in the building next door. Two phones, one in the living room and one in the north bedroom. Same two stairways, front and rear, leading to the basement. There's no way onto the roof from inside, although there is a small attic space, and nowhere to go even if he made it to the roof. But unless we can persuade him to give up his hostage and surrender, he can stay there for a week or two before he runs out of food. We won't force the issue as long as the hostage is there and unharmed."

"Have you talked to her?"

"Where's the mother now?"

"Her mother is in one of the other apartments. She's been in touch with the hostage and established that she's okay. Being in a life-threatening situation, of course, the girl is naturally terrified. So's her mother."

The detective ignored a flurry of questions.

"The other mother, in case you're interested," he went on, raising his voice to be heard, "is on her way from Flossmoor. She ought to be here any time now, and we'll get her on the line with the doctor as soon as we can. Meanwhile the officers in that building and the other buildings will do nothing until some decision is reached in this one, across the hall. The commander is over there. He'll speak to you later if you wish. For now, we just wait. And talk to the doctor."

"Have you established any reason he's out to get Channel 2 anchor people?" Reporters glanced Jimmy's way.

"We haven't discussed that. All we know is he wants to come out, otherwise he says he'll kill his hostage, but he knows he's going to jail. Let's leave it at that."

"Is the chief coming over?"

"The chief is being kept apprised of everything that happens. He has no plans to leave his office until this is over. Okay, that's all." Kirkpatrick turned away, and fending off further questions went back across the hall, closing the door. Gradually the living room began to empty.

Jimmy found Ginko in one of the bedrooms, sitting on the bed with his back to the wall. Ginko eyed Jimmy's bandaged wrist. "So you finally met up with him."

Jimmy nodded. He leaned against an old-fashioned mirrored chest of drawers, wanting very much to lie down.

"Well," the detective said, "he's got one more victim to go, and whatever he does to her we've got him now. He hurt you much?"

"Mainly I just feel lousy."

Ginko got off the bed. "Where's the anchor lady?"

"Probably in the newsroom. They're about ready to go on the air."

"Oh, by the way, Clara Turner's back in the hospital. The pressure got too much, so her doctor checked her in."

"Where?"

"Downtown. Northwestern Memorial. She'll be out in a few days."

Jimmy wanted to tell him about Karen taking the razor blade from her pocket. He wanted to tell him about her eyes. But he didn't know where to start. Did any of it mean anything?

A young reporter from Channel 7 popped into the doorway. "Could you give us a couple of minutes on tape, Jimmy? We have a camera setup downstairs. How you feeling?" She looked concerned and full of energy.

"Fuck off," Ginko said. "He'll be down later. He has to lie down, doctor's orders."

"Oh," she said. "Of course." She said to Jimmy, "Second floor, the other side," and disappeared.

"Thanks," Jimmy said. He sat down on the bed. "You doing all right?"

"I don't like this waiting. It's gonna happen, so let it happen."

"You want to go in?"

"Take the bastard, put him away. First Kirk wants him to talk to his mother. Soften him up, see what he does."

"I wish you luck."

"Do you really?" Ginko looked away, smiling sardonically. "Sometimes I wonder why I came to this fucking country. If I'd stayed home, I could probably have a nice little apartment by now, and a car. I'd have a woman picking up after me. I miss the old ways." He looked down and kicked at the rug. "Fucking Communists."

"They screwed up things for you."

"Yeah. It's better to screw them up yourself, like they're doing over there now. But it's still a good country. It's home." He started for the door. "I'd better check in. See you, Jimmy."

"See you, Ginko."

He closed the door and stretched out on the bed, closing his eyes. His head throbbed gently but firmly, and colorful little arcs of light appeared and gradually evaporated. He didn't sleep. He could hear voices from the next room, and outside the windows. It sounded like an armed camp out there. The room was small and he felt securely enclosed, but he knew that any minute the whole place could explode.

The doctor's mother was speaking to her son by phone for the third time when, shortly after five o'clock, the girl came out of a bedroom window. She was in her underwear and it was twenty-five or thirty feet to the ground, but fortunately she landed in the grass rather than on the sidewalk. The grass was very thick and green and the ground relatively soft, but she broke her ankle anyway. She sat there crying and holding herself while, in a window across the courtyard, her mother screamed and, from high in the adjacent building, heavy automatic firing erupted, knocking out window glass and dislodging wood and bricks and mortar. This was dangerous to the girl, for some of the debris fell in her direction, but it was considered necessary to keep the doctor at bay while two or three uniformed cops lifted and carried her around to safety and medics came running with a stretcher.

At that point, while the doctor's mother was sobbing into a silent telephone, the cops who had been crouched for hours on the stairs broke down the living-room door. Seeing the doctor leap half-naked across the small hallway between bedrooms, they opened fire, hitting him in the legs and knocking him down. He crawled into the bathroom, locked the door and, to keep things tidy—a dedicated and thoughtful physician to the last—climbed into the bathtub, drawing the shower curtain between him and the rest of the world.

The first in was Ginko. He moved into the little hallway past the others and shot the lock off the door, then made it to the tub just as the doctor was blowing his own brains out.

This is what Ginko told the young woman from Channel 7 who had been waiting on the lawn with a camera crew for the commander to come down. Jimmy thought Ginko looked ravishing with the trickle of blood on his tanned forehead, from the doctor's brains splashing off the tile.

As the detective stepped away from the camera, he smiled cockily. "You see what can happen when you cross the line," he said to Jimmy. He was still greatly excited.

"No hard feelings," Jimmy said. "About Acapulco."

Ginko laughed, really charged up. "Christ," he said, and clapped him on the shoulder. "You know I got trouble with the language. Is that like an avocado or something?"

He walked away, skirting a small group of civilians who were escorting the doctor's mother down the sidewalk toward the street. She no longer reminded Jimmy of a cheerleader. She was weeping uncontrollably and looked about to collapse.

31

Jimmy left his car in the garage at about seven o'clock. He went upstairs, took a couple of the big red pills the nurse had given him, flopped on his bed, and dialed Patricia. "I'm okay," he told her. "I suppose you saw it."

"I certainly did. You looked awful."

"They ran that interview? No, I meant the doctor."

"Yes, how horrible!"

"Dutch had me worried today. How's he doing?"

"He's playing cribbage with Billy. I think Billy's letting him win. When he's winning he sounds insane. You know, like Dr. Frankenstein inventing something. Tell me how you are."

"I ache all over. I'm going right to sleep."

"About time. Aren't you supposed to check in with your doctor?"

"I'll call him tomorrow, when I get rid of this headache."

"Call him now. Take the pills. That's what they're for."

"I did. Mike there?"

"No." There was a pause. "Let's have an arrangement. If

you don't ask about Mike, I promise to tell you when the ax falls."

"Okay. Sorry. Did you see Karen Kohl on the air?"

"I'm not sure. I don't remember which channel I was watching."

"I'll give you a ring tomorrow. Good night."

He put the receiver down, seeing messages blinking on the machine. Deciding they could wait, he unplugged the phone, lay back and felt fatigue flow over him like surf over sand.

The pounding on the door awakened him and he sat up, surprised to find himself in street clothes. It was just after midnight. Getting out of bed and staggering drunkenly into the foyer, he shouted through the door, "Who is it?"

"The doorman, Mr. Gillespie. Your phone won't answer and you have callers. It's the police."

He unlocked the door and opened it, seeing the doorman and then Kirkpatrick and his partner. He turned away, heading for the living room.

"Sorry, Gillespie," Kirk said, following him. Jimmy heard the door close as he sank down on the couch. The two detectives began looking around.

"Nice place," Ginko said.

Kirk concentrated on the near wall, maybe counting the picture frames. There were more than fifty, mostly old news photos and scenes of the city going back to the early part of the century. "We're asking around about Miss Kohl," he said without turning around. "Ginko thought she might be here."

Jimmy looked darkly at the partner. "Why would she be here?"

Kirk said, "She's been missing since early this afternoon. She was last seen in your company."

He thought about that. "She was headed downtown."

"Never showed up. Missed two newscasts, never went home. What do you make of it?"

Jimmy sat up and put his head in his hands. It was swimming. "I think maybe I'll make a drink."

Ginko said, "Didn't they tell you no drinking? At the hospital?"

"I don't remember them saying that."

"Well, I'm telling you. Till the doctor says so, stay off the booze."

He looked up at Kirk. "You think something happened to her in the park? The doctor could still have been there."

Kirk shrugged. He was still perusing the photographs.

Ginko said, "Something happened somewhere. That newscast is her favorite TV show. She wouldn't miss it. She tapes it, she told me once. Says she learns something new every time she watches it, but I think it's vanity. She can't get enough of herself." He sat down on the couch beside Jimmy. "So where would she go?"

He shook his head. "I think I need my pills."

"I'll get them," Ginko said, getting to his feet. "Where are they?"

Jimmy thought for a moment. "In the kitchen, beside the sink. Round plastic bottle."

The detective went into the kitchen and Jimmy heard tap water running. Kirk was still looking over the pictures on the wall. "Here's one of you with the legendary columnist. Who's that, Kup's wife?"

Jimmy groaned and settled back on the couch. "Since I'm up, I'll tell you. It's a long story. Mrs. Kup got mad at me once. Some cameraman I sent out for some reason said something rude to her, I forget what. He was wrong and I apologized, but she was unforgiving. Then I ran into her at a Channel 5 party. We were seated side by side, as a matter of fact. She ignored me for a while and then she said, 'Oh, what the hell.' We wound up having our picture taken."

The sergeant said, "Some classy-looking broad." He moved over to another group of photographs.

Jimmy said, "So was the park searched?"

"The Skokie cops looked around. Seems odd, her disappearing on the day the doctor got it. The commander thought so. That's why we're here, anyway. He said go, and we went."

Ginko came back with the pill bottle and a glass of water and sat down, waiting for Jimmy to pop a couple. "She have any other boyfriends?"

"You mean besides you and me?" He drank.

"Well, judging by the past . . ."

Jimmy put the glass on the floor. "The last time I said something like that, you were shocked."

"Was I?"

Ginko looked up at the sergeant, and Kirk said, "Ginko's talking about Acapulco. She was down there with somebody interesting."

"Who?"

Kirk moved to a chair and sat down. "Marlee Roberts's boyfriend. Remember him, the one from Miami? Miami called us. It looked like he was on his way to a meeting, so we sent Ginko down there to see who."

Ginko said, "They were together the whole weekend. Whoever told you he didn't speak English must have meant he had an accent. But from what I could see, they communicated pretty good."

"So what was it about? Lust? Money?"

Kirk said, "It seems likely that Ernie Escobar simply picked up where he left off with Marlee Roberts. Karen was the next local celebrity in line, only younger and snazzier."

"You think she could be in Miami?"

"No trace of her down there. Scranton either. They picked up Escobar for us, but he won't talk to them. Her parents don't know anything." He looked at Ginko. "I'm tired. It's been a long day, and I have to see the lieutenant before I can go home."

When they had left, Jimmy remembered. He went into the bedroom and checked the answering machine. Only one surprise, a message from Kathleen. She sounded much the same as in their last conversation, tentative and a little worried. Or just tired, he couldn't tell. He saved the tape so he could replay her voice in the morning. He would call back then.

"She's here," Kathleen said. "She called me last night, wanting to use my car. I told her I needed it, and she said okay, forget it. But she sounded so hurt and angry, I said she could have it. Well, she's just out of the hospital. Anyway, she was completely upset by then, said I was some kind of weird friend and hung up. But then it dawned on me. She hadn't even heard what I'd said about the car. I know what it's like to be completely distraught because I've been there. Not hysterical. Hopeless. Do you know the difference, how it sounds? No inflections, nothing at all. Jimmy, I'm worried. She's not at the hotels I called and not at her parents', and I don't know what to do. I'm afraid."

"Listen," Jimmy said, "before we get into this, I want you to know how much I—"

"Oh, God!" she broke in. "That was one of the things she

said, 'Don't tell anyone I'm here or I'll tell them about Jimmy Gillespie.' My God, Jimmy, did you tell her about us?"

"No. She's guessing."

"It didn't seem like that. Are you sure?"

"Not a word." He was wondering what else she and Dutch might have talked about. Did Dutch ask her about some married lady in Wilkes-Barre?

"Well, it scared the hell out of me, and then I thought, So what, she's in trouble. I'm not sure I'd have called you, though, if I'd waited. Nothing, Jimmy, nothing must happen to my marriage, do you understand?"

He decided he had no comment on that. All he cared about was wanting her here. "So what do you want me to do?"

"I don't know. Think of something. I'm worried."

"Well, if she rented a car, that should be easy but wouldn't do us much good. A taxi would be better. Does Wilkes-Barre have taxis?" Apparently she had no comment on that. It was Saturday morning, two days before he was due back at work. His head felt better. His wrist probably needed to be looked at, but that could wait. He said, "I'm coming out. If I can make it, I'll be there this afternoon."

"No, I don't want you here. It's too—it feels too threatening."

He thought a while. "Well, let's see, you could call the police or hire a private investigator, but who knows what she might tell them? Who can you trust to keep his mouth shut besides me?"

"If you did."

"For Christ's sake, Kathleen, we're having our first argument, that's all. I'll just nose around, and you won't know I'm there unless I find her, and then I'll figure out some way to let you know and keep her quiet. Stay cool. Go to work. Paint a picture." Paint a leaf, he almost said. "Did she say where she was calling from?"

"No, she wouldn't tell me. She just said downtown."

"Okay, we start from scratch. Now, will you be all right? Are we okay on this?"

He could hear her breathing. After a while she said, "I'm all right. I hope—" Suddenly she began laughing. "Oh, Jimmy, I don't believe it! Right this minute, there's a cardinal at my kitchen window. He keeps knocking against the glass, trying to get in. There he goes. Oh, my God, Jimmy, was that you?"

"Kathleen, I love you. I won't let anything happen to your marriage, so stop worrying."

"I can't."

"Okay, one thing. If you hear from her, call my house. Leave a message, because I'll be checking in with the machine."

"All right. I appreciate what you're doing. I love you."

"Well, of course you do. See you, Kathleen."

His head was aching again. He took another pill and tossed the bottle into an empty suitcase. He called the airline and made a reservation for two hours away. Then he took off his clothes and tied an industrial-size plastic bag around his left arm to keep the hospital dressing dry and got into the shower.

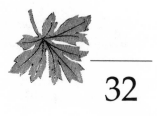

32

The plane put him down about 3:00 P.M. He rented a dark Oldsmobile and drove into downtown Wilkes-Barre, where he spent half an hour checking out the car rental agencies to make sure she hadn't rented one, and then the hotels and the taxicabs parked outside the hotels. It was after five o'clock before he found the right driver, an older man with a crewcut and a lined, freckled forehead, and eyes so squinted they had permanently wrinkled his nose.

"Where did you take her?"

The cabbie stared up at him, scratching an angular jaw. "That's kind of her business, isn't it?"

"Look, I'll triple her fare. Where'd she go?"

The man considered the question and then said, "Out toward Route 81 South, just outside of town. That's partly how I remember, because it was after dark and I was leaving her out there on the highway. But I didn't argue with her. I could tell she was—something wasn't quite right about her."

"Highway to where?"

"You her husband?"

"No."

"Well, it goes to Harrisburg and points in between. I dropped her off in Ashley, on the way to Sugar North. Who knows where she was going after that? Maybe she lives out there, how do I know? Maybe meeting somebody. People do all kinds of things."

"You said she was wearing a dark jacket and pants. Could it have been a running suit?"

"Running suit?" He laughed. "Maybe she was going jogging."

"Any luggage?"

"No. That's one reason I thought—"

"She all right? No sign of an injury?"

"Injury? No, she looked all right." He glanced up at the head of the line, where the first cab was taking on passengers. As it pulled away, he eased the cab ahead, and Jimmy tagged along. "Like I say, she acted funny."

"How do you mean?"

"Well, you know the homeless?" He took the cab out of gear. "Not many of them around here, but every once in a while you pick up somebody who can't pay. I was afraid she was one of those. They act peculiar. Staring, she was. Wouldn't talk, wouldn't smile, wouldn't answer my questions. Short with me. Reminded me of the ones who walk down the street talking to themselves or Jesus. Angry, that's how she acted."

"How far out is this Ashley?"

"It's just outside of town a couple of miles. Not much out there. A bank, a post office, that's about it."

"All right, now listen. We're going to get my car and I'll follow you out there. Here's a twenty. I'll give you another one when we get there." The cabbie nodded, folding the bill and putting it in his shirt pocket. "First I have to make a phone call, okay? Then you can take me to my car."

Jimmy went into the hotel, found a pay phone in the lobby and called the bookstore. Kathleen had gone home. He found the number on the back of her card, put in another quarter and dialed.

She wailed and then began whispering. "How could you call me here? My husband will be home any minute. Are you in town? Have you found her?"

He could hear children's voices in the background. "No, but she took a cab out to Ashley last night. I don't even know where that is. Can you think of any reason she'd go out there?"

"Out by the breaker." She had stopped whispering.

"Where?"

"Where we went that morning, the day of the wedding."

"It's out that way?"

"It's right out Main Street. We went up on the other side of it, beyond it up the hill. Just a minute." She spoke to one of her children. "David, put that down. Dinner in a second." Back on the phone, she said, "I'm trying to feed my kids. I can only talk a second."

"Why would she go out there?"

It took her a while to answer. "Oh, well, if she's in some kind of trouble, I guess I should tell you. The friend who offered to—you know."

She didn't want anyone to overhear, so he said it for her. "Help you kill yourself."

"Yes. That was Karen."

The hesitation marks, the wrists, the blood on the walls. Was there a connection? "I thought he was a guy. Why didn't you tell me?"

"She asked me never to tell. I promised her."

"So what does that have to do with the breaker?"

"That's where she told me to go home and get the—you know."

"The razor blade."

"Yes."

"My God, so that's where you were." He pictured the breakers he had been inside, their bleakness, the grime that covered everything. He pictured the stark abandoned building they had seen on the side of the hill. "Is there some way to get in?"

"There used to be. A hole in the fence, at the back, on the uphill side. Then a kind of opening at one corner of the breaker you could squeeze through. Lots of kids did it all the time."

"I don't know, Kathleen, it seems like such a long shot. Isn't there any other reason she'd go out there? Somebody she knows?"

"I don't think so." She gasped. "David, no! Mommy's coming."

"Okay, I'll have a look around. Thanks, Kathleen."

He followed the taxi out of downtown Wilkes-Barre and onto the highway, and after a few minutes saw it up ahead, the long rise leading toward the mountains and the breaker shed. About halfway up, the cab pulled over and stopped. Jimmy parked behind it, got out, and went over to the driver. "This is where you let her out? Not up there?"

The cabbie was chewing something. He leaned over to the far window and spat. "Right here. Like I say, it was dark and I thought it was a mighty queer place to let somebody out, but I wasn't going to argue."

Jimmy wondered if he kept saying that because that's all he did when he wasn't driving, argue. He gave him the other twenty. "What time was this?"

"Ten o'clock, maybe a quarter after."

"There's an old coal breaker up there, isn't there?"

"Yes sir, right over the hill, down on Main Street. It hasn't been used for a long, long time. Where are you from, Philadelphia?"

"No. Anybody come out to look at the breaker these days?"

"Naw. They used to have auctions and bake sales and that, in the parking lot. That's when they were thinking of making it into a coal mine museum like some of the others around, but nobody wanted to spend the money. So there's nothing to see."

Jimmy stepped away. "Thanks. I appreciate your help."

The driver looked down at the twenty-dollar bill. "That's it?" He tucked it into his pocket and put the cab in gear. "Well, I guess I won't argue with you either."

When the cab had completed its U-turn, heading back toward the city, Jimmy drove to the top of the rise and pulled off onto the grassy shoulder. He killed the engine and sat for a while, examining the bulky black oblong down the slope. The sun, slowly dying over the greening mountains, was becoming a red ball of fire. It would set in less than an hour. Its rays struck the side of the building without leaving a trace. The breaker sat solid and opaque, a dense block of galactic matter jammed into a hill, its sole purpose to raise questions about the universe. If mankind set out to duplicate a black hole in space, he decided, it could do worse than to build a breaker.

He got out and walked down the slope toward it, thinking of suicides and attempted suicides and suicides that weren't really suicides, thinking, Ah, man's infinite variety. The ground beneath his feet seemed not to have been walked on since the place was alive. It was gritty and it crunched. It looked not so much like earth as slag, the unusable slate brought to the surface along with the coal and discarded in mountainous piles, where it burned and turned orange. That was the entire purpose of the breaker sheds, to separate chunks of slate from the black harvest. Then the rains drenched the charred hills of acid-orange slag, washing the rust down the slopes along with the coal dust, coloring the rocks and fouling the valleys, blackening the streams and rivers, killing the earth with its own detritus.

He could see the fence and the base of the breaker now, and beyond it a few business buildings and several houses on the other side of the street. The fence was about twelve feet high, topped with strands of barbed wire. The gate, apparently, was on the street side. As he came closer, he saw where the fencing had been cut and peeled back along the bottom. He stooped and crawled through, then stood up, dusted himself off and moved slowly across the parking lot.

The breaker rose more than a hundred feet above him. It looked no more inviting than you might expect of a hulking instrument of the land's demise. Nothing but blackened, rusted metal and cracked, blackened glass, and, where the windows were broken, blackest of all.

At one corner of the building he found a narrow, angular opening about head-high, where one edge of a metal panel had been forced inward. He looked through it, seeing only a long stretch of dark concrete floor and, rising from it, three or four inclined gravity chutes, the final step in the process that began up high, near the ceiling. Involuntarily, he crossed himself, then slipped inside.

Pale shafts of filmy light from the broken windows penetrated the interior darkness, making a vast, angular interplay of opposites that began at the highest point, tracking downward in a vertical complexity of screens and rollers and conveyors and troughs, remnants of nineteenth-century mechanical wizardry.

The topmost of these, a large sloping platform, loomed just beneath the dark ceiling. This was the head of the breaker, where the wet, shiny slabs of mixed coal and slate and clay from the mine were dumped from cars and the process of sorting began. It was also where the corrosive sulfuric-acid water from the mine had misted down, and the haze of coal dust, and the little light, while the fearsome noise of the machinery had shaken the building.

Beneath the platform, cascading downward like a giant mobile, hung several tipped cylindrical screens of cast iron filled with sharp steel teeth, fat acrobatic goblins that long ago had feasted and slept. Once these had rotated noisily, cracking the coal into smaller and smaller sizes as it tumbled inside them, spewing out the vast black clouds that permeated the air. The chunks spilled from one to the other, to be screened and washed and chewed again by the rollers, the crushers, the masticators, for these were the breakers themselves. Spat out, the coal and what was left of the slate crashed and rattled down the final chutes past the scrabbling hands of the breaker boys, fingers cut and bleeding, throats choked with dust. Working like scores of tiny slavey devils, the slate pickers separated the burnable from the dross as the lumps tumbled steadily downward all day long into the hoppers above the waiting railroad cars.

Standing before the sloping chutes, Jimmy could make out only the vaguest outlines of this in the pervasive gloom. At his feet, though, where waning sunlight accumulated, he noticed the tiny white cylinders dotting the blackened cement floor. Cigarette butts, lots of them. Fresh ones. He picked one up and examined it. A Camel.

Looking up, he called out, "Karen!" The name echoed faintly. "Karen, where are you?"

Nothing moved that he could see. Scanning the overhead spaces and keeping an eye out for whatever might be down below, he sidled over toward the far wall. There were more butts along the way. Had she smoked through the night, then moved on, or was she watching? The other possibility, that her body lay somewhere in this dark labyrinth, was something he didn't think he could handle right now.

"Karen, I'm going outside and get the others. We'll search the place. We'll find you. Come on out." He waited, seeing nothing, hearing nothing. I'm talking to myself, he thought. She's gone, maybe for cigarettes. Has she eaten lately? "We've got food, hot food. Cigarettes. Candy bars. Whatever you want. Karen, come on down."

He moved a few steps toward the hole in the wall and heard a voice, faraway and scratchy but strong. "Who's there?" It came from high up, twanging his nerves. Echoing. Or was it a snicker?

He waited. Nothing.

Peering upward and moving slowly toward the thin triangle of sunlight that was the only exit, he said casually, "It's Jimmy. You all right?"

This time it was unmistakably a laugh, a tiny giggle.

Then he saw her, a black shape moving against the dark, way up where the coal cars were tipped and emptied. Instantly, she was gone.

A wind, creaking. A moaning sound, not human. Then a sharp crack, as if the building had split in two. A black haze drifted and settled over everything, old coal dust sifting, falling, and they came swooping down, the bats. He ducked. He would have said dozens, but there may have been only a few. They swung trapeze-like, gliding and arcing upward, vanishing.

From somewhere, her laughter, brittle yet almost merry.

Then, high up at the top of the breaker where he had glimpsed her, a light. It splashed off the ceiling and sprayed downward, casting a dim glow over the screens and chutes and rollers suspended beneath it, a crazed, thin waterfall of light trickling down over an ancient rockface.

What was it, a lantern? A flashlight? Could a flashlight do that?

He saw her as she stepped into the light, her face illuminated from below. And leaped.

33

She came spilling from the top of the breaker, dropping down from the sloped platform along a steeply pitched conveyor shaft onto a high wooden trestle. Ran along it and tripped or fell, hanging for a moment from the metal mesh of the topmost grinder like an acrobat on a swing, then came tumbling over the next horizontal cylinder, clinging for a moment, then dropped and came sliding head-first down one of the narrow sorting chutes, her body bumping against its supporting structure, until she finally came to rest at the bottom, curled up in front of him, seeming to hide. Maybe more than than that, or less. Dazed, unconscious, dead, or wide awake?

A grimy black shape in a black running suit. Coal black. She didn't move. Neither did he.

Then he heard her say in tiny voice, "I'm hurt, Jimmy. Help me." It sounded like a voice from a cave.

He leaned over the table-like surface between them and said her name.

Her face flared up, dusted with soot, eyes and teeth flashing, and she screamed. Fingers lashed out, nails biting into his throat.

He fell away from the glint of a knife blade, and she was suddenly up and running with a limp along the sorting surface, laughing hilariously. She took the last chute, clambering upward holding its edges, boosting herself along. At the top she paused and glanced back.

"Don't come after me! I'll slice you up, Jimmy!" Her voice was harsh.

Getting to her feet, she gave him a hard look, then smiled. "I used to do this all the time. Don't be worried. Scared the high school boys to death. Mother used to scream at me, coming home so filthy."

Then she was gone, disappearing behind the nearest roller. He heard her footsteps running up stairs.

He yelled, "Karen!" but thought, What's the use?

She kept going, mounting higher. A couple of bats skittered across the heights. Dust drifted and floated. He could feel it on his skin.

He could go up after her, but what for? Where could she go? She hadn't done anything he could swear to except possibly leave her senses. Had she killed? Who knew? She had looked at him on the chute as if she might have, scratching him and flashing the knife, and it had nearly scared him out of his skull. But had she meant him harm? The bats had scared him, too, and she might be no more guilty of anything than they were.

High up, her steps slowed, and soon the creaking stopped. He waited, starting to cough from the spreading dust.

When she finally reappeared, she was on the shadowy platform, and he could barely make her out. It was like a stage with a single footlight illuminating only downstage center, leaving the wings dark.

"Jimmy," she said sharply, matter-of-factly, and coughed deep in her chest. She was breathing hard. "Jimmy, what you're about to see here isn't the real me. I'm an anchorperson." She tittered, and there was a witchy echo. "What we have here, though, is a coal miner's daughter. That's a pun. Do you like puns, Jimmy?" She drew a heavy breath and choked, a harsh rattle in the emptiness of the building.

"I like puns," he called back. "That's a perfect pun."

"I know. Here's one. Almost perfect. I like things almost perfect, don't you? This one's a pun on Jimmy. Think of a pun on Jimmy." He tried, but he couldn't think of one. "Hard, isn't it? Well, here's a clue. It's an old song I used to sing with Kate, when we were going to be a team. Of course, it wasn't a pun then, because we didn't know you, and we weren't trying to be clever, just talented. I like being talented, don't you? Okay, you ready?"

"Ready," he said.

Stepping downstage along the gentle incline, into the light, she began to dance. The dance wasn't meant to have a lot of class. It was kind of a sexy dance-hall-girl's dance, and it began to have a lot of serious, vigorous movement, her knees pumping, her elbows swinging. The platform shook beneath her feet. She began to sing. Her voice was obviously in bad shape, but it seemed to fit the style of the dance hall, and she gave it a certain husky Flora Dora style.

"Oh, I wish that I could Jimmy like my sister Kate—" She stopped and peered down at him. "Jimmy, shimmy. You like it? That's a pun."

He called out, "Karen, we were worried about you."

She tittered, sounding vaguely coquettish. "Who? You and Kate?" She began singing and dancing again. "She Jimmys just like jelly on a plate—"

"Kate," she said, and sniffled, then coughed. "Kate was

like a sister to me, but not any more. She didn't Jimmy very well, not back then. I guess she does now, is that right, Jimmy?" She coughed, hacking. "I could kill Kate. She's a slob, a twig, a boring, boring child. I should have killed her then, when I had a chance. Right about where you're standing, Jimmy. Nobody would have known a thing."

He said, "You're not a killer, Karen. I know you're not. Who found the doctor for you? Was it Escobar?" He waited, then went on. "Kirk knows about Acapulco. Ginko saw you down there. Was it Escobar hired the doctor? Was that what the money was for?"

Her hips shifted, dance-hall style. She said, "Dream on." Suddenly the knife blade flashed and vanished, then reappeared. She seemed to be using it for something. Was she trying to clean her nails?

"The police," he said, and cleared his throat, "the police are talking to Escobar right now, down in Miami." A stray thought hit him. Did she know about the doctor? She must have left town before the siege began. "Kirk's talking to the doctor. He's confessed."

"He's lying," she said, and coughed. "He tried to kill me."

"You're tired, Karen. You're confused. You faked the attack in your apartment. You took him to the prairie. They found him in a place on Ridge Boulevard. He's told them everything."

She brought her hands up to her chest and backed away a little. The knife flickered. Was she going to jump, for Christ's sake?

He moved to his left, where he could see her better. "Killing Marlee, that had to be a tough choice."

"Tough," she said. "No. She was like Kathleen, all that hair, all that goodness. She didn't get it. She didn't know what was going on."

"But it had to look like a serial killer, right? Did you think about what you were doing, those two girls?"

She had turned partly away. The knife was gone. "They were dead, anyway," she said in that low alto, Lady Macbeth. Her voice rasped deep in her throat, almost a growl. "They had nothing to live for."

"Marlee did. But all it took was money, is that it? Until the money ran out?"

For a moment he thought he had lost her. But she had only retreated into the shadows. Her back to him, she seemed gathered into herself, elbows tight against her ribs. Then she was moving. She seemed to be dancing again, but it was a dance without rhythm. She coughed and spat, her head tossing from side to side. The dancing became erratic, bobbing and weaving, faster and faster. She gasped and moaned, writhing as if she were in mortal combat. He heard a hideous sound that seemed to go on and on.

"Karen, no!"

He was up on the chute when he heard the knife fall, then her body, coal dust drifting and spreading. He was climbing upward as she fell, her body striking the topmost cylinder and then the last, and tumbling into the adjacent chute, wedged in ten feet above him, her head and one arm thrown back. She lay still.

He started to climb into the chute where she lay when he saw the black dust that layered it shifting slightly. As he watched, the dust began to glisten, gathering what little light remained, and then it moved downward a bit faster, trickling nighttime rivulets.

Backing away from the other chute, he climbed upward until he was just above her. She lay sidewise, her head away from him, her knees drawn up awkwardly so that he couldn't see her face. By leaning over her, he could see the jagged wound at the base of her arched, begrimed throat. Blood had welled up and pooled there in the hollow, then spilled into the chute.

The blood had stopped running. Leaning closer, he reached out and touched her throat just below the jaw. No pulse. He raised up, arching his body until he could see her eyes. They gazed up, empty.

Outside in the twilight, he lunged through the gap in the fence, hearing his jacket rip, then scrambled to his feet and ran up the hill toward the car.

Halfway up, in the light of one of the street lamps, he saw the red Corolla, and Kathleen standing beside it. She waved, and he stopped where he was. He didn't have to raise his voice much in the quiet of early evening.

He called out, "Go home." He waved his arms, signalling for her to leave.

For a moment she didn't move. Then her lifted arm came down and she turned and ran to her car, slamming the door and gunning the engine, the tires kicking up slag and gravel as she circled back onto the highway and was gone.

He turned to listen. A car went by on the street below, but nobody was in sight. The breaker shed looked even more abandoned with the street lights behind him pitting its surface, tiny chunks of light trying to get in.

He walked the rest of the way and sat in the Olds for a long time, getting himself together, thinking about what he would say to the police.

34

"How could a person do that? How could she do that to herself?"

Kirkpatrick sounded as if he didn't believe she had. "Except the examiner says he saw it done once, in a flophouse on West Madison. An old guy. He took a steak knife and went into the jugular notch at the top of the breastbone, and he twisted and twisted the knife until he got the aortic arch. That's the only way you die almost instantly with a knife, sever a major artery."

"It was awful," Jimmy said.

"Hell," Kirk said, "you can walk a mile even with a cut jugular. But the aorta, that will kill you, all right, drops your blood pressure and you're dead."

They were sitting across a desk in the otherwise empty work area at Violent Crimes, the sergeant leaning back in his chair fiddling with a well-chewed pencil. "Did she ever have a long talk with him, the medical examiner?"

"I don't know," Jimmy said. "She may have."

"I'll have to ask him sometime whether he told her that. You don't do something like that unless somebody told you, or you read up on it. But I don't know for sure where you'd go to read up on it." He sighed and leaned forward, planting his elbows on the desk. "What a fucking way to die. How was she able to do that?" Glancing past Jimmy toward the lieutenant's office where Ginko had gone, he said, "She didn't tell you anything, though. The doctor, Escobar, nothing about the money."

Jimmy shook his head. He had slept until noon but he was still tired. He had Wilkes-Barre on his mind, the good and the bad of it. He hadn't talked to Kathleen since the breaker. He had no immediate plans to do so.

"Well," Kirk said, "it doesn't matter. We put together the posse and rode out and came back with the doctor's body. We'd make you an honorary deputy if the commander wasn't so ticked off that you went out to Wilkes-Barre without telling us. Vigilantes and fate always screw up the works. You can use that on the air, if you ever get back on the air. When is your vacation over, anyway?"

"I go back to work tomorrow."

"You know they were going to hold you yesterday, don't you? In Pennsylvania? Until they talked to me? They were sure you did it. This one detective thought you represented his fame and fortune. He already had the book written. They didn't believe a word you told them, and I can understand that. What would Karen Kohl call you for, tell you where she was? How could she kill herself that way?"

"The money. She said she needed money to get where she was going." He hadn't mentioned Kathleen and didn't intend to.

"Unhuh. She say how much she needed exactly?"

"No. She was pretty sure I could come up with it."

"Would you have?"

"Probably not."

"She would have been very disappointed."

"No doubt."

"So she knows you can get it, but when you tell her the doctor's signed a confession she kills herself but doesn't say why. And we don't know if Escobar's in it, we don't even know what they had for breakfast in Acapulco." He leaned back in his chair and gazed off across the room. "Ginko bugged the room, but the tape malfunctioned, can you believe it? Geez, I'd like to nail that Escobar. So would Miami."

"He denies he was there?"

"Same old story. All day Sunday he was out in the boat off the Florida coast. Fishing, wrestling a marlin that got away. The night before he was seen downtown, seen here, seen there. There's always somebody to say, yes, Scout's honor, three fingers up, he was with me or I saw him and it was 10:53 P.M. and look, I got a calendar watch so I know what day it was. Miami must be a wonderful place to go get your memory back." He broke the pencil, fidding with it. "Forget him. Forget Escobar. But I can't get over the stink of him. He should be arrested just for that. He smells like a vat of cheap Mexican cologne."

Jimmy shifted in his chair. "How long will this take?"

"Your statement will be ready in a minute, and you can sign it and depart with my blessing." He was leaning on the desk again. "And all that stuff about looking up the cabbie and asking where she was, they didn't go for that. She either told you or she didn't, so why go looking for the cabbie? It's no wonder they didn't believe you."

"She was confused. I couldn't get her to explain exactly where she was."

Kirk laughed. "Well, I'll tell you quite honestly, I had half a mind to let them keep you because you gave me a hard time, all day yesterday."

"Me?"

"Yes, you, Gillespie. I couldn't believe it when the newsroom called me and said you were missing."

Jimmy smiled and shook his head. "Sorry about that. I forgot to call Pat. Who called you, the assignment manager?"

"No, the other guy. You know, the little shit that rolls his eyes."

"Howard?"

"Howard, yeah. The news director. Direct from Hollywood and Vine. Your sister called him because she didn't hear from you, and he called me. Yeah, well, what with Karen Kohl disappearing and then you, I got a little apprehensive myself. We checked out the health club and your shitty little tavern. We even checked out some old girlfriends your father told us about."

"You called Dutch?"

"Is that what you call him? Feisty old bird. Anyway, it's a good thing you nearly got yourself arrested, so we knew where you were."

Kirk's having fun with this, Jimmy decided. He might not have much of a sense of humor, but he enjoys his work. What he's got is a sense of adventure.

The sergeant said, "He's coming now."

Jimmy looked around, seeing Ginko coming toward them from the lieutenant's office, smiling cheerfully and waving a small sheaf of papers. He dropped the typed statement on the desk and sat down at the next one, taking some note cards from his pocket and looking through them.

Kirk riffled the pages of the statement. "Well, this looks about right."

"Another chunk of the file," Jimmy said.

"Yes, and not the last." Kirk yawned.

The lieutenant appeared in the doorway of his office and stood for a moment watching them. It was Sunday afternoon. He usually wasn't here on Sunday. Jimmy guessed he was here for him, wanting to be in on the wrap-up: the doctor dead and Karen seriously implicated by Jimmy's testimony. As Kirk tossed the statement aside, the lieutenant returned to his office.

Kirk said to Ginko, "You saw him down there in Acapulco, right? All weekend. But he says he didn't go down there. How about that guy?"

Ginko shuffled the index cards and stacked them. "I saw him twice, once on Friday and again on Sunday. I know him, don't I? It's in the report."

"You're sure. It couldn't have been somebody else."

"Well, it was all eyeball. He wasn't using his own name or address, and I didn't bother with prints, and they let me go down there with a busted recorder. Plus nobody was down there pointing him out and saying, 'There's Ernie Escobar, the big Miami drug dealer I've known since grade school.' And if you want to get specific, yeah, it could have been somebody else down there. Somebody who looked exactly like him."

"And smelled of cheap cologne?"

Ginko looked puzzled. Then he smiled and nodded. "That too, yeah. But it's not like I was seeing him for the first time. They were lovebirds, just like in Miami."

Jimmy looked up. "Karen was in Miami? When?"

"Last fall," Kirk said. "We had it from the homicide

bureau down there. They were seen together on three separate occasions."

"Before Marlee was killed." Jimmy said to Ginko, "You saw them together in Acapulco?"

"Yeah. Twice. Once on Friday—"

Kirk broke in. "But you knew him from when he was brought up here, after Marlee Roberts died."

Ginko laid three of the index cards out on the desk and studied them. "No, remember? I had time off then. But I know what he looks like. I've seen mug shots."

Kirk laughed, leaning back in his chair and crossing his legs. "You mean we sent you down there and all you had to go on were mug shots?" He shook his head. "That's right, you were off, I'd forgotten that." He glanced at Jimmy. "What some guys won't do for a weekend in the sun, huh."

"I know him!" Ginko slapped down two more cards. "How could I forget the guy? The way he struts around. The way he smells of bad cologne."

Kirk said sharply, "You told me you knew the guy! Why'd you tell me that?"

"I know the guy!" Ginko looked over, red in the face. "I saw him down there!"

The sergeant jumped to his feet. "Yeah, and what happened in the bathroom, with the doctor? Why do we see your prints all over the gun?" He was shouting.

Astonishment spread across the detective's face. "The son of a bitch had the gun in his mouth. I was trying to get it away from him."

"Oh, no. Oh, no, that's not what the backup said. He told us you were making him eat it."

Ginko started to get up. "He couldn't see! How could he see? I was alone in there."

Kirk was on him, pushing him back in the chair. Index

cards flew and scattered on the floor. Jimmy got up, staring in disbelief.

"Nobody can see, is that it?" Kirk was yelling, his furious face in Ginko's horrified one. "So if nobody sees, you can do what you want! Well, what if I told you Escobar smells like a rose. He uses only the finest perfume. Chanel, okay?" Ginko's face was going gray. "And what if I told you further that you were seen down there in Mexico, going in and out of Karen Kohl's hotel room?"

"I had to plant the bug! I had to—"

"Not once, you scumbag. The whole weekend, shacked up with her. Escobar wasn't down there, you lying son of a bitch! But you sure as hell were. Miami was down there, waiting for Escobar, but he didn't show. But you did, so they did us a favor and let us know."

Ginko was shaking his head, his eyes bugged out. "What the hell are you doing?" He jumped up and went around the desk, beseeching Jimmy, "Tell them, we were just friends, me and her." To Kirkpatrick, the desk between them, he cried, "You got no reason to do this! I haven't done anything."

Kirk turned to Jimmy, "And you, Gillespie. You have no way to prove what happened in Pennsylvania. Was there some reason you didn't take the local cops in with you? You didn't want any witnesses?"

Jimmy stared at him. "What the hell are you talking about?"

"I'll tell you something you don't know. They almost read you your rights there in Pennsylvania. They would've, if they hadn't talked to me. They didn't believe anyone would kill themselves like that. I'm starting to wonder why I didn't let them keep you." What's he doing, Jimmy wondered, repeating what he'd said earlier?

Casually, Kirk picked a piece of broken pencil off the desk. "You're in trouble, my friend. How do we know you didn't kill her? Maybe you were telling her what to do all along, but then in Pennsylvania she cracked. She became a little too dangerous to let live."

Ginko cried, "Yeah, he must be the one that told her what to do! She told me. She said he put her onto the doctor."

Kirk looked at him. "She told you that?"

"Yeah, in Acapulco. She saw me down there and said come up to her room. She said he was going to kill her if she didn't get the money."

The sergeant turned on Jimmy in a towering rage. "So where did you find the doctor?" Jimmy gaped, and Kirk said to Ginko, "Where did he find the doctor?"

"Out on Roosevelt Road somewhere, I forget where she said. He paid the guy to do the killings from what he collected from her. That and more, he got from her. Lots more. Fifty, sixty thousand."

"Where would she get that kind of money?"

"How do I know? Escobar?"

Kirk said quietly, "Oh yeah, the guy you knew what he looked like. So why wasn't that in your report?"

Ginko looked at Jimmy and gave his head a little toss. "I said we had to find a way to stick him with it, and she should wear a wire. I was waiting to set that up." He said to Kirk, "She told me not to tell anyone or she wouldn't do it, not even you."

The sergeant smiled. "Well, that's what good friends are for." He tossed the piece of pencil back on the desktop. It rolled off onto the floor, among the index cards. "Ginko, you stupid cluck." He turned and walked away, then turned back and called out, "You had enough of this shit, lieutenant?"

The lieutenant stepped out of his doorway and came down between two rows of desks. "Please sit down, gentlemen," he said. "Ginko, take a seat and I'll read you your rights."

Ginko, watching him approach, cried, "This is a joke. A joke! What is this? I'm no criminal!"

"Your departmental rights," the lieutenant said, adjusting his shell-rimmed glasses as he approached them, "for when your case comes up before the police board."

"You got nothing! What have I just been telling you?" the detective screamed. "I don't have to stand here—"

"Sit down." The lieutenant gave him a little shove, and Ginko backed away into a chair. Jimmy sat down, too.

"I don't have to take this," the detective grumbled.

"No, we'll take it from here." The lieutenant reached out and removed the pistol from Ginko's shoulder holster. "I'll take this, and then after we take your badge we'll ship you back. They'll read you your criminal rights over there, the government of Poland."

"Ship me back! You out of your minds? I'm a fucking citizen!"

The lieutenant handed the automatic weapon to Kirk, who sat down at the desk and put it carefully into a drawer, then looked up at Jimmy. "That's how we got onto this guy."

"Got onto me?" Ginko shouted. The lieutenant wagged a finger at him, then put it to his lips.

"Things didn't add up in Acapulco," Kirk went on, "so we asked the Polish consulate to look up our man here, prints and pictures and all, you know? And never mind the name, which was a good thing because three days ago they came up with a different one, same guy. His name isn't Ginko, though, it's not even Gruszczynski. You know what he did? He's been wanted over there for seventeen years, for embezzlement and suspicion of murder." He looked at Ginko, who wasn't looking at anybody now. His hands were clamped between his knees. "That about right, my friend? Embezzling funds belonging to the Polish people is the way I think they put it. Way back in seventy-six you were twenty-five and worked in the shipyard at Gdansk, pretty hard labor, I'd imagine. You were also a clerk for some kind of labor organization, right? Solidarity? Or wasn't that alive yet? The old government, the Communists, they must have hated you, though, didn't they? It was a tough go, and it wasn't worth it. So you stole from the union treasury, killed whoever he was that got in the way, and hopped a boat in the harbor. Seventy-six is the year you entered this country, I believe. And believe me, they don't think of you over there as some kind of Robin Hood. They hate your guts, Ginko. And what for? What was it, three thousand four hundred dollars?"

Ginko looked up. "Not that much. I had to split it with the captain of the ship." He jerked his head forward and spat on the floor.

"Ah-ah-ah," the lieutenant said, taking off his glasses and pointing a stem down at the glob of spit. "Don't get insubordinate, officer, or we'll start looking deeper into the suicide in the bathtub and sundry other goddamn fucking matters, like how good you've always been with money. Is that what you got from her, fifty or sixty thousand? There's about twenty-five grand in your bank account. We can't account for all of it. Can you? And there's your new Mitsubishi, very slick. It must have set you back a bundle." He leaned back against a desk and smiled at Jimmy. "You getting all this?"

Kirk said, "What we don't know is who killed who. What

do you know, Ginko? You found the doctor down on Roosevelt Road, that what you're saying? When was this? September? October? She didn't come to Chicago until September. She didn't meet Clara Turner until late that month. She didn't meet you until sometime in October, after the first one was killed. Does that mean she's the one who found the doctor? How could she find him that fast? He'd disappeared from the face of the earth. Come on, Ginko."

Ginko said, "Why should I say anything? A lawyer would say stay mum."

"Because," the lieutenant said, "we can send you back or we can keep you. Which do you prefer? Or we can even cut a deal, try you on a lesser charge. You know how it works. It's up to you. Cooperation, that's the answer. You know how much we appreciate that."

The detective raised his eyes and lowered them. "For God's sake, don't send me back." He nodded several times. "I found him for her. It took me till the middle of December, but I found him."

"December!" Kirk looked up at the lieutenant, then back at Ginko. "So if he killed Roberts, who killed the first two?"

"She did."

"Go on! That fresh-faced youngster? Comes to town and within two months she's killed two people? Makes it look like suicide? Makes sure it doesn't, so we can start looking for a serial killer? Pays the doctor, has him do a third one, just to be absolutely convincing? All that? She does all that? You kidding me?"

"She's a devil," Ginko said. "Look what she did to me, getting me to do that, find the doctor, make him do what she wanted. Look at how she killed herself." He looked at Kirk.

Kirk sat back in his chair, smiling. "Ginko, you know something? That's the first time you did that. Looked straight at me."

The lieutenant said, "Did she, Ginko? Did she do it?"

"She did. But the only thing I knew at first was she knew a lot about the cuts."

"Go on."

"The first one, she said she questioned the landlady very closely, because she's the one found the body. And then she asked me try to remember how deep the cuts were, and were they straight across, like slashes, you know, and how many. She said it didn't sound like suicide. Remember? I asked you, Kirk, what you thought."

Kirk glanced at the lieutenant. "I don't remember that."

"I did. I asked you that. The second, she wondered if it might be the same. She said her friend Clara had mentioned the doctor and was scared of him. That's the first I heard of him. You know, I brought it up with you, how it might be murder."

"To me?" Kirk searched his memory. "My God, I think you did."

"Sure, I did. I could see it later, how she was calling attention. Using me, to put the idea in your mind."

"But did she kill them, for Christ's sake?"

"She did. She told me."

Kirk's face went a kind of purple. "My God, man—!"

"Not then! She didn't tell me till a couple of months ago, and by then I would have done anything she wanted. I didn't care what she'd done—"

"All right, all right." The sergeant's eyes looked sad. "And at some point, it occurred to you that she might be good for a new car and then some. But why would you go in with her, put all you have on the line?"

Ginko's head was down. "I was crazy about her. I was seeing some real money. But there was the other thing. I was no better than she was. I'd killed somebody, too."

The lieutenant cleared his throat. "What about her alibis?"

Ginko shrugged. "You go out of town, you can fly back in. Fly out again. Come home like you've been on vacation. You return some phone calls, you don't have to be home. You can retrieve your messages from anywhere and call back from anywhere. She called from the girl's apartment. The second one, right after she killed her."

Kirk said, "What? A blow on the head, a few cuts, spread the blood around, put her in the tub and finish the job?" He looked at the lieutenant, nodding. "And then put it in my mind. She did! She put it in my mind. Shit." He said to Ginko, "So then in Acapulco you made your first collection and made sure the tape recorder didn't work, and later, when the opportunity presented itself, you took care of the doctor. I guess she was happy to pay for services rendered. What else? What made her kill herself like that?"

"She said she was going to."

"When did she say that?"

"From the start. She had this thing about suicide. It was almost a kind of religious act to her. She'd talk about her sister, about her whole family, as if they were all doomed, but she could make it all right by killing herself. She told me she had it all planned out. I didn't believe her, of course. But that's when I knew how cuckoo she was."

"But she paid you off anyway? Why?"

Ginko shook his head. "She was nuts. She just laughed. She said she wanted to go out when she was ready and not before."

"On her own terms." Kirkpatrick said to Jimmy, "So she

arranged it. She made sure you knew exactly where you could find her. It was all part of the show."

"The show?" the lieutenant asked.

"She was a show girl. An exhibitionist. And I thought when I met her she was just an objectionable little upstart. Maybe you'd like to take my badge, too."

Ginko smiled up at him, grimacing. "You know, that's what I was thinking, coming to America, the show girls, the movie stars. I thought how it would be to marry one."

Kirk winced. "By God, that would be funny if it wasn't so pathetic." He looked up at the lieutenant. "Well, she's not here to say no. What do you think?"

"Just one thing I'm not sure about. Why Marlee Roberts?"

Ginko said, "The reason she did everything. She wanted her job. At least that's what she told herself, why she did it all."

Kirk said to the lieutenant, "Got enough?"

The lieutenant nodded, and Kirkpatrick took the automatic pistol out of the desk drawer and put it in his pocket. Then he took out a tape recorder and turned it off. The lieutenant turned around and shouted, "Okay, gentlemen."

The door to the commander's office opened and two uniformed officers came down the room and escorted Ginko away, reciting his rights as they went.

The lieutenant looked down at the tape recorder. "You sure it works?" He winked at Jimmy and went after Ginko, first going into his office for his jacket, then stopping off to have a word with the commander before going downstairs.

Looking weary, the sergeant put on his coat and asked Jimmy if he needed a lift. Jimmy said no, he was driving. But first, he added, he needed to use a phone.

"Sure, help yourself." The sergeant pushed Jimmy's

statement across the desk. "Sign this before you go. You can leave it with the commander. Oh, the commander would like to see you before you leave, if you have a minute. Good night, Gillespie." He made no move to go. "You tired? I'm tired. I have to stop by the lab and the evidence room. Then I'm going home and get into a hot tub. I think I'll skip the news tonight." He picked up the tape recorder. "See you around."

Jimmy watched Kirkpatrick lumber out and go down the stairs. Then he signed the copies of his statement, took it over and knocked on the commander's door. It opened and the captain stood there in his hat and coat.

Jimmy handed him the statement and said, "You wanted to see me, Art?"

"Oh yeah, come in. Sit down a minute." The captain went around his desk, removing his hat and coat and hanging them on the rack. He sat down.

Jimmy dropped into one of the two chairs in front of the desk. "Nice job, commander. Life is full of surprises."

"Don't I know it!" the captain said. "Say, Gillespie, did I ever tell you, back when I was in Property Crimes, how I cracked the case of the three-fingered carpenter?"

Jimmy tried to remember. "Thumb prints?"

"Naw. This is going to surprise you, Gillespie. You'll find a way to work it into your report."

"Art, I'd like to hear it, but first I wonder if I could use the phone. This case is pretty important."

The commander pushed his phone across the desk and got up. "Damn right it's important. And we gave it to you, don't forget that." He strolled around the desk. "I'll wait. I'll be back in a couple. Take your time." He went out the door.

Jimmy picked up the receiver and dialed the newsroom.

When he had finished dictating the bulletin, he sat back and waited for the commander to return. The case of the three-fingered carpenter? Well, it was Sunday, his last day of vacation. He figured he had twenty minutes or so to spare.